Gerald Massey

My Lyrical Life

Poems Old and New

Gerald Massey

My Lyrical Life
Poems Old and New

ISBN/EAN: 9783744776806

Printed in Europe, USA, Canada, Australia, Japan

Cover: Foto ©Andreas Hilbeck / pixelio.de

More available books at **www.hansebooks.com**

MY LYRICAL LIFE:

Poems Old and New.

BY

GERALD MASSEY.

FIRST SERIES.

London:

KEGAN PAUL, TRENCH & CO.,

1 PATERNOSTER SQUARE.

1889.

RICHARD CLAY & SONS, LIMITED,
LONDON & BUNGAY.

Dedication.

Good Friend Of Mine, To Me Unknown,
Save For The Secret Friendship Shown,
Accept, In Your Sequestered Nook,
The Dedication Of My Book.

EXPLANATORY.

I saw myself described the other day as being the most unpublished of Living Authors. There were reasons for this. It happens that I have not hitherto had a Publisher to keep my books before the public. There has never been a collected edition of my poems; and the four separate volumes have been out of print for many years. Thus their old friends have been passing away without the chance of my making new ones. Meantime another generation of readers has arisen to whom my poems may prove to be "as good as MS." To these I have to introduce myself, or rather the writings of my other, earlier, self, who is now almost a stranger to myself!

These two volumes contain the better part of the earlier four, together with a hundred pages of additional matter. I give them the title of

"MY LYRICAL LIFE,"

because that only includes one half of my literary life.

By "Poems Old and New" it is not meant that all the new ones are recently written, but that they will be new to the readers of the Volumes previously printed.

With some obvious exceptions the poems earliest written are collected in the Second series, whilst those that were written latest appear in the First volume. They are not rigidly arranged upon any set plan or system, although there is at times a sort of sequence in the grouping, either of subjects or in accordance with the chronology.

I have done what I could in that way to eke out the reader's interest by giving as much variety as was possible within the limited scope of lyrical poetry, which cannot have the advantage of a cumulative interest.

It should be remembered, that the writer of lyrical poems is not always the speaker of them! The Lyrist has the liberty if not the latitude of the dramatist in representing other characters, situations, standpoints, or moods, than those which may be strictly personal to himself. Hence Robert Browning's descriptive title of "Dramatic Lyrics." Many of my Lyrics are also dramatic in the sense of the writer being moved and the poetry written on behalf of other people. As a matter of fact, the poem of "Babe Christabel" was not founded on a personal sorrow of my own. But I do not say this with the object of shirking any personal responsibility for the contents of these volumes. Nor am I about to put forth a private theory of poetry such as might supply the most suitable frame for my own portrait.

I am, as a matter of course, aware that in the estimation of some readers, including a few personal friends, the " *Last Lyrics* " in these volumes may suffice to damn all the rest! But that cannot be helped.   It has been my luck all along the line of my Lyrical Life to fight upon the weaker side— the side, however, that I have lived to see at times victorious.

I was a Home-Ruler thirty years ago!   Also it was my lot to start in life with something of

> *The spirit that can stand alone*
> *As the Minority of one;*
> *Or with the faithful few be found*
> *Working and waiting till the rest come round.*

No one will dare to impugn my patriotism, or doubt that I am English to the heart-roots, even though my latest lyrics are devoted to the cause of another nationality than ours—even though I do think there are other ways of wooing and winning than by brute conquest and brutal coercion, whether in the individual, social, or national life; and that the time has come for humaner methods to be applied.   Still, it is possible that if we have no sympathy with the subject-matter, be it political, patriotic, domestic, or spiritualistic, we are more or less incapable of justly appraising the poetry.

Much of my verse is bound up with the political and patriotic life of our time.   Some of the pieces, such as "Havelock's March," published in 1860, and others on the "Second Empire," are more properly historic photographs, rather than Poems in the Esthetic sense.   But they are national; and such things may have their place as illustrations in historic records.   Whatsoever the matter might be, I have always written *for* the subject with all my heart.

Also, for the truth's sake I ought to explain that the kind of Spiritualism, Gnosticism, or Neo-Naturalism to be found in my poetry is no delusive Idealism derived from hereditary belief in a physical resurrection of the dead!   Neither am I making a new attempt to cheat the ignorant by false pretences of knowledge.   My faith in our future life is founded upon facts in nature and realities of my own personal experience; not upon any falsification of natural fact.   These facts have been more or less known to me personally during forty years of familiar face-to-face acquaintance-ship, therefore my certitude is not premature; they have given me the proof palpable that our very own human identity and intelligence do persist after the blind of darkness has been drawn down in death. The Spiritualist who has plumbed the void of death as I have, and touched this solid ground of fact, has established a faith that can neither be undermined nor overthrown. He has done with the poetry of desolation and despair; the sighs of unavailing regret, and all the passionate wailing of unfruitful pain. He *cannot be bereaved in soul!* And I have had ample testimony that my poems have done welcome work, if only in helping to destroy the tyranny of death, which has made so many mental slaves afraid to live.

I see myself referred to at times as a poet who has not fulfilled the promise of his early work!

It is true that some twenty years ago my singing on the old lines ceased. First, there was the insuperable difficulty of living by the poetry that one would gladly have lived for! No one lives by poetry in England except the Laureate. Not even those who have been most generously assisted by such a Prince amongst publishers as was Alexander Strahan, who did his best (I fear) to ruin his own business in trying to help poets and others to live by their writings. Independently of this difficulty I had then almost ceased to look upon the writing of poetry as the special work of my literary life; and since that time, instead of nursing ancient delusions by poetizing misinterpreted Mythology, I have been strenuously seeking to get rid of them by Explanation.

Hence it has been said of me, my life and work, by a friendly singer—

" Behold a Poet who could even forego
The joy peculiar to the Singer's Soul,
His pleasant dream of fame, his proffered seat
Upon the heights to which his Spirit soared,
To dive for treasures where but few could breathe,
And dredge the old sea-bottoms of the Past.
Lover of Beauty who gave up all for Truth !
　　*　　*　　*　　*　　*　　*　　*
And having wrought through years of sacrifice,
And brought his message to the unwelcoming world,
He, calm, contented, leaves the rest with God ;
As if he recked not, though the Bark were wrecked,
The treasure being landed safe on shore." [1]

The result of this change, which I hope to fully justify before my day's darg is done, is that these volumes contain the lush-leafiness of the Spring-time, alluded to so warmly by Walter Savage Landor, with something of the Summer's bloom, but do not show the ripened tints of Autumn's gold. My *"Lyrical Life"* may contain the flower, but the fruit of my whole life has to be looked for elsewhere by those who are in sympathy with my purpose.

[1] *Sheen and Shade,* by J. R. and B. M. R.　Printed by Richard Clay and Sons, 1887.

I had not attained the larger, more objective out-
look of my later life when called away from poetry
to "prospect" for other treasures in my search
for truth. Possibly this fact of my breaking-off
midway in life may be thought to give me a kind of
right to rank with those Poets who died young, and
thus invited a gentler judgment for their verse.

It was not that I felt the fount and source of
song had dried up within or without. Nor was it
owing to any spiritual lassitude from lack of faith
in man, or woman either. I had neither lost
heart in the present, nor hope for the future; nor
had I begun to think that human life had come to
the dregs of its days. Although I am growing
old myself—at least the years say so—I cannot
bewail the changes going on around us fast and
faster, for it is by change the world renews and
must renew its youth, unheeding all the lamenta-
tions of old age, the cries of warning and prophecies
of woe that proceed from those who keep on calling
for double drags to be put on, whilst we are ascending the hill, because they fear lest the summit
ahead of us should only reveal a precipice beyond.

We are in the pangs of sloughing; but we are
getting good riddance of much impedimenta bequeathed to us as the burden of the past, which
the race has been so painfully, and, as was thought,
most dutifully, lugging along!

b *

The false faiths are fading; but it is in the light of a truer knowledge. The half Gods are going in order that the whole Gods may come. There is finer fish in the unfathomed sea of the future than any we have yet landed.

It is only in our time that the data have been collected for rightly interpreting the Past of Man, and for portraying the long and vast procession of his slow but never-ceasing progress through the sandy wilderness of an uncultivated earth into the world of work with the ever-quickening consciousness of a higher, worthier life to come. And without this measure of the human past we could have no true gauge of the growth that is possible in the future!

Indeed it seems to me that we are only just beginning to lay hold of this life in earnest; only just standing on the very threshold of true thought; only just now attaining a right mental method of thinking, through a knowledge of Evolution; only just getting in line with natural law, and seeking earnestly to stand level-footed on that ground of reality which must ever and everywhere be the one lasting foundation of all that is permanently true.

It is only of late that the Tree of Knowledge has begun to lose its evil character, to be planted anew, and spread its roots in the fresh ground of every Board-School, with its fruits no longer accursed, but made free to all.

I sometimes think the genuine passion for essential truth is growing, with our keener moral sense, so that one may almost expect to see the time when the Writer can earn his living by telling the truth!

We are beginning to see the worst evils now afflicting the human race are man-made, and do not come into the world by decree of Fate or fiat of God; and that which is man-made is also remediable by man. Not by man alone! For Woman is about to take her place by his side as true help-mate and ally in carrying on the work of the world, so that we may look upon the Fall of Man as being gradually superseded by the Ascent of Woman. And here let me say parenthetically, that I consider it to be of the first necessity for women to obtain the Parliamentary Franchise before they can hope to stand upon a business footing of practical equality with men; and therefore I have no sympathy with those would-be abortionists, who have been somewhat too "previously" trying to take the life of Woman-Suffrage in embryo before it should have the chance of being brought to birth.

Some of the most generous critics of my early volumes prophesied that they contained immortal verse. Whether they did or not remains to be tested by that fierce furnace and crucible of the future, which await the work of all. Doubtless these will reduce to cinders much of the poetry of the present, and consume to ashes many of the artificial *Immortelles* that friendly hands have fondly placed upon the brows of the

"*Immorta's prematurely brought to birth.*"

Personally I form no overweening estimate of the value of my verse. The Prefatory lines of twenty years ago were written in all sincerity. I think the poems real so far as they go, but their range is very limited. They will not let me speak proudly of them; yet I do not think they are outgrown and superseded, or I should not have reprinted them.

On looking back at these Writings of my more youthful years, I cannot help wishing that they had been worthier, but I also feel thankful to find they are no worse. I am glad to know the ghost of my former self, now raised, is not appalling as it might have been. And after all the brooding patience of long research, and the painful labour spent in writing big books to stand on library shelves, I feel no shame in confessing the fact that it is very pleasant to come at last and nestle near the warm heart of one's lovers and friends in a Pocket Edition of one's poetry.

July, 1889. GERALD MASSEY.

CONTENTS.

PAGE

A GREETING.

ANNIE BESANT, brave and dear,
May some message, uttered here,
Reach you, ringing golden-clear.

Though we stand not side by side
In the front of battle wide,
Oft I think of you with pride,

Fellow-soldier in the fight!
Oft I see you flash by night,
Fiery-hearted for the Right!

You for others sow the Grain:
Yours the tears of ripening rain;
Theirs the smiling harvest-gain.

Fellow-worker! we shall be
Workers for Eternity;
Such my faith. And you shall see

Life's no bubble blown of breath
To delude the sight till death;
Whatsoe'er the Un-Seeing saith.

Love that closes dying eyes,
Wakes them too, in glad surprise:
Love that makes for ever wise.

Soul—whilst murmuring "*There's no soul*"—
Shall upspring like flame from coal:
Death is not Life's final goal.

Bruno lives! Such Spirits come,
Swords, immortal-tempered, from
Fire and Forge of Martyrdom.

You have Soul enough for seven;
Life enough our earth to leaven,
Love enough to create heaven.

One of God's own faithful Few,
Whilst unknowing it, are you,
Annie Besant, bravely true.

PREFATORY POEM.

A singer sang in sleep, and, sleeping, dreamed
He sang divinely, while his spirit seemed
So far in Music's heaven to soar and sing,
They could not follow who stood listening!
For him, the soul of sweetness found a voice,
For them, the Singer only "made a noise."

Such is the difference in the uttered strain,
From that fine music passing through the brain.
Such sumless treasures we possess in dreams,
To find at waking only mirrored gleams.
No revelation of the written word
Will render all the spirit saw and heard.

So fresh they breathed; so faded now they look;
My few poor withered flowers in a book.
Gone is the glory that once gleamed from them;
The Spirit of Light imprisoned in the gem!
Now the winged life hath settled down in words,
These seem but stuffed instead of Singing Birds.

Feelings brimful of warmth as is a rose
Of its June-red, have lost their perfumed glows;
The heaven-revealing thoughts that star-like shone,
The daily kindlings of eternal dawn,
All darkened down, like Meteors that have birth
In Heaven, to flash and quench them cold in earth.

We grasp at diamonds visible in the dew,
And open empty tear-wet hands to you!
We clasp at heart the daughters of the skies,
Their shadow stays with us; the substance flies.
Glimpses divine will peep; pictures will pass,
That leave no likeness in the Seer's glass.

The Poet's best immortally will lurk
In that rare motion of his soul at work.
Bee-like, he brings you one gold honey-drop;
But the full-swing, high on the flower-top,
'Twixt Heaven that rained itself in sweetness
    down,
And Earth—all bloom for him—is ne'er made
    known.

MY poem was in the making. These are your
Warmth-needy nurslings. Reader! mine no more.
The life I gave will no more fill my breast
Than the flown birds come back to last year's nest:
And if these live again, 'tis you must give
The reflex thrill to them by which they live.

You must make out the music from the hint
Prelusive: I but tune the instrument.
The glory or the gladness or the grace
Must shine for me re-orient in your face.
The seed, that in my life took secret root,
In yours must bud, and flower, and bear you fruit.

MY LYRICAL LIFE.

BABE CHRISTABEL.

It fell upon a merry May morn,
    All in the prime of that sweet time
    When daisies whiten, woodbines climb,—
The dear Babe Christabel was born :

When Earth like Danaë bares her charms,
    That for the coming God unfold,
    Who, in the Sunshine's shower of Gold
Leaps warmly into her amorous arms ;

When Beauty dons her daintiest dress,
    And, fed with April's mellow showers,
    The woods laugh out all leaves and flowers
That flush for very happiness ;

And Spider-Puck his wonder weaves
    O' nights : and nooks of greening gloom
    Grow rich with Violets that bloom
In the cool dusk of dewy leaves ;

Green fields transfigure, like a page
    Of Fable to the eye of Faith ;
    Where cowslips and primroses rathe
Bring back a real Golden Age ;

When Rose-buds drink the fiery wine
  Of Dawn, with crimson stains i' the mouth,
  All thirstily as yearning Youth
From Love's hand drinks the draught divine;

When fainting hearts forget their fears,
  And in the poorest Life's salt cup
  Some rare wine runs, and Hope builds up
Her rainbow over Memory's tears,—

It fell upon a merry May morn,
  All in the prime of that sweet time
  When daisies whiten, woodbines climb,—
The dear Babe Christabel was born.

————

All night the Stars bright watches kept,
  Like Gods that look a golden calm;
  The Silence dropped its precious balm,
And the tired world serenely slept.

The birds were darkling in the nest,
  Or bosomed in voluptuous trees:
  On beds of flowers the happy breeze
Had kissed its fill and sank to rest.

All night beneath the Cottage eaves,
  A lonely light, with tremulous Arc,
  Surged back a space the sea of dark,
And glanced among the shimmering leaves.

And when the Morn with frolic zest,
  Unclosed the curtains of the night,
  There was a dearer dawn of light,
A tenderer life the Mother's pressed.

And she at all her suffering smiled.
　　The Star new-kindled in the dark—
　　Life that had fluttered like a Lark—
Lay in her bosom a sweet Child!

How she had felt it drawing down
　　Her nesting heart more close and close,—
　　Her rose-bud ripening to the Rose,
That she should one day see full-blown!

How she had throbbed with hopes and fears,
　　And strained her inner eyes till dim,
　　To see the expected glory swim
Through the rich mist of happy tears;

For it, her woman's heart drank up,
　　And laughed at, Sorrow's darkest dole:
　　And now Delight's most dainty soul
Was crushed for her in one rich cup!

And then delicious languors crept,
　　Like nectar, on her pain's hot drouth,
　　And feeling fingers—kissing mouth—
Being faint with joy, the Mother slept.

————

Babe Christabel was royally born!
　　For when the earth was flushed with flowers,
　　And drenched with beauty in sun-showers,
She came through golden gates of Morn.

No chamber arras-pictured round,
　　Where sunbeams make a gorgeous gloom,
　　And touch its glories into bloom,
And footsteps fall withouten sound,

Was her Birth-place that merry May-morn ;
        No gifts were heaped, no bells were rung,
        No healths were drunk, no songs were sung
When dear Babe Christabel was born :

But Nature on the darling smiled,
        And with her beauty's blessing crowned :
        Love brooded o'er the hallowed ground,
And there were Angels with the Child.

And May her kisses of love did bring ;
        Her Birds made welcoming merriment,
        And all her flowers in greeting sent
The secret sweetnesses of Spring.

In glancing light and glimmering shade,
        With cheeks that touched and ripelier burned
        May-Roses in at the lattice yearned,
A-tiptoe, and Good Morrow bade.

No purple and fine linen might
        Be hoarded up for her sweet sake :
        But Mother's love will clothe and make
The little wearer bravely dight !

Wide worlds of worship are their eyes,
        Their loyal hearts are worlds of love,
        Who fondly clasp their cooing Dove,
And read its news from Paradise.

Their looks praise God—souls sing for glee :
        They think if this old world had toiled
        Through ages to bring forth their child,
It was a glorious destiny.

BABE CHRISTABEL.

O HAPPY Husband ! happy Wife !
　　The rarest blessing Heaven drops down,
　　The sweetest blossom in Spring's crown,
Starts in the furrows of your life !

Ah ! what a towering height ye win,
　　Who cry, " Lo, my beloved Child ! "
　　And, life on life sublimely piled,
Ye touch the heavens and peep within.

Look how a star of glory swims
　　Down aching silences of space,
　　Flushing the Darkness till its face
With beating heart of light o'erbrims ;

So brightening came Babe Christabel,
　　To touch the earth with fresh romance,
　　And light a Mother's countenance
With looking on her miracle.

With hands so flower-like soft, and fair,
　　She caught at life, with words as sweet
　　As first spring violets, and feet
As faëry-light as feet of air.

The Father, down in Toil's mirk mine,
　　Turns to his wealthier world above,
　　Its radiance, and its home of love ;
And lights his life like sun-struck wine.

The Mother moves with queenlier tread :
　　Proud swell the globes of ripe delight
　　Above her heart, so warm and white
A pillow for the baby-head !

Their natures deepen, well-like, clear,
    Till God's eternal stars are seen,
    For ever shining and serene,
By eyes anointed Beauty's seer.

A sense of glory all things took,—
    The red Rose-Heart of Dawn would blow,
    And Sundown's sumptuous pictures show
Babe-Cherubs wearing their Babe's look !

And round their peerless one they clung,
    Like bees about a flower's wine-cup ;
    New thoughts and feelings blossomed up,
And hearts for very fulness sung

Of what their budding Babe should grow,
    When the Maid crimsoned into Wife,
    And crowned the summit of some life,
To bear the morning on her brow !

And they should bless her for a Bride,
    Who, like a splendid saint alit
    In some heart's seventh heaven, should sit,
As now in theirs, all glorified.

'Twas thus they built their Castles brave
    In faëry lands of gorgeous cloud ;
    They never saw a wee white shroud,
Nor guessed how flowers will mask the grave.

She grew, a sweet and sinless Child,
    In shine and shower,—calm and strife ;
    A Rainbow on our dark of Life,
From Love's own radiant heaven down-smiled !

In lonely loveliness she grew,—
  'A shape all music, light, and love,
  With startling looks, so eloquent of
The spirit whitening into view.

At Childhood she could seldom play
  With merry heart, whose flashes rise
  Like splendour-wingèd butterflies
From honeyed hearts of flowers in May:

The fields in blossom flamed and flushed,
  The Roses into crimson yearned,
  With cloudy fire the wall-flowers burned,
And blood-red Sunsets bloomed and blushed,—

And still her cheek grew pale as pearl,—
  It took no tint of Summer's wealth
  Of colour, warmth, and wine of Health:
Death's hand so whitely pressed the Girl!

No blush grew ripe to sun or kiss
  Where violet veins ran purple light,
  So tenderly through Parian white,
Touching you into tenderness.

A spirit-look was in her face,
  That shadowed a miraculous range
  Of meanings, ever rich and strange,
Or lightened glory in the place.

Such mystic lore was in her eyes,
  And light of other worlds than ours,
  She looked as she had gathered flowers,
With little maids of Paradise.

And she would talk so weirdly-wild,
    And grow upon your wonderings,
    As though her stature rose on wings!
And you forgot she was a Child.

Ah! she was one of those who come
    With pledge and promise not to stay
    Long, ere the Angels let them stray
To nestle down in earthly home:

And, through the windows of her eyes,
    We often saw her saintly soul,
    Serene, and sad, and beautiful,
Go sorrowing for lost Paradise!

Our Lamb in mystic meadows played:
    In some celestial sleep she walked
    Her dream of life, and low we talked,
As of her waking heart-afraid.

In Earth she took no lusty root,
    Her beauty of promise to disclose,
    Or round into the Woman-Rose,
And climb into Life's crowning fruit.

She came,—as comes the light of smiles
    O'er earth, and every budding thing
    Makes quick with beauty — alive with
        Spring;
Then goeth to the golden Isles.

She came—like music in the night
    Floating as heaven in the brain,
    A moment oped, and shut again,
And all is dark where all was light.

MIDNIGHT was trancèd solemnly
　　Thinking of dawn: Her Star-thoughts
　　　　burned ;
　　The Trees like burdened Prophets yearned,
　Rapt in a wind of prophecy :

When, like the Night, the shadow of Woe
　　On all things laid its hand death-dark,
　　Our last hope went out as a spark,
And a cry smote heaven like a blow.

We sat and watched by Life's dark stream,
　　Our love-lamp blown about the night,
　　With hearts that lived as lived its light,
And died as died its precious gleam.

In Death's face hers flashed up and smiled,
　　As smile the young flowers in their prime,
　　I' the face of their gray murderer Time,
And Death for true love kissed our child.

She thought our good-night kiss was given,
　　And like a flower her life did close.
　　Angels uncurtained that repose,
And the next waking dawned in heaven.

They snatched our little tenderling,
　　So shyly opening into view,
　　Delighted, as the Children do
The primrose that is first in Spring.

WITH her white hands clasped she sleepeth; heart
     is hushed, and lips are cold;
  Death shrouds up her heaven of beauty, and a
     weary way we go,
Like the sheep without a Shepherd on the wintry
     norland wold,
  With the face of Day shut out by blinding
     snow.

O'er its widowed nest my heart sits moaning for
     its youngling fled
  From this world of wail and weeping, gone to
     join her starry peers;
And my light of life's o'ershadowed where the dear
     one lieth dead,
  And I'm crying in the dark with many fears.

All last night-tide she seemed near me, like a lost
     beloved Bird,
  Beating at the lattice louder than the sobbing
     wind and rain;
And I called across the night with tender name
     and fondling word:
  And I yearned out through the darkness, all
     in vain.

Heart will plead, " Eyes cannot see her: they are
     blind with tears of pain;"
  And it climbeth up and straineth for dear life
     to look and hark
While I call her once again: but there cometh no
     refrain,
  And it droppeth down, and dieth in the dark.

In this dim world of clouding cares,
    We rarely know, till wildered eyes
    See white wings lessening up the skies,
The Angels with us unawares.

And thou hast stolen a jewel, Death !
    Shall light thy dark up like a Star,
    A Beacon kindling from afar
Our light of love, and fainting faith.

Through tears it streams perpetually,
    And glitters through the thickest glooms,
    Till the eternal morning comes
To light us o'er the Jasper Sea.

With our best branch in tenderest leaf,
    We've strewn the way our Lord doth come ;
    And, ready for the harvest-home,
His Reapers bind our ripest sheaf.

Our beautiful Bird of light hath fled :
    Awhile she sat with folded wings—
    Sang round us a few hoverings—
Then straightway into glory sped.

With sense of Motherhood new-found
    Some white-winged Angel nurtures her,
    High on the heavenly hills of myrrh,
With all Love's purple glory round.

Through Childhood's morning-land, serene
    She walked betwixt us twain, like Love ;
    While, in a robe of light above,
Her watching Angel walked unseen,

Till Life's highway broke bleak and wild ;
    Then, lest her starry garments trail
    In mire, heart bleed, and courage fail,
The Angel's arms caught up the child.

Her wave of life hath backward rolled
    To the great ocean ; on whose shore
    We wander up and down, to store
Some treasures of the times of old :

And aye we seek and hunger on
    For precious pearls and relics rare,
    Strewn on the sands for us to wear
At heart, for love of her that's gone.

O weep no more ! there yet is balm
    In Gilead ; Love doth ever shed
    Rich healing where it nestles,—spread
O'er desert pillows, some green Palm !

God's ichor fills the hearts that bleed ;
    The best fruit loads the broken bough ;
    And in the wounds our sufferings plough,
Love sows its own immortal seed.

Strange glory runs down Life's cloud-rents,
    And through the open door of Death
    We see the hand that beckoneth
To the beloved going hence.

———

COUSIN WINNIE.

THE glad spring-green grows luminous
  With coming Summer's golden glow;
Merry Birds sing as they sang to us
  In far-off seasons, long ago:
The old place brings the young Dawn back,
  That moist eyes mirror in their dew;
My heart goes forth along the track
  Where oft it danced, dear Winnie, with you.
A world of Time, a sea of change,
  Have rolled between the paths we tread,
Since you were my "*Cousin Winnie*," and I
  Was your "*own little, good little Ned.*"

There's where I nearly broke my neck,
  Climbing for nests! and hid my pain:
And then I thought your heart would break,
  To have the Birds put back again!
Yonder, with lordliest tenderness,
  I carried you across the Brook;
So happy in my arms to press
  You, triumphing in your timid look:
So lovingly you leaned to mine
  Your cheek of sweet and dusky red:
You were my "*Cousin Winnie*," and I
  Was your "*own little, good little Ned.*"

My Being in your presence basked,
  And kitten-like for pleasure purred;
A higher heaven I never asked
  Than watching, wistful as a bird,

To hear that voice so rich and low;
    Or sun me in the rosy rise
Of some soul-ripening smile, and know
    The thrill of opening paradise.
The Boy might look too tenderly,
    All lightly 'twas interpreted :
You were my "*Cousin Winnie,*" and I
    Was your "*own little, good little Ned.*"

Ay me, but I remember how
    I felt the heart-break, bitterly,
When the Well-handle smote your brow,
    Because the blow fell not on me !
Such holy longing filled my life,
    I could have died, Sweet, for your sake ;
But never thought of you as Wife ;
    A cure to clasp for love's heart-ache.
You entered my soul's temple, Dear,
    Something to worship, not to wed :
You were my "*Cousin Winnie,*" and I
    Was your "*own little, good little Ned.*"

I saw you, heaven on heaven higher,
    Grow into stately womanhood ;
Your beauty kindling with the fire
    That swims in proud old English blood :
Away from me,—a radiant Joy !—
    You soared ; fit for a Hero's bride :
While I, a Man in soul, a Boy
    In stature, nestled at your side !
You saw not how the poor wee Love
    Pined dumbly, and thus doubly pled :
You were my "*Cousin Winnie,*" and I
    Was your "*own little, good little Ned.*"

And then that other voice came in !
   There my Life's music suddenly stopped.
Silence and darkness fell between
   Us, and my Star from heaven dropped.
I led Him by the hand to you—
   He was my Friend—whose name you bear :
I had prayed for some great task to do,
   To prove my love.   I did it, Dear !
He was not jealous of poor me ;
   Nor saw my life bleed under his tread :
You were my " *Cousin Winnie*," and I
   Was your " *own little, good little Ned.*"

I smiled, Dear, at your happiness—
   So Martyrs smile upon the spears—
The smile of your reflected bliss
   Flashed from my heart's dark tarn of tears !
In love, that made the suffering sweet,
   My blessing with the rest was given—
" *God's softest flowers kiss her feet*
   On Earth, and crown Her head in Heaven !"
And lest the heart should leap to tell
   Its tale i' the eyes, I bowed the head :
You were my " *Cousin Winnie*," and I
   Was your " *own little, good little Ned.*"

I do not blame you, Darling mine ;
   You could not know the love that lurked
To make my life so intertwine
   With yours, and with mute mystery worked.
And, had you known, how distantly
   Your calm eyes would have looked it down,
Darkling with all the majesty
   Of Midnight wearing her star-crown !

Into its virgin veil of cloud,
  The startled dearness would have fled.
You were my "*Cousin Winnie*," and I
  Was your "*own little, good little Ned.*"

I stretch my hand across the years ;
  Feel, Dear, the heart still pulses true :
I have often dropped internal tears,
  Thinking the kindest thoughts of you.
I have fought like one in iron, they said,
  Who through the battle followed me.
' I struck the blows for you, and bled
  Within my armour secretly.
Not caring for the cheers, my heart
  Far into the golden time had fled :
You were my " *Cousin Winnie*," and I
  Was your " *own little, good little Ned.*"

I sometimes see you in my dreams,
  Asking for aid I may not give :
Down from your eyes the sorrow streams,
  And helplessly I look and grieve
At arms that toss with wild heart-ache,
  And secrets writhing to be told :
I start to hear your voice, I wake—
  There's nothing but the moaning cold !
Sometimes I pillow in mine arms
  The darling little rosy head.
You are my " *Cousin Winnie*," and I
  Am your " *own little, good little Ned.*"

I bear the name of Hero now,
  And flowers at my feet are cast ;
I feel the crown upon my brow—
  So keen the thorns that hold it fast !

Ay me, and I would rather wear
  The cooling green and luminous glow
Of one you made with Cowslips, Dear,
  A many golden Springs ago.
Your gentle fingers did not give
  This ache of heart, this throb of head,
When you were my "*Cousin Winnie*," and I
  Was your "*own little, good little Ned.*"

Alone, unwearying, year by year,
  I go on laying up my love.
I think God makes no promise here
  But it shall be fulfilled above;
I think my wild weed of the waste
  Will one day prove a flower most sweet;
My love shall bear its fruit at last—
  'Twill all be righted when we meet;
And I shall find them gathered up
  In pearls for you—the tears I've shed
Since you were my "*Cousin Winnie*," and I
  Was your "*own little, good little Ned.*"

HESPER.

WE called her Hesper; for it seemed
Our Star of Eve had on us beamed,
Like Hesper, from the Heaven above,
To latest life a Lamp of love.

But for a little while withdrawn
She heralds an Eternal Dawn,
Above these mists of mortal breath,
Our Hesper in the dark of death!

Beyond the Shadow of the night
That parted us, she lifts her light
To beacon us the Homeward way,
Where we shall meet again by day.

The Star of Eve may set, but how
It shines, the Star of Morning now,
And smiles with look of love that dries
All tears from our uplifted eyes!

APOLOGUES.

THE YOUTH AND THE ANGEL.

ONCE on a time, when Immortals
  To earth came visibly down,
There went a Youth with an Angel
  Through the gates of an Eastern Town:
They passed a Dog by the roadside,
  Where dead and rotting it lay,
And the Youth, at the sickening odour,
  Shuddered and turned away:
He gathered his robes about him
  And hastily hurried thence;
But nought annoyed the Angel's
  Clear, pure, immortal sense.

By came a Lady, lip-luscious,
  On delicate tinkling feet:
All the place grew glad with her presence;
  The air about her sweet;
For she came in fragrance floating;
  Her voice most silverly rang;
And the Youth, to embrace her beauty,
  With all his being sprang.
A sweet, delightsome Lady!
  And yet, the Legend saith,
The Angel, while he passed her,
  Shuddered and held *his* breath.

SUNBEAM AND ROSE.

" Pretty Rosebud, are thy emerald
   Curtains still undrawn ?
Odalisque of Flowers,—
   Tender soul o' the fervid South !
I am dainty of thy beauty,
   All this dewy dawn ;
I am fainting for the ruddy
   Kisses of thy mouth."

Sweetly sang the Sunbeam,
   With a voice made low to win ;
Round the Rose-heart playing,
   Till it touched the tenderest strings ;
" Pretty Rose-bud, ope thy lattice,
   Let thy true love in."
And for Heaven down-wavering warm,
   She waved her leafy wings !
Listen, Maidens, to my Legend of the Sunbeam
   and the Rose.

Out she sprang, kiss-coloured,
   In her eyes the dews of bliss ;
All her beauty glowing
   With a blush of bridal light ;
Gave her balm and bloom for banquet
   To the Tempter's kiss ;
Proudly oped each chamber
   For a princelier delight.

Soon the Snake of Sweetness,
   Sated, could no longer stay ;

And away he went, a-wooing
  Every flower that blows!
'Twas the reign of Roses
  When her Lover passed to-day:
Lonely in her rifled ruin
  Drooped the dying Rose!
Listen, Maidens, to my Legend of the Sunbeam
    and the Rose.

LOVE-LONGING.

LIKE a tree beside the river
  Of her life that runs from me,
Do I lean me, murmuring ever
  In my love's idolatry:
Lo, I reach out hands of blessing;
  Lo, I stretch out hands of prayer;
And, with passionate caressing,
  Pour my life upon the air.
In my ears the siren river
  Sings, and smiles up in my face;
But for ever and for ever
  Runs from my embrace.

Spring by Spring the branches duly
  Clothe themselves in tender flower;
And for her sweet sake as truly
  All their fruit and fragrance shower:
But the stream, with careless laughter,
  Fleets in merry beauty by,
And it leaves me yearning after,
  Lorn to droop, and lone to die.

In my ears the siren river
  Sings, and smiles up in my face;
But for ever and for ever
  Runs from my embrace.

I stand mazèd in the moonlight,
  O'er its happy face to dream;
I am parchèd in the noonlight
  By that cool and brimming stream:
I am dying by the river
  Of her life that runs from me,
And it sparkles past me ever,
  With its cool felicity.
In my ears the siren river
  Sings, and smiles up in my face;
But for ever and for ever
  Runs from my embrace.

THE NEST.

I BUILT my Nest by a pleasant stream,
That glided along with a smile in its gleam,
  Bringing me gold that was sumless;
Ah me! but the floods came drowning one day,
Swept my Nest with its wealth away,
  And I in the world was homeless!

I built my Nest in a gay green tree,
And the summer of life went merrily
  With us—we were Birds of a feather!
But the leaves soon fell, and my pretty ones flew,
And through my Nest the bitter winds blew;
  'Twas bare in the wildest weather.

I built my Nest under Heaven's high eaves;
No rising of floods, no falling of leaves,
   Can mock my heart's endeavour.
Waters may wash, breezes may blow,
In the bosom of Rest I shall smile, I shall know
   My Nest is safe for ever.

HUNT THE SQUIRREL.

It was Atle of Vermeland
   In Winter used to go
A-hunting up in the pine-forest,
   With snow-shoes, sledge, and bow.

Soon his sledge with the soft fine furs
   Was heaped up heavily,
Enough to warm old Winter with,
   And a wealthy man was he.

When just as he was going back home,
   He looked up into a Tree;
There sat a merry brown Squirrel, that seemed
   To say—" *You can't shoot me!* "

And he twinkled all over temptingly,
   To the tip of his tail a-curl!
His humour was arch as the look may be
   Of a would-be-wooed sweet Girl,

That makes the Lover follow her, follow her,
   All his life up-caught,
A-dreaming on with sleeping wings,
   High in the heaven of thought.

Atle he left his sledge and furs;
　All day his arrows rung,—
The Squirrel went leaping from bough to
　　bough,—
　Only himself they stung.

He hunted far in the dark forest,
　Till died the last day-gleams;
Then wearily laid him down to rest,
　And hunted it through his dreams.

All night long the snow fell fast,
　And covered his snug fur-store;
Long, long did he strain his eyes,
　But never found it more.

Home came Atle of Vermeland,
　No Squirrel!　No furs for the mart!
Empty head brought empty hand;
　Both a very full heart.

Ah, many a one hunts the Squirrel,
　In merry or mournful truth;
Until the gathering snows of age
　Cover the treasures of Youth.

Deeper into the forest dark
　The Squirrel will dance all day;
'Till eyes go blind and miss their mark,
　And hearts will lose their way.

My Boy! if you should ever espy
　This Squirrel up in the tree,
With a dancing devil in its eye,
　Just let the Squirrel be!

THE GLOW-WORM.

The Apes found a Glow-worm,
　Smiling in the night,—
A little drop of radiance
　Tenderly alight.

" *Ho! ho!* " shivered the Apes,
　Grinning all together,
" *We'll make a fire to warm us;*
　'Tis jolly cold weather."

With dry sticks and dead leaves,
　All the Apes came ;
Piled a heap and squatted round
　To blow it into flame !

But fire would not kindle so—
　Vain their wasted breath !
Only they blew out the glow,
　And put the worm to death !

Glow-worms were meant to shine,—
　Apes can't blow them hot,
Just to warm their foolish paws,
　Or boil their own flesh-pot.

So the world would serve the Poet,
　With his light of love :
Probably his use may be
　Better known above.

THE SUNKEN CITY.

By day it lies hidden. and lurks beneath
    The ripples that laugh with light ;
But calmly and clearly and coldly as death
    It looms into shape by night,
When—the awful Heavens alone with me !—
I look on the City that's sunk in the sea.

Many a Castle I built in the air ;
    Towers that gleamed in the sun ;
Spires that soared up stately and fair,
    Till they touched heaven, every one,
Lie under the waters that mournfully
Closed over the City that's sunk in the sea.

Many fine houses, but never a home ;
    Windows, and no live face !
Doors set wide where no beating hearts come ;
    No voice is heard in the place ;
It sleeps in the arms of Eternity—
The silent City that's sunk in the sea.

There the face of a dead love lies,
    Embalmed in the bitterest tears ;
No breath on the lips ! no smile in the eyes,
    Though you watched for years and years :
And the dear drowned eyes never close from me,
Looking up from the City that's sunk in the sea.

Two of the bonniest birds of God
    That ever warmed human heart
For a nest, till they fluttered their wings abroad,
    Lie in their chambers apart—

Dead! yet pleading most piteously
In the lonesome City that's sunk in the sea.

Oh, the brave Ventures there lying a wreck,
   Dark on the shore of the Lost!
Gone down with every hope on deck,
   When all-sail for a glorious Coast!
And the waves go sparkling splendidly
Over the City that's sunk in the sea.

Then I look from my City that's sunk in the sea,
   To that Star-Chamber overhead;
And torturingly they question me—
   " What of this world of the Dead
That lies out of sight? and how will it be
With the City and thee, when there's no more sea ?"

HOW IT SEEMS.

STARS in the Midnight's blue abyss
So closely shine, they seem to kiss;
But, Darling, they are far apart;
They close not beating heart to heart:

And high in glory many a Star
Glows, lighting other worlds afar,
Whilst hiding in its breast the dearth
And darkness of a fireless hearth.

All happy to the listener seems
The singer, with his gracious gleams;
His music rings, his ardours glow
Divinely: ah, we know, we know!

D

For all the beauty he sheds, we see
How bare his own poor life may be ;
He gives Ambrosia, wanting bread ;
Makes balm for Hearts, with ache of head.

He finds the Laurel budding yet,
From Love transfigured and tear-wet ;
They are his life-drops turned to Flowers,
That make so sweet this world of ours !

THE WILD-FLOWER.

A VAGRANT Wild-Flower sown by God,
  Out in the waste was born ;
It sprang up as a Corn-flower
  In the golden fields of Corn :
The Corn all strong and stately
  In its bearded bravery grew—
Gathered the gold for harvest
  From earth and sun and dew ;
And when it bowed the head,—as Wind
  And Shadow ran their race,
Like influences from Heaven
  Come to Earth, for playing place,—
It seemed to look down on the Flower
  All in a smiling scorn,
"*Poor thing ! you grow no grain for food,
  Or garner,*" said the Corn.

The bonny Flower felt lonely,
  Its look grew tearful-sad ;
But there came a smile of sunshine
  And its beauty grew so glad !

Ah, bonny Flower! it bloomed its best
  Contented with its place;
A blessing fell upon it
  As it looked up in Heaven's face;
And there they grew together
  Till the Reapers white-winged came—
All their Sickles shining!
  All their faces were a-flame;
The Corn they reaped for earthly use,
  But an Angel fell in love
With that Wild Flower, and wore it
  At the Harvest-Home above!

THE BIRD OF MORN.

Up out of the Corn the Lark carolled in light,
Like a new splendour sprung from the dark hush
    of Night;
Green light shimmered laughing o'er forest and sod;
The rich sky was full of the presence of God.
A fountain of rapture he lavished around
His wealth of bird-fancies in blithest of sound:
All through the Morn's sun-city, sea-like his psalm,
With melodious waves dashed the bright world of
    calm:
But heavily hung the drooped ears of the Corn:
Gathering gold in the dewy morn.

And he sang, as on heaven's fire-grains he had fed,
Till his heart's merry wine had made drunken his
    head.

How he sang! as his honey in Life's cells ne'er
    dwindled,
And bonfires of Joy on all Life's hills were
    kindled:
He sang, as he felt that to singing was given
The magic to build rainbow-stairways to heaven!
And he could not have sung with more lusty cheer,
Had all the world listened a-tiptoe to hear!
    All the while heavily hung the Corn,
    Its drowsy ears heard not the minstrel of Morn.

A BIRD OF NIGHT.

Sing, Birdie, concealed in your Bower,
Sing, Birdie, for this is the hour,
Shake round you the musical shower,
    Like Larks from their cloud in the Spring:

The Star of the twilight is twinkling,
The bicycle bells are a-tinkling,
And I have a prescient inkling
    That Birdie is going to sing.

She sings not for laud or for Lover;
She sings all unseen as the Dove, or
The Nightingale hid in her cover;
    She sings—her delight is to sing!

I seek not my supper or pillow,
My bosom will heave like a billow,
I hang up my harp on the Willow,
    And listen like anything.

Sing, Birdie, when days have been dreary,
Sing, Birdie, when hearts are a-weary,
Sing, Birdie, till spirits grow cheery,
 Sing, Birdie, that never takes wing !

Sing, Birdie, in Spring or September,
From New Year to last of December;
Sing, Birdie, and never remember,
 That any one's listening !

THE LADY OF LIGHT.

STAR of the Day and the Night !
 Star of the Dark that is dying ;
 Star of the Dawn that is nighing,
 Lucifer, Lady of Light !

Still with the purest in white,
 Still art thou Queen of the Seven ;
 Thou hast not fallen from Heaven,
 Lucifer, Lady of Light !

How large in thy lustre, how bright
 The beauty of promise thou wearest !
 The message of Morning thou bearest,
 Lucifer, Lady of Light !

Aid us in putting to flight
 The Shadows that darken about us,
 Illumine within, as without, us,
 Lucifer, Lady of Light !

Shine through the thick of our fight;
  Open the eyes of the sleeping ;
  Dry up the tears of the weeping,
    Lucifer, Lady of Light !

Purge with thy pureness our sight,
  Thou light of the lost ones who love us,
  Thou lamp of the Leader above us,
    Lucifer, Lady of Light !

Shine with transfiguring might,
  Till earth shall reflect back as human
  Thy Likeness, Celestial Woman,
    Lucifer, Lady of Light !

With the flame of thy radiance smite
  The clouds that are veiling the vision
  Of Woman's millennial mission,
    Lucifer, Lady of Light !

Shine in the Depth and the Height,
  And show us the treasuries olden
  Of Wisdom, the hidden, the golden,
    Lucifer, Lady of Light !

LITTLE PEARL.

" Poor little Pearl, good little Pearl ! "
  Sighed every kindly neighbour ;
It was so sad to see a girl
  So tender, doomed to labour.

A wee bird fluttered from its nest
  Too soon, was that meek creature ;
Just fit to rest in mother's breast,
  The darling of fond Nature.

God shield poor little ones, where all
  Must help to be bread-bringers !
For once afoot, there's none too small
  To ply their tiny fingers.

Poor Pearl, she had no time to play
  The merry game of childhood ;
From dawn to dark she went all day,
  A-wooding in the wild-wood.

When others played she stole apart
  In pale and shadowy quiet ;
Too full of care was her child-heart
  For laughter running riot.

Hard lot for such a tender life,
  And miserable guerdon ;
But, like a womanly wee wife,
  She bravely bore her burden.

One wintry day they wanted wood,
  When need was at the sorest ;
Wee Pearl, without a bit of food
  Must up and to the forest.

But there she sank down in the snow,
　All over numbed and aching;
Poor little Pearl, she cried as though
　Her very heart was breaking.

The blinding snow shut out the house
　From little Pearl so weary;
The lonesome wind among the boughs
　Moaned with its warnings eerie.

A Spirit-Child to wee Pearl came,
　With footfall light as Fairy;
He took her hand, he called her name,
　The voice was sweet and airy.

His gentle eyes filled tenderly
　With mystical wet brightness:
" *And would you like to come with me,*
　And wear the robe of whiteness ? "

He bore her bundle to the door,
　Gave her a flower when going;
" *My darling, I shall come once more,*
　When the little bud is blowing. "

Home very wan came little Pearl,
　But on her face strange glory;
They only thought, " *What ails the girl ?* "
　And laughed to hear her story.

Next morn the Mother sought her child,
　And clasped it to her bosom;
Poor little Pearl, in death she smiled,
　And the rose was full in blossom.

———

THE MAIDEN MARRIAGE.

She sat in her virgin bower,
   Half sad with fancies sweet,
And wist not Love drew softly nigh,
   Till she nestled at his feet.
"*Arise, arise, thou fair Maiden;*
   And adieu, adieu, thou dear!
But meet me, meet me at the Kirk,
   In the May-time of the year."

Up in her face of holy grace
   The startled splendour broke;
Her smile was as a dream of heaven
   Fulfilled whene'er she spoke.
She felt such bliss in her beauty,
   Such pleasure in her power
To richly clothe her perfect love
   For a peerless marriage dower.

"*Now kiss me, kiss me, Mother dear;*
   He calls me, I must go!"
She went to the Kirk at tryste-time,
   In raiment like the snow.
But he who clasped her there was Death;
   And he hath led her where
No voice is heard, there is no breath
   Upon the frosty air.

THOU SHALT LOVE THY NEIGHBOUR AS THYSELF.

To love our neighbour, we are told,
"*Even as thyself.*"   That Creed I hold;
But love her more, a thousand-fold!

My lovely Neighbour; oft we meet
In lonely lane, or crowded street;
I know the music of her feet.

She little thinks how, on a day,
She must have missed her usual way,
And walked into my heart for aye.

Or how the rustle of her dress
Thrills through me like a soft caress,
With trembles of deliciousness.

Wee woman, with her smiling mien,
And soul celestially serene,
She passes me, unconscious Queen!

Her face most innocently good,
Where shyly peeps the sweet red blood:
Her form a nest of Womanhood!

Like Raleigh—for her dainty tread,
When ways are miry—I could spread
My cloak, but, there's my heart instead.

Ah, Neighbour, you will never know
Why 'tis my step is quickened so ;
Nor what the prayer I murmur low !

I see you 'mid your flowers at morn,
Fresh as the rosebud newly born ;
I marvel, can you have a thorn ?

If so, 'twere sweet to lean one's breast
Against it, and, the more it pressed,
Sing like the Bird that sorrow hath blessed.

I hear you sing !   And through me Spring
Doth musically ripple and ring ;
Little you think I'm listening !

You know not, dear, how dear you be ;
All dearer for the secrecy :
Nothing, and yet a world to me.

So near, too ! you could hear me sigh,
Or see my case with half an eye ;
But must not.   There are reasons why.

AN APOLOGUE.

It was a goodly Apple,
  The topmost on the Tree,
That golden grew, and sweet all through,
  As Fruit that few could see.

Soft in God's smile it glistened,
  A Crown that might be given,
To man, if he would soar and win
  The Woman nighest Heaven.

Ah! many sighed with longing,
  To see the fruitage drop,
But no one climbed to gather it
  From off the tall tree-top!

And many ran for Apples
  That were rolled along the sod;
But this, which did but tempt toward Heaven,
  Was left alone for God.

The dear ones who are worthiest of our love
Below, are also worthiest above.
Too lofty is his place in glory now,
For hands like ours to reach and wreathe his brow :
A few poor flowers we plant upon his tomb,
Watered with tears to make them breathe and bloom.
The gentle soul that was so long thy ward,
Now hovers over thee, thine Angel-Guard :
And, as thou mourn'st above his dust so dear,
Thy happy Comforter draws smiling near.
　Look up, dear friend, our Doves of Earth but rise,
　Transfigured into Birds of Paradise.

IN MEMORIAM.

APPARELLED richly in presence of the Gods,
With crown upon his brow, the old Greek stood,
And offered up his soul at Sacrifice.
Even then the tidings came,—"THY SON IS DEAD."

They saw the sharp words pierce him through and
　　through,
The firm lip quiver, and the face grow white ;
They saw the strong man tremble to the knees :
Slowly the big drops gathered in his eyes :
Slowly he took the crown from off his head,
And let it fall to the ground, as one who feels
Heart-broke all over,—for his pride of life
Hath faded ; all his strength spilled in the dust.

But, when the Messenger went on to tell
The exulting story—how the valiant youth
Had lost a life to win a country's love;
How bravely he had borne him in the battle;
How well he fought, how gloriously he fell;
The weeping Father put his war-look on,
And rose up with the stature of his soul—
All his life listening at the hungry ear—
Eyes burning with the splendour of quenched
          tears—
His pillared chin firm-set, his brave mouth clenched
In calm resolve to bear, and on his face
A smile as if of Sword-light!
                              Then he stooped,
And gently took the crown up from the ground;
Softly replaced it on his brow, and wore
It proudly, as the visible symbol of
That other awful crown which darkened down.

So, when the word came that our friend was
          dead,
We bowed beneath the burden of our loss,
And could have grovelled straightway, prone in
          dust.
But looking on the happy death he died,
And thinking of the holy life he lived,
And knowing he was one of those that soon
Attain their starry stature, and are crown'd,
We could not linger in the dust to weep,
But were upborne from earth as if on wings;
A sunbeam in the soul dried up the tears,
In which the sorrow trembled to be gone;
For his dear sake we could afford to smile.

Why should we weep, when 'tis so well with him ?
Our loss even cannot measure his great gain !
Why should we weep when death is but a mask
Through which we know the face of Life beyond ?
Grief did but bow us at his grave to show
Far more of Heaven in the landscape round !

For such a vestal soul as his,—so pure,
So crystal-clear, so filled with light, we looked
As at some window of the other world,
And almost saw the Angel smiling through—
'Twas but a step from out our muddy street
Of earth, on to the pavement all of pearl.

Why should we weep?   We do not bury love;
The dust of earth but claims its kindred dust ;
We do not drop our jewels in the grave,
And have no need to seek our treasures there.
We do not bury life, and cannot feel
The grave-grass grow betwixt our warmth and
      him ;
Death emptieth the House, but not the Heart :
That keeps its darlings safe though out of sight.

Let us uplift the eyelids of the Mind,
And see the living Love who dwelt awhile
In that frail body, now a spirit of Light,
All jubilant upon the hills of God.
This gloom we feel, this mourning that we wear,
Is but the Shadow of his lordlier height.

Why should they weep who have another friend
In death ; another thread to guide them through
Life's maze ; another tie to draw them home ;
A firmer foothold in the infinite ;

Another kinsman on the spiritual side ;
Another grasp to greet them through the Void ;
Another face to kindle with its life
The pale impersonality of God ?

The dearest souls, you know, must part in sleep,
Though lying hand in hand, or side by side,
And death is but a little longer night.
A little while, and we shall wake to find
The clasp unbroken by the dark, and see
Our lost ones with us face to face, and feel
All years of yearning summed up in a kiss.

Why should we fear the Grave ?   It is the bed
Where the Kings lay in State with Angels round,
And hallowed it for evermore to us.
Why should we fear the Grave ?   It is the way
The Conquerors went, and made the very dust
Grow starry with the sparkle of their splendour,
And left the darkness conscious of their presence.
We can look down upon the Grave now they
Have plumbed it, spanned it, one foot on each side.

Through their dear love who have abolished death,
We may shut up our Graveyards of the heart,
That looked so grim of old, and plant anew
This garden of our God to smile with flowers.

Why do we shrink so from Eternity ?
We are in Eternity from Birth, not Death !
Eternity is not beyond the stars—
Some far Hereafter—it is *Here*, and *Now !*
The Kingdom of Heaven is within, so near
We do not see it save by spirit-sight.

We shut our eyes in prayer, and we are *There*
In thought, and Thoughts are spirit-*things*—
Realities upon the other side.
In death we close our eyelids once for all
To pass for ever, and seem far away.
And yet the distance does not lie in death ;
No distance, save in dissimilitude !
Death's not the only door of spirit-world,
Nor visibility sole presence-sign :
The Near or Far is in our depth of love
And height of life : We look WITHOUT, to learn
Our lost ones are beyond all human reach :
We feel *Within*, and find them nestling near.

Flow soft, ye tears, adown my Lady's face,
And bathe the broken spirit with your balm,
And melt the cloud about her into drops
That glister with the light of Heaven's own smile.
And thou, God, whisper as the tears do fall,
No cloud would rise to rain but for Thy Sun !
She sorroweth not as those who have no hope,
Nor is her House left wholly desolate.
O Grief, lie lightly on my Lady's brow :
She gave her best of life in love for him !
A crown of glory wears the dear bowed head
That hath grown gray in noble sacrifice.

Ah me, I know the heart must have its way.
I know the ache of utter loneliness ;
The severance between those that were so near .
The silence never broken by a sound
We still keep listening for ; the spirit's loss
Of its old clinging-place, that makes our life
A dead leaf drifting desolately free :

The many thousand things we had to say ;
And on the dear still face that hushing look.
As though it bade us listen and be still ;
As though the sweet life-music still went on,
Though too far off for hearing—(as it doth).
Thrice have I wrestled and been thrown by Death,
Thrice have I given my dear ones to the grave ;
And yet I know—see it in spite of tears :
Say it, even while the heart breaks in the voice :
These are His ways to draw us nearer Him.
We climb our heavens by pathways of the cloud.

He breaks the image to reveal Himself !
He takes our dearest things to woo us with ;
Takes, for a little while, the gift He gave
For ever : but to better still our best.

Feeling for that which fled, our finite love
Is caught up in the clasp o' the Infinite,
Palpably as though God did press the hand
And make the heart well up and flood the eyes
With that proud overflow of fuller Heaven !

O Lady, let mine be the songbird's part,
That singeth after rain, and shakes the drops
Down, with his thrillings from the drooping spray,
And sets it softly springing nigher Heaven
That 'twixt the blown-clouds smiles with gladdest
  blue,
As with the eye of bliss that is to be.
Your love-ties have but lengthened to release
The shadowed soul that needed far more sun.
So the fair Valisneria down the dark
Beside his lover, yearneth towards the light,

And lives up faster, till he springs afloat,
To sun him on the surface of the stream :
And now he draws up, even by the root,
His Love left pining on the earth below,
Lifting her to his side again, full flower ;
And 'tis her Heaven to die and get to him !

What did we ask for him, with all our love,
But just a little breath of fuller life,
To float the labouring lungs ?   And God hath
      given
Him Life itself ; full, everlasting Life.
What did we pray for ?   Rest, even for a night,
That he might rise with Sleep's most cooling dews
Refreshed, to feel the morning in his s ul ?
And God hath given him His Eternal Rest.
We could not offer freedom for one hour
From that dread weight of weariness they bear
Who try for years to shake Death's Shadow off :
And God hath made him free for Evermore.

Before me hangs his Picture on the wall,
Alive still, with the loving, cordial eyes.—
How tenderly their winsome lustre laughed !—
The fine pale face, pathetically sweet,
So thin with suffering that it seemed a soul :
We feared the Angels might be kissing it
Too often, and too wooingly for us :
The hands, so delicate and woman-white,
That day by day were gliding from our gra p,
They used to make my heart ache many a time.

I see another picture now.   The form
Ye sowed in weakness hath been raised in power ;

A palace of pleasure for a prison of pain.
The beauty of his nature that we felt
Is featured in the shape he weareth now!
The same kind face, but changed and glorified;
From Life's unclouded summit it turns back,
And sweetly smiles at all the sorrows past,
With such a look as taketh away grief:
No longer pale, and there is no more pain.
His face is rosed with Heaven's immortal bloom,
For he hath found the land of Health at last;
The One Physician who can cure all ills:
And he hath eaten of the Tree of Life,
And felt the Eternal Spring in brain and breast
Make lusty life that lightens forth in love.

Indeed, indeed, as the old Poet saith,
He was a very perfect, gentle Knight!
A natural Noble, by the grace of God:
Affection in the dearest human form.
Yet, gentle as he was, how gallantly
He bore his sufferings, kept the worst from sight,
Having the heroic flash of English blood.
How freely would he spend his little hoard
Of saved-up strength with spirit lordly and blithe,
To enrich a welcome and make gladder cheer!

And to the Poor he was all tender heart.
The very last time that he talked with me
His trouble was to know how poor folk lived
Upon so small a pittance, and he sighed
For life, for strength to do more than he might,
And in his kingly eyes great sorrow reigned.

No sighs, no weakness now, in that glad world
Where yearning avails more than working here,

And to desire is to accomplish good :
For Wishes get them Wings of power, and range
Rejoicing through illimitable life ;
And we shall find some Castles built in Air
Stand good ; are habitable after all !

To me, his life is like the innocent Flower
That springs up for the light and spreads for love ;
Breathes fragrantly in gratitude to God,
And in sweet odours passes from our sight.
But there's no jot of all his promise lost :—
Each golden hint shall have fulfilment yet—
All that was heavenliest perfected in heaven.

All the shy modesties of secret soul
That breathed like violets hidden in the dusk ;
The folded sweetness, the unfingered bloom ;
The unsunned riches of his rarer self ;
With all the Manhood, coyly unconfessed ;
Are shut up softly to be saved by Him
Who gave us of the Flower, but keeps the fruit.

The best his life could grow on earth is given ;
The rest can ripen till ye meet in heaven.

And, dear my Lady, little can we guess
What God hath planned for those He loves so
      much
And beckons home so early to Himself !
May some full foretaste of His perfect peace
Fall on you, solacing with solemn joy.
Of such as he was, there be few on Earth ;
Of such as he is, there are many in Heaven ;
And Life is all the sweeter that he lived,
And all he loved more sacred for his sake :

And Death is all the brighter that he died,
And Heaven is all the happier that he's there.

So, one by one the dear old faces fade.
Hands wave their far farewell while beckoning us
Across the river all must pass alone.
We stand at gaze upon their shining track,
Until the two worlds mingle in a mist,
And the two lives are molten into one ;
Familiar things grow phantom-like remote ;
Things visionary draw familiar-near ;
The pictures that we gaze on seem the Real
Looking at us ; and we the Shadows that pass.

And yet 'tis sweet to feel—as underfoot,
OUR path slopes for the quiet place apart ;
Day darkens in the Valley of Death's shade—
Our best half landed in the better life ;
The balance leaning to the other side ;
The peaceful evening comes that brings all home,
And we are weaning kindly to leave go
Our hold of earth ; the Home-sigh of the soul
Is daily deepening ; and as the gloom
Gathers, and things are growing all a-dusk,
We know our Stars are smiling overhead,
In their eternal setting high and safe
Where they can look down on our passing night,
Glad in the loftier lustre of a sun
We may not see, with steadfast gaze of love
Unfathomable as Eternity :
Dear memories of Hesper gentleness
That are the Phosphor hopes of coming day,
And death grows radiant with our Shining Ones.

Blessed are they whose treasures are in Heaven !
Their grief's too rich for our poor comforting.
Let us put on the robe of readiness,
The golden trumpet will be sounding soon,
That calls us to the gathering in the Heavens !
Let us press forward to their summit of life
Who have ceased to pant for breath and won their
    Rest,
And there is no more parting, no more pain !

CARMINA NUPTIALIA.

WEDDED LOVE.

This little spring of life, that feeds the root
  Of England's greatness, giveth, undergroun l,
Bloom to the Flower, and freshness to the Fruit ;
  Then wells and spreads, with golden ripples
    round,
In circling glory to a sea of might,
  Embracing Home and Country of our love :
Half-mirroring the beauty beyond sight,
  To take some likeness of the abode above.

THE WEDDING.

ALL Women love a Wedding ! old
    Or youthful ; Mother, Widow, or Wife :
It lights with precious gleam of gold
      The river of poorest life :

For one, the gold is far and dim ;
    For one, a glimpse of things to be ;
But here it sparkles, at the brim
      Of full felicity !

And they will cluster by the way ;
    Crowd at this Eden-gate, with eyes
That run, and pray that this Pair may
      Keep their new Paradise.

Green is the garden, as at first ;
    As smiling-blue the happy skies,
Where float the bubble-worlds that burst,
      And leave us smarting eyes.

They seem to think that these *must* clasp
    The jewel turned to dew or mist :
The glamour they could never grasp,
      Though wedded lips have kissed ;

That this gold Apple of promise, crowned
    With redness on the sunny side,
Will gradually grow ripe all round ;
      That this new Lover and Bride

Must reach the breathing Magic Rose
  Such cunning spirits hold in air,
On which our fingers could not close,
  Even when we knew 'twas there !

This nest of hopes will bring forth young
  Unto the brooding heart's low call—
Not merely pretty birds'-eggs, strung
  To hide a naked wall !

So many start thus, hand-in-hand—
  Few only reach the blessed goal ;
But *these* shall surely see the land
  Hid somewhere in the soul.

And delicate airs creep sweetly through
  Old bridal-chambers dusty and dim :
Down from a far heaven warm and blue,
  The mellow splendours swim.

The Woman's eyes grow loving wet ;
  They dazzle with the morning ray :
The Woman's longing will beget
  Her own dear wedding-day !

In his network of wrinkles, Age
  May veil their virgin beauties now ;
Faces be furrowed—a strange page
  Of writing on the brow :

The smiling soul cannot erase
  The sad life-lines it shines above ;
Yet, imaged in the dear old face,
  You see their own young love !

The sleeping Beauty wakes anew
   Beneath the drops of tender tears ;
The Flower unfolds. to drink the dew,
    That seem'd dead for years.

All hearts are as a grove of birds
   Spring-touched and chirruping every one ;
And each will set the Wedding-Words
    To a music of her own.

Some withered remnant of old bliss
   Flushing on faded cheeks they bring,
Telling of times when Love's young kiss
    Was a fire-offering ;

And spirits walk in white, as starts
   This bridal-tint that blooms anew ;
And so, with all their Woman-hearts,
    They fling Good Luck's old shoe !

———

SERENADE.

" Awake, sweet Love, for Heaven is awake,
And waiting to be gracious for thy sake !
*   All night I saw thy fairness gleam afar*
*   With fresh, pure sparkle of the Morning-Star :*
*   Awake, my Love, and be the veil withdrawn*
*   From Beauty bathèd at the springs of Dawn.*

" Awake, sweet Love, for Heaven is awake
And waiting to be gracious for thy sake.

A touch upon some silver-sounding string,
As all the harps of heaven were vibrating
Within me, woke me, bade me rise and say,
' Awake, my Love, this is our Wedding-day.'

" Awake, sweet Love, for Heaven is awake,
And waiting to be gracious for thy sake.
It is the tender time when turtle-doves
Begin to murmur of their vernal loves :
Spirits that all night nestled in the flowers
Shake perfume from their wings this hour of
    hours.

" Awake, sweet Love, for Heaven is awake,
And waiting to be gracious for thy sake.
Thy presence sets my cloudland round about
Glowing as heaven were turning inside out :
And all the mists that darkened me erewhile
Are smitten into splendours at thy smile.

' Awake. sweet Love, for Heaven is awake
And waiting to be gracious for thy sake.
To feel thee mine my faith is large enough,
And yet the miracle needs continual proof !
One minute satisfied, the next I pine
For just one more assurance thou art mine.

" Awake, sweet Love, for Heaven is awake,
And waiting to be gracious for thy sake.
Our great sunrise of life begins to glow,
And all the buds of love are ripe to blow ;
And all the Birds of Bliss are gaily singing,
And all the Bells of Heaven for bridal ringing."

ARGUING IN A CIRCLE.

" WHEN first my true Love crowned me with her
*   smile,*
Methought that heaven encircled me the while !
When first my true Love to mine arms was given,
Ah, then methought that I encircled Heaven."

AN APRIL WEDDING.

O APRIL Wedding,
    Sad-smiling, shadowy-bright ;
The Grave at foot, and overhead
    The merry Bird of Light !

O April Wedding,
    The conscious ear at times
Detects the Bell that tolled the knell
    Among the Marriage-Chimes !

O April Wedding,
    Thy hues together run,—
Through wet eyes seen,—as Red and Green
    Will dazzle and grow one !

O April Wedding,
    Where Love is crowned in tears,
And on a ground of deepest gloom,
    Hope's brightest Bow appears !

O April Wedding,
  Thy clouds go all in white;
Those that darkliest wept are now
  Most glorified in light!

O April Wedding,
  Glittering in sun and showers
The very grave looks glad To-day,
  And dead hands offer flowers!

LEAVE-TAKING.

When the wings are feathered,
  The birds forsake their nest;
So the Bride will leave her Home
  Leaning to her Lover's breast.
The tear was in her eye,
  But the soul was smiling through,
Brimful of sunshine
  As a drop of summer dew.

AS THEY PASSED.

Within Love's chariot, side by side,
Sweetness and Strength did never ride
More perfectly personified:
  One of the dearest Angels out
  Of Heaven, the Bride was, beyond doubt;
And his a Manhood fit to be
The mortal Mansion of some deity.

All eyes, like jewels, on them hung
  Glowing with precious life,
As at her Husband's side she clung,
  The nestled, new-made Wife!
Glad were they in the happiness they gave,
But in their own proud pleasure they were grave.

EVOË.

In the presence of Spring, *our* beautiful Spring,
Blithe bird of the bosom! the heart will sing.
A Spirit of Joy in the oldest breast
Is stirring, and making it young as the rest:
Quickens new life to leap in each limb,
And laugh out of eyes that were wintry and dim;
So the old Wine stirs in his winter gloom,
And wants to waken, and climb, and bloom,
As he used to do in the world outside,
When the grapes grew big in their purple of pride.
He would laugh in the light, he would flush in the
    foam;
In a care-drowning wave he would rosily roam;
For his blood is so mellow, so merry, so warm,
Into spirit of joy it would fain transform,
Rioting ruddily, ripple and play,
And in human life keep holiday—
Break on the brain in a luminous spray,
Tinting with heaven our earthiest clay;
In a fiery chariot mount on his way,
With spirit-company, lordly and gay,
And pass like a soul that is lost in day.

So the Spirit of Joy in the oldest breast
Is stirring, and making it young as the rest ;
Wakes a new life to leap in each limb,
And laugh out of eyes that were wintry and dim.
Blithe bird of the bosom ! the heart will sing
In the presence of Spring, *our* beautiful Spring.

ENGLISH John Talbot, Shakspeare's terribly brave,
Great Fighter, lay in his forgotten grave.
It was but yesterday they found his dust,
The sheath of that old Sword long gone to rust
In English earth ; his burial-place recover
In lands owned by a certain Lordly Lover.
And, lo ! a Rose had sprung from out his tomb,
And climbed about the Lover's life to bloom :
A peerless flower of the old Hero's stock—
The tenderest gush from that heroic rock.
Not oft doth Fate vouchsafe so plain a sign,
Prefiguring the lives that are to twine.
All sweetness to this wedded life be given ;
Its root so deep in earth, its perfect flower in
    heaven.

A WAYSIDE WHISPER.

" *SEVEN years I served for you,*
   To Love, our lord of life,
Ere he made me a Master
   And I won you for my wife,—

So faithfully, so fondly,
  Through a world of doubts and fears,
Seven long years, Belovèd!
  Seven long years.

" Seven years you beaconed me—
  My leading, crowning star,
To climb the Mount of Manhood,
  As you drew me from afar:
You made my gray hours golden,
  You glistened through my tears,
Seven long years, Belovèd!
  Seven long years.

" Sometimes you shined so near me—
  Wide as we dwelt apart—
I hardly sought you with my arms,
  You were so safe at heart!
Sometimes you dwined so distant,
  I bowed with solemn fears;
Seven long years, Belovèd!
  Seven long years.

" I built my Arch of Triumph
  For you to ride through;
I kept my lamps all lighted
  That the warring winds outblew:
I worked and I waited,
  And I fought down my fears,
Seven long years, Belovèd!
  Seven long years.

" Now the perils are all over,
  And the pains all past,

My fortune's wheel full-circle comes
In your dear eyes at last!
For such a prize the winning
Most brief and poor appears,
Yet, 'twas seven long years, Belovèd!
Seven long years."

THE WELCOME HOME.

Warm is the Welcome! 'tis our way to grasp
  The hand in love or greeting till it ache;
  But to a tender heart our love doth take
The happy pair it doth so proudly clasp.

And very tender in its love To-day
  Is every heart touched with a thought of Him
  Low-lying in the Cypress-shadow dim,
From which we came to waft you on your way,

And the still face, that looks from Ashridge towers
  With smile more regnant in its touching ruth,
  And sad hoar-frost upon the dews of youth.
And Widow's weeds to mix with bridal-flowers.

Through Him we lost, we have more love to give.
  As some fond Mother yearningly hath breathed
  Her life out in the new life she bequeathed,
Our dearest died that this great love might live.

These darling Violets eloquently mute,
  Are rich in sadder bloom and sweeter breath,
  And that pathetic sanctity of death,
Because our buried joy was at their root.

These Roses blush with a more vital glow
   Of crimson—like pale buds, whose tips are red,
   As though the flower's heart, in breaking, bled—
Because of looks so lately wan with woe.

These are our Jewels! tears that purged our sight
   Like Euphrasy; they lay above the Dead
   All drear and dim; but the sad drops we shed
Now live with twinkling lustres in Your light!

The love that darkly wept at heart hath risen
   Transfigured. See its sunburst in each face!
   As Earth, with all her flowers, smiles embrace
To Spring, rejoicing from her wintry prison.

These Voices, mounting merry as Larks up-spring,
   But now were praying on the low, cold sod:
   The night is past—they soar in praise to God;
They make the old English greeting rarely ring.

We lean and look to You, thinking of Him.
   Warm welcome for the sake of One that's gone;
   Warm welcome for your own! Pass on, pass on;
We wave our hands, and shout till sight grows dim:

And, ere the shouts cease ringing in your ears,
   We drink a health—all standing—drink to you,
   While in our eyes the tears are standing too:
Old tears, that wanted to be wept for years:

But keep a holy hush 'mid all the noise,
   To match the silent music your hearts make:
   Pass on into your faëry heaven, and take
Our gentlest blessing on your wedding joys.

F 2

The dawn *will* rise, though golden days be set ;
　The birds sing merrily, in spite of Death ;
　　Young hearts will love while lasts this human
　　　　breath ;
Rainbows bridge Earth and Heaven for eyes tear-
　　　　wet.

Pass *gaily* on in glory through the gate
　Of your new life, beneath this Bridal-Dawn ;
　And when from future days the veil is drawn
All happy fortunes for you lie in wait !

And, looking on your bliss, with proudest flush
　May the dear Mother's face be glorified.
　　We, now the sound hath ceased, will stand
　　　　outside
Your Portals—all hearts praying 'mid the hush.

THE BONNY BRIDELAND FLOWER.

　In the Brideland sleeping,
　　Nestled Beauty's Flower ;
　Came the Lover peeping
　　Into her green bower ;
　On her face hung tender
　　As a drop of dew ;
　With her virgin splendour
　　Thrilling through and through.

　Now, the shy, sweet maiden
　　Softly droops her head :
　All her heart is laden
　　With his coming tread !

Now the new dawn breaketh
    In a blush of bliss ;
The Belovèd waketh
    At her Troth-love's kiss.

In our dull gray weather
    We have seen her bloom ;
Fain as Exiles gather
    Round some flower from Home ;
Seen the face that never
    Fades away, but gleams,
With its still smile, ever
    Through the land of Dreams.

Fair befall the bonny,
    Bonny Brideland flower !
All things dear and sunny
    Bless her bridal bower !
Truest love e'er given
    Feed her new life-root ;
And thou God in heaven,
    Crown the flower with fruit.

A LOVER'S SONG.

" One so fair—none so fair.
    In her eyes so true
Love's most inner Heaven bare
    To the balmiest blue !

" One so fair—none so fair.
    In the skies no Star
Like my Star of Earth so near—
    They but shine afar.

" One so fair—none so fair.
All too sweet it seems :
Wake me not, O world of care,
If I walk in dreams.

" One so fair—none so fair.
O my bosom-guest,
Love ne'er smiled a happier pair
To the bridal-nest.

" One so fair—none so fair.
Lean to me, sweet Wife :
Light will be the load we bear :
Two hearts in one life."

THE MARRIED LIFE.

O HAPPY love of weans and Wife,
Ye make a man's heart dance ;
Kindle the desert face of life
With colours of romance :

A Land of Promise sparkles where
Your rosier light hath shone ;
Too distant to attain, but near
Enough to tempt us on.

'Tis here that Heaven striketh root
To give the Immortal birth,
Man tastes the unforbidden fruit
That deifies on earth.

All ye that such a Garden own,
  Of wingèd thieves beware,
And trifles, light as thistle-down,
  That sow the seeds of care.

Only in singleness of heart,
  Ye keep the heaven ye win!
When Wife and Husband pull apart
  The Serpent glideth in.

VIA CRUCIS VIA LUCIS.

SPITE of the Mask Eternal Love doth wear
At times, that makes us shrink from it in fear,
Because the Father's face we cannot find,
Nor feel the presence of His love behind,
Nature at heart is very pitiful.

How gentle is the hand doth kindly pull
The coverlet of flowers o'er the face
Of Death, and light up his dark dwelling-place!
With fingers and with foot-fall soft and low
She comes to make the quiet mosses grow:
Safe-smiling, draws the Snowdrop through the snow.
Busy in sun and rain, she strives to heal,
Doing her best to comfort or conceal:
With tenderest grass makes green the saddest
    grave,
And over death her flags of life *will* wave.
She is the Angel, waiting by the prison,
That saith, "*He is not here, he is arisen,*"

When lorn in soul we seek the face we knew,
And dream of buried sweetness coming through
The earth in spring-time, every flower a smile
Of that dear Presence we have lost awhile.

Thus, on our old Crimean battle-ground,
A poor, unknown, dead Soldier's bones were
  found—
(*Known* with those noble Englishmen of ours!)
When the next May came with her sweet Wild
  Flowers,
Nestled they lay above-ground in a grave
Of tall, plumed grass, funereally a-wave
In the West wind that breathed of Home: and
  tender
There rose from earth a dawn of such spring-
  splendour,
As if the heavens were breaking through the tomb:
The Wild Flowers had so buried them in bloom.

And, if we lift our eyes up from the ground,
We see how surely life is compassed round
With the Divine, that doth so kindly bound
The pitiless blaze of fires that soon would scorch
To ashes and put out our tiny torch
Of being; veil the vastness of the Whole,
As with drooped eyelids for the naked soul.
The silent Ministers of Healing crowd
About the broken heart and spirit bowed,
To stay the bleeding with immortal balm,
And still the cries with lips of blessèd calm;
Out of the old death make the new life spring,
Our earthly-buried hopes take heavenward wing;
And to each blinding tear that dimmed our sight,
They give a starrier self; a Spirit of Light.

No matter in what separate lives we range,
We feel a rootage deeper than all change.
We know the roses flower to fade : We know
The roses also fade again to blow.
Death is Life's Shadow!

                Mute the music looks,
And dark and dead when shadowed forth in books :
Do but interpret it, all heaven will roll
The Life of Music through the echoing soul.

So we grow friends, familiar friends, with Death ;
Can look up in his face with firmer faith,
To see the frowning brows shade tender eyes,
Like sunny openings into Paradise.

Through all the gloom and stillness of distress,
With life all muffled up in silentness,
We voyage on — ice-locked, snow-blind, frost-
    bound—
Like Sailors with the Arctic winter round,
Who thought they stranded in the dark, and found
The solid water all one floating ground ;
And drifted through the night, divinely drawn,
Out to the open sea, where daylight shone.

The Shadow of Death is changed into the Dawn,
That radiant Angel of Eternity !
The mourners look up from the grave to see
The dark, that bowed them by its awfulness,
Fell from the Father's hands, spread out to bless.
So, in His own good season, God hath given
This beautiful Joy-Bringer from His Heaven,
To bear His benediction from above,
And be the smiling Presence of His love !

Though heaviness endureth for a night,
Joy cometh with the morning.   Lo! the Light.
Gone is the winter from our spirit-clime;
This is the herald of our golden time.
In all the beauty of promise, Spring is here—
Our Spring—that will be with us all the year.

O, beautiful Joy-Bringer! everywhere
Happiness smiles around you, like an air
Of glory, which you dwell in—Starrily-fair!
The lives that have in mourning darkling lain
Now gather colour; sun them once again.
The tender shine that cometh after rain
Illumes the eyes of old heart-ache : the pain
Of loss transmuted to all-golden gain.

Just now we are in the shadow of great change,
And faces darken, and old things grow strange ;
And from the new Unknown a many shrink.
Our world is getting tilted, Sages think.
" *The wine of life is drawn, and the mere lees*"
All that is left us.   Shame on fears like these!
Whate'er Eclipse may come, storm-signals threat,
We are English yet, my friends, true English yet.
We are standing in the shadow of some sublime
Wide-wingèd Angel of the coming time.
No need to wring our own hands.   Let us clasp
Each other's strongly with a manlier grasp.
No fear the pillars of the house will fall
Because we brush our cobwebs from the wall.
Exultingly, O storm-winds, rise and roll
All misty blight from off the stagnant soul,
And lift its trailing wing to winnow through
The cloudy heaven, and bare it to the blue.

As in the very heart of Hope we'll ride,
Borne on the ninth wave of our triumph's tide,
That with its new life heaves Old England's
    breast,
To lift the lowly, succour the oppressed ;
Only be loyal to the Loftiest.
Arise and crown old sanctities anew,
By nobler conquest make your lordship true ;
Awake the spirit in our English blood,
That slowly brightens to the fervid flood,
And does not flash till the leap comes that shows
Power all the lustier for its long repose.
And if the proudest Nobles have to bow,
Then let it be as Rowers bend to row
A sturdier stroke ; and faint not, though ye know
Not under what dark arch we have to go :
But win the nod of an approving soul,
Even though ye never reach your chosen goal.

O ! young hearts, dancing to the rise and fall
Of life's most winsome tune at festival,
Looking on your new world wherein ye move
With all the large, sweet wonder of young
    love,
The moments thronging with the life of years ;
Crowded with happiness and quick to tears ;
New smiles of greeting in each minute's face ;
New worlds of pleasure brimming every space ;
This is no winter-withered earth to you.
Love comes, and life is deified anew !
And hearts grow larger than their fortunes are,
The horizon lifts around, sublime and far,
With god-like breathing-space—an ample scope
For loftier life, and glorious ground for hope.

Turn, happy Lovers, turn on those below
A little of the light in which ye glow;
A little of your sunshine round you shed,
And make our old world blossom where ye tread.
Bring back a little seed from Eden-bowers
To sow our fallows with immortal flowers.
Ah ! Nobles, what a chance is yours to be
The founders of a lordlier Chivalry !
And, with the proud old fire this people lead.
When they were weak. I threatened; now I plead,
Give eyes to their blind strength, for great the
    need.

The *Word* of *Life* is well-nigh preached to death ;
The Flower of all sweetness withereth,
Crushed in the grip of many that handle it,
As though they thought Life would but yield its
    sweet
In giving up the breath ; shut the live flower
In a dead Book, and kill it every hour
By reason of their clasp :
                      We want the Book
Translated into life, not the mere look
Of Life embalmed and shrouded in the Book.
We want the life indeed, quick in the lives
Of Fathers, Mothers. Children, Husbands, Wives.
We need the life itself—lived in the Home
On Week-days, ere, the Sabbath-rest will come
To many a homeless hungerer for home.

We pray " *Thy Kingdom Come.* "   But not by
    prayer
Can it be ever built of breath in air.
In life through labour, must be brought to birth
The Kingdom ; as it is in heaven, on Earth.

The light that left Heaven centuries ago
Hath not yet reached dark myriads here below:
Your lives should be the lamp that bears this light,
Still burning, as the stars through all the night.
Because ye are looked up to, they would mark
Your shining!
        O, the spirits lying dark
To-day, as jewels waiting but the spark
Of splendour that to Love's dear smile is given,
To brighten with the best that brighten Heaven!
Look down, you Shining Ones, look kindly down,
And save them, set as jewels in your crown.

How beautiful upon the mountain height,
The feet of them that bring the Lowly light —
O'ershadowing, on wings of gentle Love,
The faults and failings that they soar above!
How beautiful the face of those whose smile
Doth make rare sunshine in the heart of Toil;
In low, sick rooms a presence as of Health;
The true Rich folk, in whom the Poor have wealth!
A beautiful life begets itself anew
In other lives, as perfume stealing through
The sense creates the flower to live again;
Its spirit re-embodied in the brain.

Heartfull of shining love and singing hopes,
Come down where life, blind-folded, gnome-like
    gropes.
We house the Poor to lie and die.   But give
Them room to stand in; house the Poor to live;
A little touch of clasping hands might prove
Mightiest of all the languages of Love.

Give them a glimpse of kindlier, sweeter grace,
And be the model of a nobler race—
The living Poem that we may not write;
The Picture that we cannot paint to sight;
The Music that we dream but do not get;
The Statue marble never mirrored yet.

Now while the Thrush upon the barest bough
Stands piping high in azure, telling how
The Spring-wind wanders where the Children go
A-violeting by the warm hedge-row;
Daily more rich the Sallow-palms unfold
And change their silver-gray for sunny gold;
" *Good-bye, Old Winter*," the blue heavens laugh;
" *The flowers shall write you a kindly epitaph*,"
Far on a sea of Light the twinkling Lark
Is launched, and floating like a heaven-bound
        bark,
In which some happy spirit sails and sings,
And stirs us in a dream of waking wings,
With homeward yearnings, heavenward flutterings,
As all about the inner life there plays
A breath of bliss from out old innocent days,—
Now, while the Spring mounts somewhere up the
        blue,
We bring our firstling flowers to offer you!
Violets, dim and tender; glad Primroses,
That promise, ere the happy prospect closes,
Ye, hand in hand, through rosier days shall tread
Green earth, with richer glories garlanded;
Where the wild Hyacinths, all a-dreaming, lean,
In peeps of deep sea-azure through the green;
And Summer sets that Golden Age of hers
A-bloom, in mellow miles of yellow Furze;

While, smiling down the distance, Autumn stands,
The ripened fruitage glowing in his hands.

And, if among the flowers some few appear
Sacred to woe, and leaning with the tear
Still in the eyes, I did but seek the leaf
Of Healing—gather Heartsease for the grief :
Nor are they tears, but rather drops of dew
From heaven, that hidden Love is looking through.

As, after death, our Lost Ones grow our Dearest,
So, after death, our Lost Ones come the nearest :
They are not lost in distant worlds above ;
They are our nearest link in God's own love—
The human hand-clasps of the Infinite,
That life to life, spirit to spirit knit !
They fill the rift they made, like veins of gold
In fire-rent fissures torture-torn of old ;
With sweetness store the empty place they left,
As of wild honey in the rock's bare cleft.
In hidden ways they aid this life of ours,
As Sunshine lends a finger to the flowers,
Shadowed and shrouded in the Wood's dim heart,
To climb by while they push their grave apart.

They think of us at Sea, who are safe on Shore ;
Light up the cloudy coast we struggle for !
The ancient terror of Eternity—
The dark destroyer, crouching in Life's sea
To wreck us—is thus Beaconed, and doth stand
As our Deliverer, with a lamp in hand.
We would not put them from us when we are sad ;
We will not shut them from us when we are glad ;

Nor thrust our Angel from the Marriage Feast,
Although he comes, not clothèd like the rest
In visible garment of a Wedding-Guest.

Now pray we.
                    Lord of Life, look smiling down
Upon this Pair; with choicest blessings crown
Their love; the beauty of the Flower bring
Back to the bud again in some new spring!
Long may they walk the blessèd life together
With wedded hearts that still make golden weather,
And keep the chill of winter far aloof
With inward warmth when snow is on the roof;
Wed in that sweet for-ever of Love's kiss,
Like two rich notes made one in bridal bliss.

We would not pray that sorrow ne'er may shed
Her dews along the pathway they must tread:
The sweetest flowers would never bloom at all
If no least rain of tears did ever fall.
In joy the soul is bearing human fruit;
In grief it may be taking divine root.

Come joy or grief, nestle them near to Thee
In happy love twin for eternity!
They take our Darling's place; long may they be
As glad and beautiful a hope as he
Hath left a bright and blessèd memory:
Their day fulfil the promise of his dawn—
That, as with Thee, he may with us live on.

ANCIENT EGYPT.

Egypt ! how I have dwelt with you in dreams,
So long, so intimately, that it seems
As if you had borne me ; though I could not know,
It was so many thousand years ago !
And in my gropings darkly underground
The long-lost memory at last is found
Of Motherhood—you Mother of us all !
And to my fellow-men I must recall
The memory too ; that common Motherhood
May help to make the common brotherhood.

Egypt ! it lies there in the far-off past,
Opening with depths profound and growths as vast
As the great valley of Yosemité ;
The birthplace out of darkness into day ;
The shaping matrix of the human mind ;
The Cradle and the Nursery of our kind.
This was the land created from the flood,
The land of Atum, made of the red mud,
Where Num sat in his Teba throned on high,
And saw the deluge once a year go by,
Each brimming with the blessing that it brought,
And by that water-way, in Egypt's thought,
The Gods descended ; but they never hurled
A Deluge that should desolate the world.

There the vast Hewers of the early time
Built, as if that way they would surely climb

G

The heavens; and left their labours without name—
Colossal as their carelessness of fame—
Sole likeness of themselves—that heavenward
For ever look with statuesque regard,
As if some Vision of the Eternal grown
Petrific, was for ever fixed in stone!
They watched the Moon re-orb, the Stars go round,
And drew the Circle; Thought's primordial bound.
The Heavens looked into them with living eyes,
To kindle starry thoughts in other skies,
For us reflected in the image-scroll
That night by night the stars for aye unroll.

The Royal Heads of Language bow them down
To lay in Egypt's lap each borrowed crown.
The light of Asia was of Afric born;
Africa, dusky Mother of the Morn;
She bore the Babe-Messiah meek and mild,
The Good Lord Horus, the Eternal child:
The unhistoric Saviour,—hence divine—
Buddha in India; Christ in Palestine!
The glory of Greece was but the After-glow
Of her forgotten greatness lying low.
Her Hieroglyphics buried dark as night,
Or coal-deposits filled with future light,
Are mines of meaning; by their light we see
Through many an overshadowing mystery.

The nursing Nile is living Egypt still,
And as her lowlands with its freshness fill,
And heave with double-breasted bounteousness,
So doth the old Hidden Source of Wisdom bless
The nations; secretly she brought to birth,
And Egypt yet enriches all the earth.

EGYPTIAN ELYSIUM.

Wʜo ploughed and sowed as Mortals, and their
 furrows straightly drew,
They are Gods that reap, says Horus, in the Aah-
 en-Ru.

The bark of Khepr bears us, with the good fruits
 that we grew ;
Let them sweat who have to tow it to the Aah-
 en-Ru !

The Gods at rest are hailing the endeavours of our
 Crew,
As the Solar Bark goes sailing for the Aah-en-Ru.

Strike the Ap-Ap monster breathless ; break his
 bones, in pieces hew
The coils he rings them with who voyage to the
 Aah-en-Ru !

We can never die again ; we shall soar as spirits do ;
No more turning into Reptiles in the Aah-en-Ru.

We shall make our Transformations, and in linen
 pure of hue,
We shall work in white for ever in the Aah-en-Ru.

We shall find the old lost faces and the nestling
        young that flew
Like Hawks divine, gold-feathered, to the Aah-
    en-Ru.

We shall see the good Osiris and his son the Word-
    made-True,
Who died and rose—the Karest!—in the Aah-en-
    Ru.—

He who daily dies to save us, passing Earth and
        Hades through ;
Lays his life down for a pathway to the Aah-en-Ru.

Lo! the Cross of life uplifted in the region of
        Tattu,
With its arms outstretched for welcome to the
        Aah-en-Ru !

We shall follow in the Gateways that our God hath
        travelled through :
He will meet us, he will greet us, in the Aah-en-Ru.

Here we talk of all the glory that each morning
        doth renew,
We shall share it, we shall wear it, in the Aah-
    en-Ru.

Here we filled the Eye of Horus, here we fed the
        Eye of Shu,
To be luminous for ever in the Aah-en-Ru.

———

THE KRONIAN GODS.

AYE keeping their eternal track,
   The Deities of old
Went to and fro, and there and back,
   In boats of starry gold.

For ever true, they cycled round
   The Heavens, sink or climb;
To boundless dark a radiant bound,
   And, to the timeless, Time:

Till mortals looking forth in death
   Across the deluge dark,
Besought the Gods to save their breath
   In Light's Celestial Ark.

To the revolving Stars they prayed,
   While sinking back to Earth;
" *In passing through the world of Shade,*
   Oh, give us thy re-birth! "

And ever a Sun beyond the Sun
   Quickened the human root
With longings after life, that run
   And spring with heavenward shoot.

Their yearnings kindled such a light
   Within them, so divine,
That Death encompassed them with night,
   To show the starrier shine.

PROTOPLASM.

(PROFESSOR OF PHYSICS *LOQUITUR*.)

THE marvel of it is that when you have
Your Protoplasm perfect, Life is there
Already with its spontaneities,
Its secret primal powers all at work ;
Currents of force unfollowably swift ;
Unceasing gleams of glory ungraspable ;
Pulses of pleasure and sharp stings of pain ;
Flashes of lightning fastened up in knots,
And passion-fires bound down in prison cells.
All's there, when we can say 'tis Protoplasm.

Lymph, serum, semen, blood, or nettle-juice,
Are worlds of life, and glassy seas of life,
That heave with life, and spawn and swarm with
      life ;
A universe of life that lurks behind
The infinitely little as the large ;
Life-giving and life-taking ; fierce with life
As though the hive of life rushed forth on wings,
Or some life-furnace shed its fire in sparks ;
Moving to harmonies unutterable
Through the surrounding dark, and beautiful
As planetary wheelings in the heavens.

Nor can you have your Matter unmixed with
    Mind;
The Consciousness it comes from, with the intent
That is fulfilled in Consciousness to be!
For there's no particle of Protoplasm
Panting with life, like a bird newly caught,
As with a heart-beat out of the Unseen,
But comes with all its secret orders sealed
Within it, safe as crumpled fronds of fern,
To be unfolded in due season; all
Potentialities of tendency,
Initial forces of diversity
And modes of motion which are forms of thought;
Likings, dislikings, all are there at work
When we can say life *is* in Protoplasm.
And that's creation seen; caught in the act,
Although the Actor be invisible.

'Tis no use thrusting in the earth one's head
To be annihilated from behind.
Here is the fact that must be faced in front.
'Tis no use varnishing the face of things
Merely to see one's own reflected there!
This Matter of life will not make Life itself,
No more than Matter of thought will make the
    Thinker.
We have more Matter of thought than Shakspeare
    had,
But no more Shakspeares in our mental world.

Life is the unfathomable miracle
That mocks us mutely, while we prate of Law,
At just that distance from the surface where
Its features loom the largest as it lurks.

Form is but fossil : life's the running spring.
We see the rhythmic thrills that come and go,
But Life itself is always just beyond—
Is not precipitated, as the pearl,
Within our grasp, however deep we dive.
'Tis like the first star in the twilight heaven
You lie in wait for, never see it coming,
Catch the first twinkle ; suddenly 'tis there,
As though it watched you while you winked, and
    was
There, had been, busy, from eternity.

In vain you look for life beginning ; 'tis
But known to us in its becoming ! 'tis
Illimitable continuity !
In vain you try to untwist it to the end
That snaps off like the Periwinkle's tail.

We feel through all the universe to touch
The physical, and find it all alike,
Here underfoot the same as overhead,
Dust of the earth or glory of the star,
The Matter yields no closer clasp of Life.

We build our Babels higher than of old
Firmer, but get no nearer Heaven that way :
On the outside of things we stand to rear
Our scaffolding, while Life works from within.

Life haunts me like a Ghost that's never laid,
Yet wavering ever as a face in water.
I shift my ground, I quit my premises,
I seek an undisturbed abiding-place,
As the poor Peasant left his haunted house
To flee from its old ghostly visitant

For peace of mind ; and mid-way on the road
To his new dwelling heard the Ghost's wee voice,
From out the middle of a feather-bed,
Or God knows where, cry, " AND I'M FLITTING TOO!"

No sooner do I set my world on wheels,
Atom revolving round its fellow mite,
The universe in little grasped by Law,
Than there's a living face within the wheels,
As in the Prophet's vision.   I'm no prophet,
And had no wish to see a spirit ; wheels
Were made to run and carry, not to dazzle
And dizzy us until our eyes strike spirits—
That puts a new face on the matter, or
The Soul of things must make a face at me !

I get a good grip-hold of things themselves,
And then am lost in their relationships.
No sooner have I pitched my tent in Matter,
And feel it firm to rest on, palpable,
Tangible as a tombstone underfoot,
Than 'tis a sieve that lets the quick life through ;
There is a general rising from the Dead,
And rending of the veil ; the grave's astir
As though each atom were the womb of Life ;
Twixt each two atoms there's a gulf of God ;
My atom is afloat, adrift with me ;
It rocks and quakes like any modern throne ;
No anchorage in all Immensity !

O'erhead I draw the cloud of darkness round
About me, proof against the common light,
When lo ! the gloom begins to laugh at me ;
The life breaks in and out, darts through and
    through,

Like Lightning playing at hide-and-seek with me;
Darkness is freaked and shattered with that laugh
Zig-zagged upon the face of the Unknown.

This light within, that will break through the seen,
Cannot be phosphorescence from the dead
And luminosity of mere decay,
A corpse-light of the Grave, or else the Soul
Of all were but a gleam through a dead skull,
Lit up to show the eyeless emptiness,
And Death would be sole quickener of Life.

'Tis in the shadow cf the Sepulchre
Perchance I sit to watch and wait in vain
For that which must arise within myself
To lighten through me and illuminate
My seeing; touch mine ear to hear the voice—
"I am the resurrection and the life;
Presence that lives in light and looks through form;"
And he who hides without must bring to light
The meaning by his presence in the soul.
Perchance God speaks to us in parable,
And Matter is but symbol used by Mind,
The visible show that needs interpreting
By second-sight to read the eternal thought;
And I am as a blind man, one who feels
The letters raised, shaped to the sense of touch,
But have not learned to read what they reveal,
So miss the letter-link from soul to soul.

*He breathed the breath of life and man became
A living soul*—with power to propagate
The spark His breath yet kindles into soul?
And is He breathing yet, as at the first,

This breath of life through all things?　Is his
　　breath
Our *motion*—wave of the Eternal Will
In Evolution welling, warm with love?
Are laws that fold us arms of His embrace?
And is life visible breathing of His being?
Matter but so much breath made visible—
The cloud-mask shifting on the Protean face;
And is it need of Him that makes us breathe?
And so we live and have our life in Him
Who is the life indeed for evermore;
The heart of Life whose throbs are visible worlds
Of men and women and immortal souls?

So the voice murmurs when I shut my eyes
And lean and listen on some crumbling verge,
And hear the waters in the well of life
Sing, as they bubble with an eye to heaven,
And might know more could I but drink, but have
Nothing to draw with, and the well's so deep!

A POET'S LOVE-LETTER.

You ask me, Friend, to tell you of my Wife !
And on what stair or landing-place of life
I met, as 'twere, God's Angel coming down,
Or mine ascending, for her marriage crown.

I say you sooth, however strange it seem,
The first time that I saw her was in dream :
A vision of the night did clearly glass
Her living lineaments.   I saw her pass
Smiling, as those may smile who feel they hold
At heart safe-hidden, secret fold on fold,
The sweetest love that ever was untold.
And as it went the Vision flashed on me
A moment's look ; a lifetime's memory.
But little could I dream that this should prove
The whole wide world's one lady of my love.
I had never seen that face or form, and yet
I knew them both by daylight when we met.

Blind World ! to pass, and pass my darling by,
My lily of the vale, where she did lie
Sheathed in her own green leaves, and never see
The flower hid-in-waiting there for me,
With cloudy fragrance all about her curled ;
And yet my blessings on thee, O blind World !

It is so sweet to find with one's own eyes,
Led by divine good-hap, to her surprise,
Our Perdita, our Princess in disguise!
The eye that finds must bring the power to see;
(Says Goëthe's doctrine, comforting to me!)
And now she's found, the world would give me
    much
Could I but tell it of another such.

Is she an Angel?
            Let us not forget,
My friend, that WE are scarcely Angels yet.
At least my modest soul would not be pledged
To call itself an Angel fully fledged:
Flesh is so frail, nor am I very sure
Of being, in spirit, altogether pure!
Snags of old broken sins torment me still
With pains that Death itself will hardly kill.
If not an Angel, let the truth be told,
I have not grasped the glitter—missed the Gold.
And lucky is the man who gets the gold,
Refined and fitted for the marriage mould!
Still happier who can keep it pure to bear
The final features of immortal wear.
She is of Angel-stuff; but I'm afraid
The Angels are not given us ready-made:
In other worlds, this Wife of mine may be
The perfect public Angel all may see;
At present she's a private one for me—
My household deity of Common Things,
That into lowly ways a beauty brings,
Just as the grass comes creeping, making bright
And blessèd, with its ripples of delight
And quiet smiles, all pathways dim and bare.

Is she a Beauty?
      Well, I will not swear
A thousand beauties with her beauty blend ;
A thousand graces on her Grace attend ;
Or that she is so pitilessly fair
Each passer-by must turn, or stop, or stare,
And he on whom she looks feels instantly
As one that springs from dust to deity.
Nor can I sing of outer symbols now—
The swan-white stately neck; the snow-white brow;
The lip's live rose ; the head superbly crowned ;
Eyes, that when fathomed, farthest heaven is
  found !
I chose for worth, not show, nor chose for them
Who want the casket richer than the gem.

That Wife is poor, whate'er her dower may be,
Who hath no beauty save what all may see :
No mystery of the human and divine ;
No other face to unveil within the shrine,
Up-lighted only for one worshipper,
And to one love alone familiar :
No veil to lift from her familiar face
Daily, and show the unfamiliar grace.
Eyes shine for others, but divinely dim
And dewy do they grow alone for him !
And her dear face transfigured he doth find
All mirror to the marvel in his mind !
The beauty worn by Bird and Butterfly
Lives on the outside, lustrous to the eye :
But still as nobler grow hue, form, and face,
More inward is shy Beauty's dwelling-place.
And there's a beauty fashioned in the mould
Transmitted from the Beautiful of old,

That from some family-face its best doth win :
But my love's dawneth daily from within ;
The loveliness of love made visible,
To feature which the sculptor Form is dull :
Not the mere charms of cheek, or chin, or lip,
That vanish on a week's acquaintanceship ;
But that crown-beauty which we cannot clasp,
The beauty that eludes Death's own grave-grasp.

At forty, what we seek for in a Wife
Is a calm haven amid seas of strife :
One fresh green summit in the waste of life,
That gathers dew of heaven and tenderly
Turns it to healing drops for you or me ;
A spring of freshness in the desert sand ;
A palm for shadow in a weary land ;
A being that doth not dwell so far apart
That we can find no entrance save at heart ;
One that at equal step with us may walk,
And kiss at equal stature in our talk ;
To scale the loftiest life, still arm-in-arm,
As well as nestle in the valleys warm.

And here's my Rest, where sheen and shadow meet
O'erhead, the small flowers budding at my feet ;
Green picnic places peeping from the wood,
Where you may meet the spirit of Robin Hood
Crossing the moonlight at the old deer-chase ;
A brooding Dove the Spirit of the place ;
Gleams of the Graces at their bath of dew ;
An earthly pleasaunce ; heaven trembling through ;
My Darling sitting with her hand in mine,
Here, where amid lush grass the large-eyed kine

Ruminant, stolid, statelily behold
The milky plenty and the mellowing gold:
And with glad laugh the tiny buttercup
Its beaker of delight brimful holds up;
And prodigally glorified, the mead
Is all aglow with red-ripe sorrel-seed,
And quick with smells that make one long to be
A-gathering sweets, bloom-buried utterly.

The sylvan world's old royalties around
With all their Summer beauty newly crowned:
Broad beeches, that have caught alive the swirl
O' the wind-wave—shaped it in their branches' curl;
Proud oaks, from head to foot all feudal yet;
And whispering pines, that have in worship met,—
Their delicate Gothic sharp against the shine
Of sunset heaven's honeyed hyaline—
Black-plumed and hushed as though they were the Hearse
    Of day's departed glory, are those Firs
When Venus, glowing in the lift above,
Laughs down on lovers with the eye of Love,
And such a pulse of pleasure as is given
To those who reach the promise of her heaven,
Luminous in her loveliness, as though
The Goddess' self were coming from the glow.

I brought my Love here happy months ago,
Her winter prison, amid miles of snow.
Poor bird! she felt that she was caged at last,
Her forest far away, its freedom past:
Her eyes made mournful search, mine laughed to see,
    She would have flown, and knew not where to flee.

The little wedding-ring had grown a round
Large hoop about our lives, and we were bound !
Useless was all petitionary quest,
No outlet !—so she nestled in my breast ;
And may we always be as wise, my dear,
When things look dark around, or foes are
     near.
Peep in at window now and you may see
Her leading captive my captivity :
Contented with her prison, polishing
The grating round her in a shining ring.

And now the fragrant summer-tide hath come
And isled us in a sea of leaf and bloom.
And now the tremulous sweetness, restless grace,
Have settled down to brood in her dear face
That lightens by me, fair and privet-pale,
Soft in the shadow of the bridal-veil :
The sunny sparkle of Southern radiance
That in her English blood doth bicker and dance,
Hath steadied to the still and sacred glow
Which hath more inner life than outer show.

So many are the mishaps and the griefs
In marriage, like Beau Brummel's Neckerchiefs ;
Armfuls of failure for one perfect tie !
And *have we hit it,* do you say or sigh ?

Time was when life in triumph would have run,
And faster than the fields catch fire o' the sun,
Or light takes form and feature in the flowers,
My answer would have blossomed with the hours
I should have felt the buds begin to blow
With my love-warmth, another life-dawn glow ;

Heard all the bells in heaven ring quite plain
Because young blood went singing through my
    brain :
Like vernal impulses the verses came ;
With soul on tiptoe and my words a-flame,
I should have sung that we had reached the
    land
Where milk and honey flow o'er golden sand,
And that far *El Dorado* we had found
Where nothing less than nuggets gild the ground.
But 'tis no more the lyric life of youth,
When fancy seeméd truer than all truth,
And standing in that dawn, the sun of love
Hung dewy rainbows on each web we wove,
And to the leap o' the blood we felt it given
To scale the tallest battlements of heaven ;
Poor was the prize of wisdom's proudest dower
Beside that glory of the flesh in flower !

And now I cannot sing my ladye's praise,
Lark-like, as in the morning of those days
When at a touch the song would upward start,
And, half in heaven, empty all the heart.
'Tis August with me now and harvest-heat,
And in the nest the silence is so sweet ;
Moreover, love is such a bosom thing,
In words its nestling nearnesses take wing ;
No flower of speech could ever yet express
The married sweetness or the homeliness ;
We cannot fable the ineffable ;
The tongue is tied too, with the heart at full :
Music may hint it with her latest breath,
But fails ;—her heaven is only reached through
    Death.

The stirring of the sap in bole and bough—
Mere feeling—will not set me singing now !
I thank my God for all that He hath given
And ope the windows of my soul to heaven ;
I think, in bowed and very humble mood,
I must be better, He hath been so good.
So would I journey to the land above,
Clothed with humility and crowned with love.

I look no more Without, and think to win
The treasures that are only found Within ;
And, after many years, have grown too wise
To search our world for some Lost Paradise ;
Or feel unhappy should we chance to miss
The next life's possibilities in this.
'Tis here we follow—but hereafter find
The goal all-golden miraged in the mind.
That Age of Gold behind us, and the Isles
Where dwell the Blessèd are but as the smiles
Reflected from a heaven that onward lies,
The Gold of sundown caught in Orient skies.

And yet, if any bit of Eden bloom
In this old world, 'tis in the WEDDED HOME.
And, what a wonder-world of novel life
Do these two range through, hand-in-hand, as Wife
And Husband ; in one flesh two spirits paired ;
Their joys all doubled, all their sorrows shared :
Two spirits blending in one heavenward spire,
That soars up fragrant from an altar fire ;
Two halves in one perfection wed to prove
The perfect Oneness of immortal love !

We cannot see Love with our mortal sight,
But lo ! the singing Angels come some night

To bring His tiny image in the Child
Wherewith from out the darkness He hath smiled ;
The tender voice whereby the All-loving breaks
His silence, and in human fashion speaks ;
The gentle hand put forth to draw us near
The heart of life whose pulse is beating here.
Though seldom do we guess, so dim our eyes,
That God comes down in such a simple guise,
And yet of such the kingdom of Heaven is ;
Through them the next world is revealed in this !

And how they come to us to bring us back
What we have lost along the dusty track :
The sweetness of the dawn, the early dew,
The tender green, and heaven's unclouded blue ;
The treasures that we dropped upon the ground,
And they, in following after us, have found !

Ah, Love, my life is not so bare of leaf
But we can find a nest for shelter if
The bounteous heavens should bless us from above
And in our branches nestle some wee dove.
Nor will my darling lack a touch still warm
To finish that fine sculpture of her form ;
For if Love dwell in me, the Angel-Elf
Shall kiss her to some likeness of himself,
And little arms shall bow the pride they deck
With other bridal fetters for her neck.

At the hill-top I reach my resting-place,
To find clear heaven—feel it face to face ;
Firm footing after all the weary slips,
To hold the cup unshaken at the lips.
The meaning of my life grows clear at last,
And all my troubles smile back now they're past :

The clouds put on a glory to mine eyes,
My sorrows were my saviour in disguise :
And I have walked with angels unawares,
And upward mounted, climbing over cares,
A little nearer to the home above.
Here let me rest in the good Father's love
Embodied in these arms embracing me,
Serenely as the sea-flowers in deep sea.

'Tis true, just as we feel our foreheads crowned,
And all so glorious grows the prospect round,
It seems one stride might launch us on heaven's
        wave,
Thenceforth our steps go downward to the grave.
What then ?   I would not rest till spirit rust,
And I am undistinguishable dust :
And if Love bring no second Spring to me,
This is the fore-feel of a Spring to be ;
If no new Dawn, yet in the evening hours,
Freshly bedewed, more sweetly smell the flowers ;
And round my path the glow of love hath made
Illumination for the evening shade.

Something, dear Lord, Thou hast for me to say,
Or wherefore draw me toward the springs of day,
And make my face with happiness to shine
By softly placing this dear hand in mine
Even while I stretched it to Thee through the
        dark :
A something that shall shine aloft and mark
Thy goodness and my gratitude upon
This Mount Transfiguration when I'm gone ?
If Thou hast set my foot on firmer ground,
Lord, let me show what helper I have found ;

If Thou hast touched me with thy loftier light,
Lord, let me turn to those that walk in night
And climb with more at heart than they can bear,
Though but a twinkle through their cloud of care.
Only a grain of sand my life may be,
But let it sparkle, Lord, with light of Thee !

I ask not that my Verse should break in bloom
With flowers, to crown my love or wreathe my
        tomb ;
Nor do I seek the laurel for my brow,
But only that above my grave may grow
Some sunny grains of Thine immortal seed
That may be garnered up for human need
In Bread of Life on which poor souls can feed !

Of late my life hath gathered more at root,
Making new sap, I trust, for future fruit :
Lord, sun my harvest, set it ripening
With sheaves in autumn thick as leaves in spring !
It is my prayer at night, my dream by day,
To make some conquest for the Poor.   I pray
Thee let me have my one supreme desire,
To fill some earthly facts with heavenly fire ;
Give voice to their dumb world before I die ;
Their patient pain more piteous than a cry !
Let me work now, while all eternity
With its large-seeming leisure waits for me.

A LETTER IN BLACK.

A-FLOATING on the fragrant flood
    Of Summer—fuller hour by hour;
All the Spring-sweetness of the bud
    Crowned by the glory of the flower,—
My spirits with the season flowed,
    The air was all a breathing balm;
The lake a flame of sapphire glowed;
    The mountains lay in cloudless calm:

Green leaves were lusty; roses blushed
    For pleasure in the golden time;
The birds through all their feathers flushed
    For gladness of their marriage-prime:
Listless among the lilies I threw
    Me down, for coolness, 'mid the sheen:
Heaven, one large smile of brooding blue;
    Earth, one large smile of basking green.

A rich suspended shower of gold
    Laburnum o'er me hung its crown:
You look up heavenward and behold
    It glowing, coming in glory down!
There, as my thoughts of greenness grew
    To fruitage of a leafy dream,—
There, friend, your letter thrilled me through,
    And all the summer lost its gleam.

The world, so pleasant to the sight,
    So full of voices blithe and brave,
And all her lamps of beauty alight
    With life! I had forgot the Grave:

And there it opened at my feet,
   Revealing a familiar face
Upturned, my whitened look to meet,
   And very patient in its place.

My poor bereaven friend ! I know
   Not how to word it, but would bring
A little solace for your woe,—
   A little love for comforting :
And yet the best that I can say
   Will only help to sum your loss ;
I can but look and long, and pray
   God help my friend to bear his Cross.

I have felt something of your smart,
   And lost the dearest things e'er wound
In love about a human heart :
   I, too, have life-roots underground.
From out my soul hath leaped a cry
   For help !   Nor God Himself could save :
And tears yet start that naught will dry
   Save Death's hand with the dust o' the grave.

God knows, and we may one day know,
   These hidden secrets of His love ;
But now the stillness stuns us so ;
   Darkly, as in a dream, we move.
The glad life-pulses come and go,
   Over our head and at our feet ;
Soft airs are sighing something low ;
   The flowers are saying something sweet ;

And 'tis a merry world.   The lark
   Is singing over the green corn ;

Only the house and heart are dark,—
    Only the human world forlorn.
There, in the bridal-chamber, lies
    A dear bedfellow all in white ;
That purple shadow under the eyes,
    Where star-fire swam in liquid night.

Sweet, slippery silver of her talk ;
    The music of her laugh so dear,
Heard in home-ways, and wedded walk,
    For many and many a golden year ;
The singing soul and shining face,
    Daisy-like glad by roughest road ;
Gone ! with a thousand dearnesses
    That hid themselves for us and glowed.

The waiting Angel. patient Wife,
    All through the battle at our side,
That smiled her sweetness on our strife
    For gain, and it was sanctified !
When waves of trouble beat breast-high
    And the heart sank, she poured a balm
That stilled them ; and the saddest sky
    Made clear and starry with her calm.

And when the world with harvest ripe
    In all its golden fulness lay ;
And God, it seemed, saw fit to wipe,
    Even on earth, all tears away ;
The good true heart that bravely won,
    Must smile up in our face and fall ;
And all our happy days are done,
    And this the end.   And is this all ?

The bloom of bliss, the secret glow,
  That clothed without, and inly curled,
All gone.   We are left shivering now,
  Naked to the wide open world!
A shrivelled, withered world it is,
  So sad and miserably cold;
Where be its vaunted braveries?
  'Tis gray, and miserably old.

Our joy was all a drunken dream;
  This is the truth at waking! we
Are swept out rootless by the stream
  And current of calamity—
Out on some lone and shoreless sea
  Of solitude so vast and deep,
As 'twere the wrong Eternity,
  Where God is not, or gone to sleep.

It seems as though our darling dead,
  Startled at Death's so sudden call,
With falling hands and dear bowed head
  Had, like a flower-filled lap, let fall
A hoard of treasures we have found
  Too late! so slow doth wisdom come!
We for the first time look around
  Remembering this is not our Home.

My friend, I see you with your cup
  Of tears and trembling—see you sit;
And long to help you drink it up,
  With useless longings infinite!—
Sit rocking the old mournful thought,
  That on the heart's-blood will be nursed,
Unless the blessed tears be brought;
  Unless the cloudy sorrows burst.

The little ones are gone to rest,
　And for a while they will not miss
The Mother-wings above the nest;
　But through their slumber slides her kiss,
And, dreaming she has come, they start,
　And toss wild arms for her caress,
With moanings that must thrill a heart
　In heaven with divine distress.

And Sorrow on your threshold stands,
　The Dark Ladye in glooming pall:
I see her take you by the hands;
　I feel her shadow over all.
Hers is no warm and tender clasp;
　With silence solemn as the Night's,
And veilèd face, and spirit-grasp,
　She leads her Chosen up the heights:

The cloudy crags are cold and gray,
　You cannot scale them without scars:
So many Martyrs by the way,
　Who never reached her tower of stars;
But there her beauty shall be seen,
　Her glittering face so proudly pure;
And all her majesty of mien;
　And all her guerdon shall be sure.

Well.　'Tis not written, God will give
　To His Beloved only rest!
The hard life of the cross they live,
　They strive, and suffer, and are blest.
The feet must bleed to reach their throne,
　The brow must burn before it bear
One of the crowns that may be won,
　By workers for immortal wear.

Dear friend, life beats though buried 'neath
  A vast black vault of night ! and see
There trembles through this dark of death,
  Starlight of immortality !
And yet shall dawn the eternal day
  To kiss the eyes of them that sleep ;
And He shall wipe all tears away
  From tired eyes of them that weep.

'Tis something for the poor bereaven,
  In such a weary world of care,
To think that we have friends in heaven ;
  Who helped us here, may aid us there.
These yearnings for them set our Arc
  Of being widening more and more,
In circling sweep through outer dark
  To day more perfect than before.

So much was left unsaid.   The soul
  Must live in other worlds to be ;
On earth we cannot grasp the whole,
  For that Love has eternity.
Love deep as death, and rich as rest ;
  Love that was love with all Love's might ;
Level to needs the lowliest !
  Cannot be less Love at full-height.

Though earthly forms be far apart,
  Spirit to spirit nestles nigher ;
The music chords the same at heart,
  Though one voice range an octave higher.
Eyes watch us that we cannot see ;
  Lips warn us which we may not kiss ;
They wait for us, and starrily,
  Lean toward us from heaven's lattices.

We cannot see them face to face,
    But love is nearness; and they love
Us yet, nor change, with change of place,
    In more than human worlds above,
Where love, once leal, hath never ceased,
    And dear eyes never lose their shine,
And there shall be a marriage feast,
    That turns Earth's water to Heaven's Wine.

WIDOW MARGARET.

Poor Margaret's window is alight;
    The Widow sits alone;
Though long into the silent night,
    And far, the world is gone.
She lives in shadow till her blood
    Grows bitter and blackened all;
Upon her head a mourning hood;
    Upon her heart a pall.

The stars come nightly out of heaven,
    Old Darkness to beguile;
For her there is no healing given
    To their sweet spirit-smile.
That honey-dew of sleep the skies
    In blessed balm let fall,
Drops not on her poor tired eyes,
    Though it be sent for all.

At some dead flower, with fragrance faint,
    Her life opes like a book;
The old sweet music makes its plaint,
    And, from the grave's dim nook,

The buried bud of hopes laid low,
　Flowers in the night full-blown;
And little things of Long-Ago
　Come back to her full-grown.

Her heart is wandering in a whirl,
　And she must seek the tomb
Where lies her long-lost little girl.
　O, well with them for whom
Love's Morning-Star comes round so fair
　As Evening Star of Faith,
Already up and shining, ere
　The dark of coming death.

But Margaret cannot reach a hand,
　Beyond the dark of death;
Her spirit swoons in that high land
　Where breathes no human breath;
She cannot look upon the grave
　As one eternal shore;
From which a soul may take the wave,
　For heaven, to sail or soar.

Across that Deep no sail unfurled,
　For her; no wings put forth;
She tries to reach the other world
　By groping down through earth.
'Twas there the Child went underground;
　They parted in that place;
And ever since, the Mother found
　The door shut in her face.

Though many effacing springs have wrapped
　With green the dark grave-bed;

'Twas *there*, the breaking heart - strings
    snapped
  As she let down her dead ;
And there she gropes with wild heart yet,
  For years, and years, and years ;
Poor Margaret ! there will she let
  Her sorrow loose in tears.

All the young mother in her old.voice
  Its waking moan will make !
A young aurora light her eyes
  With radiance gone to wreck :
And then at dawn she will return,
  To her old self again;
Eyes dim and dry ; heart gray and dern ;
  And querulous in her pain.—

" *We never loved each other much,*
  I and my poor good-man ;
But on the Child we lavished such
  A love as overran
All boundaries, loving her the more
  Because our love was pent ;
Striving as two seas try to pour
  Their strength through one small rent.

" *For children come to still link hands,*
  When lives have ebbed apart ;
And hide the rift, when either stands
  At distance heart from heart.
So on our little one we'd look ;
  Press hands with fonder grasp ;
As though we closed some holy book,
  Softly, with golden clasp.

" *And as the dark earth offers up*
  Her little Winterling,
The Crocus, pleading with its cup
  Of hoarded gold, to bring
Down all the gray heaven's quickening shower
  Of Spring to warm the sod ;
So did we lift the winsome flower
  That sprang from our dark clod.

" *Our little Golden-heart, her name !*
  And all things sweet and calm,
And pure and fragrant, round her came
  With gifts of bloom and balm.
And there she grew, my flower of all,
  Pure gold and pearly white ;
Just as at Summer's smiling call
  The lily stands alight.

" *To knee or nipple, was the goal*
  Of her wee stately walk ;
The voice of my own silent soul
  Her darling baby-talk ;
Then darklingly she dwined and failed ;
  And looking on our dead,
The father wailed awhile and ailed,
  Turned to the wall and said—

" ' *'Tis dark and still, our house of life,*
  The fire is burning low ;
Our pretty one is gone, old Wife,
  'Tis time for me to go :
Our Golden-heart has gone to sleep ;
  She's happed in for the night ;
And so to bed I'll quietly creep,
  And sleep till morning light.' "

Once more the Widow Margaret rose
  And through the night passed on.
Long shadows weird of tree and house
  Made ghosts in moonlight wan!
She passed into the churchyard, where
  The many glad life-waves
That leapt of old, have stood still there,
  In green and grassy graves.

" O would my body were at rest
  Beneath this cool grave-sward :
O would my soul were with the Blest,
  That slumber in the Lord !
They sleep so sweetly underground ;
  For Death hath shut the door,
And all the world of sorrow and sound
  Can trouble them no more."

A spirit-feel is in the place,
  That makes the poor heart gasp ;
Her soul stands white up in her face
  For one warm human clasp !
To-night she sees the Grave astir;
  And as in prayer she kneels,
The mystery opens unto her :
  She for the first time feels

The spirit-world may be as near
  Us moving silent round,
As are the dead that sleep a mere
  Short fathom underground ;
And there be eyes that see the sight
  Of lorn ones wandering, vexed
Through some long, sad, and shadowy night
  Betwixt this world and next.

Doorways of fear, are eye and ear,
  Through which the wonders go;
And through the night with glow-worm light,
  The Church is all aglow!
There comes a waft of Sabbath hymn;
  She enters; all the air
With faces fills divine and dim,
  The Blessed Dead are there.

One came and bade poor Margaret sit,
  Seemed to her as it smiled,
A great white Bird of God alit
  In a forest marble-aisled.
"*Look to the Altar!*" there a spell
  Fixed her; she saw upstart,
A Woman, like a soul in hell,
  'Twas her own Golden-heart.

"*It would have been thus, Mother dear,*
  And so God took her, from
All trials and temptations here,
  To His eternal home;
And you shall see her in a place
  Where death can never part."
She looked up, and in that pure face
  Found her own Golden-heart.

The lofty music rose again
  From all those happy souls,
Till all the windows thrilled, as when
  The organ-thunder rolls;
And all her life was like a light
  Weak weed the stream doth sway,
Until it reaches the full-height,
  Breaks, and is borne away.

Her life stood still a-listening to
  The music ! then a hand
Took hers, and she was floated through
  A mystic border-land.
'Twas Golden-heart ! from that eclipse
  She drew her into bliss :
Two spirits closed at dying lips,
  In one immortal kiss.

Next day an early worshipper
  Was kneeling in the Aisle ;
A statue of life that did not stir,
  But knelt on with a smile
Upon the face that smiled with light,
  As though, when left behind,
It smiled on with some glorious sight
  Long after the eyes were blind.

***

PICTURES IN THE FIRE.

OLD Winter blows, and whistles hard,
  To keep his fingers warm, while I
Shut out the cold night, frosty-starred,
  Bleak earth and bitter sky ;
And to the Fireplace nestle nigher,
To pore on pictures in the Fire.

It has a soft, blithe, murmuring glow,
  As if it crooned a cradle-song ;
Yet whispers of some awful woe
  Are on each flaming tongue
That may have licked up human life,
Quick, ruddy as a murderer's knife !

I see the Dead Men underground,
  Just as they found them rank on rank ;
Old Mothers—Young Wives—red-eyed round
  The Corpses brought to bank ;
I see the mournful phantoms flit
About the mouth of Hartley Pit ;

And that poor Widow above the rest
  All eminent in Suffering's crown,
Who wearing sorrow's loftiest crest
  Is bowed the lowliest down ;
Poor Widow with her Coffins seven,
Look down on Her, dear God in Heaven !

I hear that crash with sinking heart—
  Eternity has broken through !
I see him play his Hero part,
  A leader tried and true,
Who faithful stood to his last breath,
And fell betwixt them and their death.

I hear him bid them trim their lamps—
  For Light hath not gone out in Heaven !
And through the dark, above the damps,
  He beacons them to haven :
Long in his eyes had lived the light
That should make starry such a Night.

I see the strong man's agony,
  That seeks to rend his ghastly shroud ;
The touch of solemn radiancy
  That kindles through the cloud ;
The trust that earned a nobler doom
Than such a death in such a tomb ;

The valour that invisibly
    Lifted the bosom like a targe;
The hidden forces that must be,
    Ready for Life's last charge!
And all the bravery brave in vain,
And all the majesty of pain:

Visions of the old Home that flash
    With all the mind's last mortal power;
The tears that burn their way, to wash
    A soul white in an hour,
When thoughts of God go deeper than
The Devil at his utmost can.

I hear the poor faint heart's low cry
    That sickens at the sight of Doom;
The prayer of those that feel it nigh,
    And groping through the gloom!
They cower together hand-in-hand
At the dark door of the dark land.

Ghostly and far away life seems
    To one returning from a swound;
And sharp the sorrow comes in dreams
    When we are helpless bound;
But deathliest swoons, or ghastliest nights,
Have no such sounds, or spirit-sights.

The waiting human world is near,
    Yet farther off than Heaven for them
Who bow the doomèd head, to bear
    Death's cruel diadem,
With farewell words of solemn cheer
And love for those who cannot hear:

Old heads with hair like spray above
    A tossed and troubled sea of life ;
Young hearts, just kissed to the quick by Love,
    That leave a one-day wife.
O pathos of a hopeless fate !
O pain of those left desolate !

'Tis brave to die in Battle's flash,
    For the dear country we adore—
Struck breathless 'mid the glorious crash,
    When banners wave before
The fading eyes, and at the ears
We are caught by following Victory's cheers !

And sailor-blood that on the waves
    Can feel the Mother's heaving breast—
True sailor-blood no wailing craves
    Over *its* place of rest,
When souls first taste eternity
In those last kisses of the Sea :

And Death oft comes with kind release
    To win a smile from those that lie
Where they may feel the blessèd breeze,
    And look up at the sky,
And drink in, with their latest sigh,
A little air for strength to die :

But 'tis a fearful thing to be
    Instantly buried alive ; fast-bound
In cold arms of Eternity
    That clasp the breathing round,
And hold them though their Comrades call
And dig with efforts useless all.

A tear for those who, in that night,
　Went down so unavailingly;
A cheer for those who fought our fight,
　And missed the victory!
Peace to the good true hearts that gave
A moral glory to that grave!

We know not how amid the gloom
　Some jewel of the just outshone;
With precious sparkle lit the tomb
　And led the hopeless on
To hope, and showed the only way
To find God's hand and reach His day.

We know not how in that quick hour
　Some poor uncultured human clod
May have put forth its one sweet flower,
　Acceptable to God:
Or how the touch of Death revealed
Some buried beauty life concealed:

We know now how the Dove of peace
　Came brooding on the fluttering breast,
To make the fond life-yearnings cease,
　And fold them up for rest;
And into shining shape the soul
Burst, like the flame from out the coal:

We only know the watch-fires burned
　Long in their eyes for human aid,
And failed, and then to God they turned,
　And altogether prayed,
And that the deepest Mine may be,
For prayer, God's whispering Gallery!

Dear God, be very pitiful
　To these poor toiling slaves of men ;
Be gracious if their hearts be dull
　With darkness of their den :
'Tis hard for flowers of Heaven to grow
Down where the earth-flowers cannot blow !

Their lives are as the Candle-snuff,
　Black in the midst of its own light !
Let hard hands plead for spirits rough—
　They work so much in night.
Be merciful, they breathe their breath
So close to danger, pain, and death.

The love-mist in a Father's eye
　Must rise, and soften much that's rude
In his poor children—magnify
　The least faint gleam of good !
O, find some place for human worth
In Heaven, when it has failed on Earth.

SONGS.

OLD FRIENDS.

WE just shake hands at meeting
  With many that come nigh ;
We nod the head in greeting
  To many that go by,—
But welcome through the gateway
  Our few old friends and true ;
Then hearts leap up, and straightway
  There's open house for you,
                              Old Friends,
    There's open house for you !

The surface will be sparkling,
  Let but a sunburst shine ;
Yet in the depth lies darkling,
  The true life of the wine !
The froth is for the many,
  The wine is for the few ;
Unseen, untouched of any,
  We keep the best for you,
                              Old Friends,
    The very best for you !

The Many cannot know us ;
  They only pace the strand,
Where at our worst we show us—
  The waters thick with sand !

But out beyond the leaping
  Dim surge 'tis clear and blue ;
And there, Old Friends, we are keeping
  A waiting calm for you,
            Old Friends,
  A resting-place for you.

SYLVIA MAY.

" *Heart of mine, so longing for rest,*
  Better to build thy love-lined Nest
On a storm-swung bough than a Woman's breast."

But this heart of mine still sayeth me, " *Nay;* "
Shows me the picture of Sylvia May ;
Wilful hearts must have their way !

" *Heart of mine, far wiser 'twould be*
  To build thy Nest on a wave of the sea,
Tossed and troubled perpetually."

But this heart of mine still sayeth me, " *Nay;* "
And whispers the name of Sylvia May :
Foolish hearts will have their way !

" *Never was love I think like mine ;*
  Never was woman so nearly divine ;
Never could lives more perfectly twine."

And this heart of mine it murmureth, " YEA ; "
Wilful hearts must have their way—
When will you marry me, Sylvia May ?

IN A DREAM.

She came but for a little while,
   Yet with a wondrous gleam;
She left within my soul her smile,
   The Darling of my Dream!

O face too clear for sorrow or tear,
   Too real for masks that seem;
I seek, but shall not find her Here,
   The Darling of my Dream!

I wonder do you wait for me
   Beside the glad Life-stream,
Or under the Leaf-of-Healing tree—
   You Darling of my Dream!

O sometimes lift your veil by night,
   And let one beauty-beam
Fill all my life for days with light,
   You Darling of my Dream!

THAT MERRY, MERRY MAY.

Ah! 'tis like a tale of olden
   Time, long, long ago;
When the world was in its golden
   Prime, and love was lord below!
Every vein of Earth was dancing
   With the Spring's new wine!
'Twas the pleasant time of flowers,
   When I met you, love of mine!

Ah ! some spirit sure was straying
    Out of heaven that day,
When I met you, Sweet ! a-Maying
    In that merry, merry May.

Little heart ! it shyly opened
    Its red leaves' love-lore,
Like a rose that must be ripened
    To the dainty, dainty core.
But its beauties daily brighten,
    And it blooms so dear,—
Though a many Winters whiten,
    I go Maying all the year.
And my proud heart will be praying
    Blessings on the day,
When I met you, Sweet, a-Maying,
    In that merry, merry May.

———

A LOVER'S FANCY.

SWEET Heaven ! I do love a Maiden,
At her feet I bow love-laden ;
When she's near me, heaven is round me,
Her dear presence doth so bound me !
I could wring my heart of gladness,
Might it free her lot of sadness !
Give the world, and all that's in it,
Just to press her hand a minute !
Yet she weeteth not I love her ;
    Never dare I tell the sweet
Tale, but to the stars above her,
    And the flowers that kiss her feet.

O ! to live and linger near her,
And in tearful moments cheer her !
I could be a Bird to lighten
Her sad heart—her sweet eyes brighten :
Or in fragrance, like a blossom,
Give my life up on her bosom !
For my love's withouten measure,
All its pangs are sweetest pleasure :
Yet she weeteth not I love her ;
   Never dare I tell the sweet
Tale, but to the stars above her,
   And the flowers that kiss her feet.

NO JEWELLED BEAUTY IS MY LOVE.

No jewelled Beauty is my Love,
   Yet in her earnest face
There's such a world of tenderness,
   She needs no other grace.
Her smiles, her voice, around my life
   In light and music twine ;
And dear, O very dear to me
   Is this sweet Love of mine.

O joy ! to know there's one fond heart
   Beats ever true to me !
It sets mine leaping like a lyre,
   In sweetest melody :
My soul up-springs, a Deity !
   To hear her voice divine ;
And dear, O very dear to me,
   Is this sweet Love of mine.

If ever I have sighed for wealth,
  'Twas all for her, I trow ;
And if I win Fame's victor-wreath,
  I'll twine it on her brow.
There may be forms more beautiful,
  And souls of sunnier shine,
But none, O none, so dear to me,
  As this sweet Love of mine.

THE TWO ROSES.

Softly stepped she over the lawn,
  In vesture light and free ;
A floating Angel might have drawn
Her hair from heaven in a glory-dawn,
  And her voice rang silverly.
Then up she rose on her tiny tip-toes,
Her white hand catches, her fingers close :
" *You are tall and proud, my dainty Rose ;*
  But I have you now," said **She**.

O so lightly over the lawn,
  Step for step went he !
Thinking how, from his hiding-place,
The war of Roses in her face,
  Dear Love would laugh to see !
Two arms suddenly round her he throws,
Two mouths, turning oneward, close ;
" *You are tall and proud, my dainty Rose !*
  But I have you now," said **He**.

SWEET-AND-TWENTY.

LIKE a Lady from a far land,
   Came my true Love brave to see !
As to heaven its rainbow garland,
   Is her beauty rich to me.

Or as some dim Mere may mirror
   One fair star that shines above,
So my life—ay growing clearer—
   Holds this tremulous star of love.

Look you, how she cometh trilling
   Out her gay heart's bird-like bliss !
Merry as a May-morn, thrilling,
   With the dew and sunshine's kiss.

Ruddy gossips of her beauty
   Are her twin cheeks : and her mouth
In its ripe warmth smileth, fruity
   As a garden of the south.

Ha ! my precious Sweet-and-Twenty,
   Husband up your virgin pride !
Just a month and this dear, dainty
   Thing shall be my wedded Bride.

THE WEDDING-RING.

Tnis old world is scarce worth seeing,
  Till Love wave his purple wing,
And we gauge the bliss of being,
  Through a golden wedding-ring;
  Heigho, the wedding-ring.

Would you draw far Eden nearer,
  And to earth the Angels bring;
You must seek the magic mirror
  Of a golden wedding-ring;
  Heigho, the wedding-ring.

As the earth with sea is bounded,
  And the winter-world with spring,
So a Maiden's life is rounded
  With a golden wedding-ring;
  Heigho, the wedding-ring.

I have known full many a Maiden,
  Like a white rose withering,
Into fresh ripe beauty redden
  Through a golden wedding-ring;
  Heigho, the wedding-ring.

As the crescent Moon rings golden,
  Her full glory perfecting,
Womanly beauty is unfolden
  In a golden wedding-ring;
  Heigho, the wedding-ring.

Fainting spirits oft grow fearless,
  Sighing hearts will soar and sing,
Tearful eyes will laugh out tearless,
  Through a golden wedding-ring;
  Heigho, the wedding-ring.

LOVE'S WESTWARD HO!

Pleasant it is, wee Wife of mine,
　As by my side thou art,
To sit and see thy dear eyes shine
　With bonfires of the heart!
And young Love smiles so sweet and sly,
　From warm and balmy deeps,
As under-leaf the fruit may try
　To hide, yet archly peeps:
Gliding along in our fairy boat,
　With prospering skies above,
Over the sea of time we float
　To another New World of Love.

One of God's Darlings is our Guide:
　Ah, how it makes us lean,
Hearts beating lovingly side by side
　That nothing may come between.
As yon brave ring of Stars doth fold
　Our world, so is it given
To this wee ring of wedding gold
　To clasp us round with heaven;
Gliding along in our fairy boat,
　With prospering skies above,
Over the sea of time we float
　To another New World of Love.

MY LOVE.

My Love is true and tender,
    Her eyes are rich with rest ;
Her hair of dappled splendour,
    The colour I love best ;
So sweet, so gay, so odorous-warm,
    She nestles here, heart-high,
A bounteous aspect, beauteous form,
    But, just a wee bit sly.

My Love is no light Dreamer,
    A-floating with the foam ;
But a brave life-sea swimmer,
    With footing found in Home.
My winsome Wife, she's bright without,
    And beautiful within ;
But—I would not say quite without
    The least wee touch of sin.

My Love is not an Angel
    In one or two small things :
But just a wifely woman
    With other wants than wings.
You have some little leaven
    Of earth, you darling dear ;
If you were fit for Heaven,
    You might not nestle here.

LULLABY.

SOFTLY sink in slumbers golden,
　Warm as nestled Birdlings lie,
Safe in Mother's arms enfolden,
　While I sing thy lullaby.
Lullaby, lullaby, lullaby, lullaby,
Sweet one, sleep to my Lullaby.

Though the night doth darken, darken,
　Light will Mother's slumbers lie ;
Still my heart will harken, harken,
　Lest her wee thing wake and cry.
Lullaby, lullaby, lullaby, lullaby,
Sweet one, sleep to my Lullaby.

At thy golden gate of slumber,
　Stands my spirit tiptoe-high,
Filled with yearnings without number,
　In thine inner heaven to fly.
Lullaby, lullaby, lullaby, lullaby,
Sweet one, sleep to my Lullaby.

In that world of mystic breathing,
　Spirit Sentinels, stand by !
Winnow, winnow, o'er my wee thing,
　Wings of Love that hover nigh.
Lullaby, lullaby, lullaby, lullaby,
Sweet one, sleep to my Lullaby.

Sleep ! and drink the dew delicious
　Till the morrow dawn is high !
Sleep with Mother near her precious,
　Wake ! with Mother waiting nigh.
Lullaby, lullaby, lullaby, lullaby,
Sweet one, sleep to my Lullaby.

AUTUMN SONG.

THE summer days are ended ;
   The after-glow is gone ;
The nights grow long and eerie :
   The winds awake to moan ;
The pleasant leaves are fading ;
   The friendly swallows flee ;
Yet welcome is the Winter
   That brings my Love to me.

No voice of bird now ripples
   The air ; no wood-walk rings !
But in my happy bosom
   The soul of Music sings ;
It sings of clearest heaven,
   And summers yet to be ;
Then welcome to the Winter
   That brings my Love to me.

A world of gathered sunshine
   Is this warm heart of mine,
Where life hath heaped the fruitage,
   And love hath hid the wine.
And though there's not a flower
   In field, nor leaf on tree ;
Yet welcome is the Winter
   That brings my Love to me.

SYRINX.

Methought to bear her branches crowned
    With fruit, my virgin vine:
Another fills her arms; around
    Another life they twine!
        So I lost the day,
    And all the night I wake,—
Bird-like singing sad sorrow away,
    Until my heart shall break.

While others gleaned Life's field for gold,
    With Flowers I made a crown;
Till, looking up alone, behold,
    The deepening night came down!
        So I lost the day,
    And all the night I wake,—
Bird-like singing sad sorrow away,
    Until my heart shall break.

Poor me! I clasped a reed, and missed
    My sweetest Syrinx fled!
Poor me! my tenderest music's kissed
    From lips of dear love dead.
        I have lost the day,
    And all the night I wake,—
Bird-like singing sad sorrow away,
    Until my heart shall break.

O LAY THY HAND IN MINE, DEAR!

O LAY thy hand in mine, dear!
  We're growing old, we're growing old;
But Time hath brought no sign, dear,
  That hearts grow cold, that hearts grow cold.
'Tis long, long since our new love
  Made life divine, made life divine;
But age enricheth true love,
  Like noble wine, like noble wine.

And lay thy cheek to mine, dear,
  And take thy rest, and take thy rest;
Mine arms around thee twine, dear,
  And make thy nest, and make thy nest.
A many cares are pressing
  On this dear head, on this dear head;
But Sorrow's hands in blessing
  Are surely laid, are surely laid.

O lean thy life on mine, dear!
  'Twill shelter thee, 'twill shelter thee.
Thou wert a winsome vine, dear,
  On my young tree, on my young tree:
And so, till boughs are leafless,
  And Song-birds flown, and Song-birds flown,
We'll twine, then lay us, griefless,
  Together down, together down.

LONG, LONG AGO.

OLD friend of mine, you were dear to my heart,
    Long, long ago, long ago.
Little did we think of a time we should part,
    Long, long ago, long ago.
Hand clasped in hand through the world we would
    go.
Down our old untrodden path the wild weeds grow !
Great was the love 'twixt us ; bitter was the smart :
    Old friend of mine long ago.

Patient watch I kept for you many, many a day,
    Long, long ago, long ago ;
Waited and wept for you far, far away,
    Long, long ago, long ago.
Merry came each May-tide, new leaves would start :
Never came my old friend back to my heart.
Lonely I went on my weary, weary way,
    Old friend of mine long ago.

Oft as I muse at the shadowy nightfall
    Over the dear Long Ago :
Borne on tears arises the dark, dark pall,
    Fallen on my heart long ago.
Love is not dead, though we wander apart ;
How I could clasp you, old friend, to my heart !
Barriers lie between us, but God knoweth all,
    Old friend of mine long ago.

A SOLDIER'S WIFE.

" *Around us the day closes dense as a wood,*
The Stars down the darkness with eerie eyes brood,
While out through the nightfall my restless thoughts
flee
To him who is fighting far over the sea.

" *Across the mirk Moorland the birds of night cry;*
A wind stirs my flesh as of ghosts gliding by;
Oh, clasp thy hands, pretty one, kneel down with
me,
And pray for thy Father far over the sea.

" *So brave is my darling, so gallant and gay,*
He'll flash through the fight in the wild, bloody
day;
He'll crest the top wave upon valour's red sea;
God shield him! God send him back safely to me!"

He's lying, poor Wife! with the valiant and
tried,
Who to-night shed their life on a reddened hill-
side:
And still she sings tenderly, " *Over the sea,*
Blow, breezes, and bring back my darling to me."

Her soul it sat smiling, all meek as a dove,
In her pure perfect face that was lighted with
love;
Her child to the full heart endearing she drew,
And bowed like a Flower 'neath its blessing of
dew.

Some luminous Presence glides over the place,
A white mist of glory ! a white spirit-face !
And a starry Shape comes slow and sweet from
    the gloom ;
God help thee, poor Widow ! thy husband is
    home !

She knows not the Spirit that hovereth nigh,
Nor whence fell the slumber that healed her
    heart's cry ;
But she weeps in her vision, and prayerfully
Still murmurs, *"God send him back safely to me!"*

ROBIN'S SONG.

Sing, Robin Redbreast,
    Though you fill our hearts with pain :
Sing, bonny Robin,
    Though our tears fall like the rain
For a Lamb far from the fold,
In the wet and wintry mould !
For a Bird out in the cold,
    Bird alane !   Bird alane !

Sing, Robin Redbreast !
    You are welcome to our door ;
Sing, darling Robin,
    Merry Larks no longer soar :
Autumn comes with feel of rain,
Mournful odours, wail of pain !
There's a Bird will come again
    Nevermore ! Nevermore !

Sing, Robin Redbreast!
    For we love your song so brave,
Though you mind us of a Robin
    Where the willows weep and wave:
To *her* little grave it clings,
Shakes the rain from its wet wings,
And for all the sadness sings
    By Her grave, by Her grave.

THE ONLY ONE.

WITH tired feet, o'er thorny ground,
    My spirit made its quest;
On wearied wing it wandered round,
    But could not find a nest;
Till at the feet of Love I found
    At last my Only Rest!

I went the downward way of Doom,
    With those that walk in Night:
I stumbled on from tomb to tomb
    Of Joys that lured my sight;
Until Love touched me through the gloom
    And smiled,—my Only Light!

O, sweet the touch of hearts, and sweet
    The tie of Child and Wife,
And blessèd is the Home where meet
    True Souls that shut out strife;
And as I nestle at Love's feet,
    I know my Only Life.

A MAIDEN'S SONG.

I LOVE! and Love hath given me
　　Sweet thoughts to God akin,
And oped a living Paradise
　　My heart of hearts within:
O from this Eden of my life
　　God keep the Serpent Sin!

I love! and into Angel-land
　　With starry glimpses peer!
I drink in beauty like heaven-wine,
　　When One is smiling near!
And there's a Rainbow round my soul
　　For every rising tear.

Dear God in heaven! keep without stain
　　My bosom's brooding Dove:
O clothe it meet for angel-arms,
　　And give it place above!
For there is nothing from the world
　　I yearn to take, but Love.

LOVE.

O LOVE! Love! Love!
　　Its glory breaks our gloom,
And there's a new Heaven overhead,
　　With all the earth in bloom.
'Tis sweet as Sunshine's golden kiss,
　　That crowns the world anew:
Sweet as in Roses' hearts of bliss,
　　Soft summer-dark drops dew.

O Love ! Love ! Love !
  May make the true heart ache ;
Pulse out its lavish life, and leave
  It mournfully to break !
But O how winsomely it starts
  The thoughts that bee-like cling,
To drain the honey from young hearts,
  And leave a bleeding sting !

O Love ! Love ! Love !
  Its very pain endears !
And every wail and weeping brings
  Some blessing on our tears !
Love makes our darkest days, sweet dove !
  All goldenly go down,
And still we'll clothe ourselves with love,
  And crown us with Love's crown.

NOW AND THEN.

O Love will make the leal heart ache
  That never ached before ;
And meek or merry eyes 'twill make
  With solemn tears run o'er.
In tears we parted tenderly,
  My Love and I lang syne ;
And evermore she vowed to be
  Mine own, aye mine, all mine !

Sing O the tree is blossoming,
  But worms are at the root ;
And many a darling flower of Spring
  Will never come to fruit.

We meet now in the streets of life ;
    All gone, the old sweet charms ;
At my side leans a loving Wife ;
    She—passes Babe-in-arms.

EMIGRANT SONG.

Behind us lies a land, all dim .
    With sighs of sorrows old ;
Before us, on the ocean's rim,
    A land that looks of gold.
        We go, a fuller life to win,
            With freedom for th' opprest—
        But won't forget the old land, in
            That new world of the West.

We cannot weep who cross the deep,
    Unfairly driven forth ;
We might not sow, we could not reap
    Our share of native earth.
        We go, a fuller life to win,
            With freedom for th' opprest—
        But won't forget the old land, in
            That new world of the West.

As Emigrants from land to land—
    From rise to set of sun,
We build the bridge till ocean's spanned,
    And all the world is one.
        We go, a fuller life to win,
            With freedom for th' opprest—
        But won't forget the old land, in
            That new world of the West.

THE SAILOR'S ORPHAN CHILD.

How happy seems the Sailor's lot,
  On Summer seas to roam,
With pleasant dreams of that wee Cot
  Where wife and weans make " home."
But he must also face the war
  Of winds and waters wild,
To fall, perchance, from home afar,
  And leave an orphan child.

The Sailor in the tempest strives
  With might and main for you ;
When raging billows race for lives,
  The Sailor brings us through.
Then succour those he leaves behind,
  As sea-drift safely Isled ;
The Sailor's orphan is a kind
  Of every parent's child.

ON DECK TOGETHER.

Out of the water the wingèd fish flew,
Flashes of light from abysses of blue,
  In the goldenest tropical weather ;
A pale still face seemed calling to me ;
Words of cheer were spoken, and we
  Were friends on deck together.

Under a still and starry night
My lady arose to her stateliest height—
  Hair without tie or tether—

And there between the sky and the sea,
She walked and talked right merry with me,
    As we trod the deck together.

We meet no more the deck to tread ;
But, when the Oceans have yielded their dead,
    I cannot help wondering whether
There will be another world where we
May voyage on some celestial sea,
    And tread the deck together.

A PEARL DIVER.

Soul of Jacoba, come forth from your shell,
My pearl of the Deep where you darklingly dwell,
The Diver hath found you, the secret is shown,
Never again will you nestle unknown ;
Nevermore feel in your loneness alone !

Soul of Jacoba, arise and shine
From the sea-green depths of her eyes divine ;
Soul of Jacoba, come forth and play
In the pale still face with a roseate ray,
And a smile that shall turn all the dark into day !

My Pearl ! that I saw by her own soft light ;
My Pearl that bejewelled the gloom of her night,
The secretly precious, the hiddenly rare ;
A prize to be won for the worthiest wear ;
My Pearl shall be set with the first of the fair !

PARTING.

Too fair, I may not call thee mine :
    Too dear, I may not see
Those eyes with bridal beacons shine ;
    Yet, Darling, keep for me—
Empty and hushed, and safe apart,
One little corner of thy heart !

Thou wilt be happy, dear ! and bless
    Thee ; happy mayst thou be.
I would not make thy pleasure less ;
    Yet, Darling, keep for me,
My life to light, my lot to leaven,
One little corner of thy Heaven !

Good-bye, dear heart ! I go to dwell
    A weary way from thee ;
Our first kiss is our last farewell ;
    Yet, Darling, keep for me—
Who wander outside in the night,
One little corner of thy light !

" FOR EVER."

" Farewell, Sweet ! may you find a nest
    Of home in haven dearer :
And safelier rest upon the breast
    Of truer love and nearer !
May favours fall, and blessings flow
    For you, and cares come never !
But kiss me, dear, before you go,
    And then shake hands for ever."

Her very heart within doth melt,
  And gathers while she lingers
A weeping warmth, as though it felt
  A wee Babe's feeling fingers:
The minutes pass, they do not part,
  And vain was all endeavour;
A touch had closed them heart to heart,
  And hands WERE clasped for ever.

SHAKSPEARE.

OUR Prince of Peace in glory hath gone,
With no spear shaken, no sword drawn,
Without one battle-flag unfurled,
To make his conquest of the world.

For him no martyr-fires have blazed,
No limbs been racked, no scaffolds raised !
For him no blood was ever shed
To dye the Conqueror's raiment red.

And for all time he wears the crown
Of lasting, limitless, renown :
He reigns, whatever Monarchs fall ;
His throne is at the heart of all.

"ALL READY AND ALL ONE."

WHAT is the News to-day, Boys ?
  Have they fired the Signal gun ?
We answer but one way, Boys :
We are ready for the fray, Boys.
  All ready and all one !

They shall not say we boasted
  Of deeds that would be done ;
Or sat at home and toasted :
We are marshalled, drilled and posted,
  All ready and all one !

We are not as driven cattle
  That would the conflict shun.
They have to test our mettle
As *Volunteers* of Battle,
  All ready and all one !

The life-streams of the Mother
  Through all her youngsters run,
And brother stands by brother,
To die with one another,
  All ready and all one !

Sydney, 1885.

ENGLAND.

THERE she sits in her Island-home,
  Peerless among her Peers !
And Liberty oft to her arms doth come,
  To ease its poor heart of tears.
Old England still throbs with the muffled fire
  Of a Past she can never forget :
And again shall she herald the World up higher ;
  For there's life in the Old Land yet.

They would mock at her now, who of old looked
      forth
  In their fear, as they heard her afar ;
But loud will your wail be, O Kings of the Earth !
  When the Old Land goes down to the war.

The Avalanche trembles, half-launched, and half-
　- riven,
　　Her voice will in motion set:
O ring out the tidings, wide-reaching as Heaven!
　　There's life in the Old Land yet.

The old nursing Mother 's not hoary yet,
　　There is sap in her ancient tree:
She lifteth a bosom of glory yet,
　　Through her mists, to the Sun and the Sea—
Fair as the Queen of Love, fresh from the foam,
　　Or a star in a dark cloud set;
Ye may blazon her shame,—ye may leap at her
　　name,—
　　But there's life in the Old Land yet.

Let the storm burst, you will find the Old Land
　　Ready-ripe for a rough, red fray!
She will fight as she fought when she took her
　　stand
　　For the Right in the olden day.
Rouse the old royal soul, Europe's best hope
　　Is her sword-edge for Victory set!
She shall dash Freedom's foes down Death's
　　bloody slope;
　　For there's life in the Old Land yet.

THE OLD LAND.

O LEAL high hearts of England,
　　The evil days draw near,
When ye, with steel in heart and hand,
　　Must strike for all that's dear!

And better tread the bloodiest deck,
   And fieriest field of fame,
Than break the heart and bow the neck,
   And sit in the shadow of shame.
Let Despot, Death, or Devil come,
   United here we stand:
We'll safely guard our Island-Home,
   Or die for the dear old Land.

O, Warriors of Old England,
   You'll hurry to the call;
And her good ships shall sail the storm,
   With their merry Mariners all.
In words she wasteth not her breath,
   But be the trumpet blown,
And in the Battle's dance of death,
   She'll dance the bravest down.
Let Despot, Death, or Devil come,
   United here we stand :
We'll safely guard our Island-Home,
   Or die for the dear old Land.

Success to our dear England,
   When dark days come again ;
And may she rise up glorious
   As the rainbow after rain.
A thousand memories warm us still,
   And, ere the old spirit dies,
The purple of each wold and hill
   From English blood shall rise.
Let Despot, Death, or Devil come,
   United here we stand :
We'll safely guard our Island-Home,
   Or die for the dear old Land.

God strike with our dear England !
　Long may the old land be
The guiding glory of the world ;
　Home of the fair and free !
Old Ocean on his silver shield
　Shall lift our little Isle
Unvanquished still by flood or field,
　While the heavens in blessing smile.
Let Despot, Death, or Devil come,
　United here we stand :
We'll safely guard our Island-Home,
　Or die for the dear old Land.

SEA-SONG.

Come, show your Colours now, my Lads,
　That all the world may know
The Boys are equal to their Dads,
　Whatever blast may blow.

All hands aboard ! our country calls
　On her Seafaring folk !
In giving up our wooden Walls,
　More need for Hearts of Oak.

Remember how that old Fire-Drake
　Would singe the Spaniard's beard ;
And think how Raleigh, Nelson, Blake,
　Into their harbours steered.

Think how o' nights we cut them out !
　'Twas many a time and oft—
Silence !—a rush—a tug—a shout—
　And the old flag flew aloft.

Be it one to seven,—be it Hell or Heaven,—
　We fought our decks red-wet !
Be it hell or heaven,—be it one to seven. —
　We fear no Foeman yet.

At every port-hole there shall flame
　The same fierce battle-face :
All worthy of the old sea-fame—
　All of the old Sea-Race.

OUR NATIVE LAND.

THIS is our Mother Country !
　　The dearest land ;
　　The rarest land.
Round which the sea keeps sentry,
　　Or Ships are manned ;
　　Or ships are manned.
Nothing but Heaven above her !
　　And here's my hand ;
　　And here's my hand.
We are brothers all who love her,
　　Our Native Land ;
　　Dear Native Land.

Afar and near they hail her,
　　With greetings warm ;
　　With greetings warm.
The famous old brave Sailer,
　　That rode the storm ;
　　Ay, many a storm.

Who would not die to save her,
    Shall bear the brand;
    The Coward's brand.
In love we never waver
    For Native Land;
    Dear Native Land.

No matter where our place is,
    We may go forth;
    We may go forth.
And turn dead frozen faces
    Home from the North;
    Home from the North.
Or sink 'neath orient Heaven,
    In burning sand;
    Waste, desert sand.
Our lives shall still be given
    For Native Land;
    Dear Native Land

Oft-times the Foe beheld us,
    All torn apart;
    All torn apart.
Although a blow would weld us
    All one at heart;
    All one at heart.
Now trust we in each other,
    A little band;
    A happy band.
As Children of one Mother!
    Our Native Land;
    Dear Native Land.

Some new heroic story
    The world shall learn ;
    The world shall learn.
If we who keep her glory
    Are true and stern ;
    All true and stern.
Come wild and warring weather,
    We ready stand ;
    All ready stand.
To fight or fall together
    For Native Land ;
    Dear Native Land.

A NATIONAL ANTHEM.

God bless our native Land,
Glorious, and grave, and grand,
    God bless our Land !
God bless her noble face,
God bless her peerless race,
Great heart, and daring hand,
    God bless our Land !

God love our native Land,
Make her for ever grand,
    God love our Land !
Robe her with righteousness,
Crown her with gifts of grace,
Throne her at Thy right hand,
    God love our Land !

If secret foes should band
To strike our dear old Land,
        God aid our Land !
Be Thou her strength and stay,
God, in the battle day ;
Strew them ashore like sand,
        God aid our Land !

Few are we, Sword in hand;
All sword in soul we stand,
        Around our Land !
And when her blood shall flow,
Green make her glory grow,
Lead her in triumph grand,
        Our leal old Land !

Here pray we hand in hand,
Tears in our eyelids stand,
        God save our Land !
Thy Watch-tower on the Sea,
Venger of Right is she,
Long let old Fear-not stand,
        God save our Land !

HAVELOCK'S MARCH.

Behold a phantom-form appears, majestic in its gloom !
Mournfully it looks across a Chasm deep as doom :
A quivering heartache seems to move its withered, wordless lips ;
Familiar eyes are kindling through their wan light of eclipse :
It is the Ancient Mother rising, Sphinx-like, 'mid her sands,
To plead with those who will not hear.   She wrings her wrinkled
      hands ;
Yearns over both.   As Brothers long ago she brought them forth,
Her dusky darlings and her great white Heroes of the North !
The Children have no memories of the Morning-Land, and yet
The Mother's heart remembers, though all the world forget.

WE look with horror, when the blood grows
    cold,
On that which stung us hotly enough of old;
Blame me not wantonly: I do but draw
Faintly the thing we felt; the sight we saw!

THE REVOLT.

"Come hither, my brave Soldier-boy, and sit you
    by my side,
To hear the tale, a fearful tale, a glorious tale
    of pride;
How Havelock with his handful, all so faithful
    and so few,
Held on in that far Indian land, to bear our
    England through
Her bloodiest pass of peril, and her reddest sea
    of wrath;
And strode like Paladins of old on their aveng-
    ing path.
Though clothes were drenched, and flesh was
    parched, or bones were chilled with cold,
The gallant hearts never gave up; they never
    loosed their hold;
But fought right on, and triumphed, till our eyes
    rained as we read
How proudly every place was filled, with living
    and with dead.

"The stillness of a brooding storm lay on that
    Eastern land;
The dark death-circle narrowed round our little
    English band:
The false Sepoy stooped lower for his spring, and
    in his eye
A bloody light was burning on them, as he
    glided by:

Old Horrors rose, and leered at them, from out
    the tide of time,—
The peering peaks of War's old world, whose
    brows were stained with crime!
The conscious Silence was but dumb, a cursèd.
    Plot to hide;
The darkness only a mask of Death, ready to
    slip aside.
Under the leafy palms they lay, and through
    their gay green crown
Our English saw no Storm roll up: no Fate
    swift-flaming down.

"At last it came. The Rebel drum was heard
    at dead of night:
They dashed in dust the only torch that showed
    the face of Right!
Once more the Devil clutches at his lost throne
    of the earth,
And sends a people, smit with plague of mad-
    ness, howling forth.
As in a Demon's dream they swarm from hor-
    rible hiding-nooks;
Red Murder stabs the air, and lights their way
    with maddening looks!
Snuffing the smell of human blood, the cruel
    Moloch stands;
Hearing the cry of '*Kill! Kill! Kill!*' and claps
    his gory hands.
At dead of night, while England slept, the fear-
    ful vision came,
She looked, and with a dawn of hell the East
    was all aflame.

" Stern tidings flashed to Havelock, of legions in
        revolt :
' *The Traitors turn upon us, and the eaters of our
        salt,*
    *Subtle as death, and false as hell, and cruel as the
        grave,*
    *Have sworn to rend us by the root; be quick, if ye
        would save ;*
    *The wild beasts bloody and obscene, mad-drunk
        with gore and lust,*
    *Have wreaked a horrible vengeance on our England
        rolled in dust.'*
And such a withering wind doth blow, such
        fearful sounds it brings,
The soul with shudders tries to shake off thoughts
        like creeping things.
A vast invisible Terror twines its fingers in the
        hair,
With one hand feeling for the throat; a hand
        that will not spare.

"They slew the grizzled Warrior, who to them
        had been so true ;
    The ruddy stripling with frank eyes of bonny
        northern blue ;
    They slew the Maiden as she slept ; the Mother
        great with child ;
    The Babe, that smiled up in their face, they
        stabbed it as it smiled !
    The piteous, pleading, hoary hair they draggled
        in red mire ;
    And mocked the dying as they dashed out,
        frantic from the fire,

To fall upon their Tulwars, hacked to Death ;
    the bayonet
Held up some child ; the demons danced around
    it writhing yet :
Warm flesh, that kindled so with life, was torn,
    and slowly hewn,
To daintiest morsels for the feast where Death
    began too soon.

" Our English girls, whose sweet red blood went
    dancing on its way,
A merry marriage-maker quick for its near wed-
    ding-day,—
All life awaiting for the breath of Love's sweet
    south to blow,
And budding bridal roses ripe with secret balms
    to flow,—
They stripped them naked as they were born ;
    naked along the street,
In their own blood they made them dip their
    delicate white feet :
With some last rag of shelter the poor helpless
    darling tries
To hide her from the cruel hell of those devour-
    ing eyes ;
Then, plucking at the skirts of Death, she prayer-
    fully doth cling,
To hide her from the eyes that still gloat round
    her in a ring.

THE AVENGERS.

" ' *Now, Soldiers of our England, let your love arise*
    in power ;
For never yet was greater need than in this awful
    hour :
Together stand like old true hearts that never fear
    nor flinch ;
With feet that have been shod for death, never to
    yield an inch.
Our Empire is a Ship on fire, before a howling
    wind,
With such a smoke of torment, as might make high
    heaven blind !
Wild Ruin waves his flag of flame, and ye must
    spring on deck,
And quench the fire in blood, and save our treasures
    from the wreck.'
Many a time has England thought she sent her
    bravest forth ;
But never went more gallant men of more heroic
    worth.

" Hungry and lean, through rain and mire, our
    War-wolves ravening go
On their long march, that shall not mete the red
    grave of the foe :
Like winter trees stripped to their naked strength
    of heart and arm,
That glory in their grimness as they tussle with
    the storm !

Only a handful few and stern, and few and stern
  their words ;
Strange meaning in their eyes that meet and
  strike out sparks like swords !
And there goes Havelock, leading the Forlorn
  Hope of our land :
The quick heart spurring at their side ; the
  banner of their band :
Kindled, but calm, along their ranks his steady
  eye doth run,
As Marksman seeks the death-line down the
  level of his gun.

" Beneath the whitening snows of age his spirit-
  ardours glow,
As glow the fragrant fires of spring in flowers
  beneath the snow.
Look in his grave and martial face, with Love's
  dear pity touched ;
A saviour soul doth sanctify the sword his hand
  hath clutched ;
A little while his silent thoughts have gone
  within to pray,
And send a farewell of the heart to the dear
  ones far away.
He prays to God to light him through the peril-
  ous darkness, when
He grapples with the beasts of blood, and quells
  them in their den.
And now his look is lifted in the light of some
  far goal ;
His lips the living trumpet of a gray-haired
  Seer's soul.

" On th' house-tops of Allahabad black, scowling
    brows were bent,
  In hate, and deep, still curses, on our heroes as
    they went
  To fight their hundred-days-long fight ; all true
    as their good steel,
  The Highlanders of Havelock, the Fusileers of
    Neil !
  A falling firmament of rain the heavens were
    pouring down ;
  They heeded not the drowning heavens, nor yet
    the foeman's frown :
  Forward they strained with hearts afire, and gal-
    lantly they toiled
  Till darkness fell upon them : then the Moon
    uprose and smiled.
  A little thing ! and yet it seemed at such a time
    to come
  Just like a proud and mournful smile from the
    very heart of Home.

" That night they halted in a Snipe-swamp; hun-
    gry, cold, and drenched ;
  With hearts that kept the blitheness of brave
    men that never blenched.
  Through flooding Nullah, slushy sand, onward
    they strode again,
  Ere Dawn, a wingèd glory, lit upon the bur-
    nished rain,
  And mists up-gathered sullenly along the rear
    of flight,
  Slowly as beaten Belooches might lounge from
    out the fight.

M 2

Then heaven grew like inverted hell ; a blazing
    vault of fire !
The Sun pursuing pitiless, to bring the brain-
    strokes nigher ;
With sworded splendours fierce in front, and
    darting down all day,
Intently as the eyes of Death a-feeding on his
    prey.

" All the day long, and every day, with patience
    conquering pain,
Our good and gallant fellows with one purpose
    forward strain ;
For there is that within each heart nothing but
    death can stop ;
They hurry on, and hurry on, and hurry till
    they drop ;
Trying to save the remnant ; reach the leaguered
    place in time
To grasp, with red-wet slaughtering hands, the
    workers of this crime.
They think of all the dead that float adown the
    Ganges' waters :
Those noble Englishmen of ours ; their gentle
    wives and daughters !
Of Fire and Madness broken loose, and doing
    deeds most pitiful ;
And then of vengeance dealt out by the choked
    and blackened city-full.

" They think of those poor things that climb each
    little eminence ;
As, from the deluge of the dark, when day is
    going hence,

The sheep will huddle up the hill, and gather
    there forlorn;
So gather they in this dread night, to wait the
    far-off morn.
Or, crouching in the Jungle, they look up in
    Nature's face,
To find she has no heart, for all her Reptilinear
    grace!
Each leaf a sword, or prickly spear, or lifted
    jagged knife!
No shields of shelter like our leaves; but threat-
    ening human life,
With ominous hints of blood; and there the
    roots go writhing round,
Like curses coiled upon the spring, that rest not
    underground.

" They find sure tokens all the day! and starting
    from their dream
At night, they hear the Pariah dogs that howl
    by Ganges' stream,
Knowing the waters bear their freight of corpses
    stiff and stark,
Scenting the footfalls on the air, as Death glides
    down the dark;
Only the Lotus with ripe lips, and arms caressing
    clings.
The silence swarms with ghostly thoughts; each
    sound with ghastly things.
There stands the plough i' the furrow; there
    the villagers have flown!
There Fire ran dancing over roofs that under-
    foot went down!

There Renaud hung his dangling dead, with but
    short time for shrift,
He caught them on their way to hell, and gave
    them a last lift.

"They saw the first sight of their foe as the fourth
    dawn grew red;
Twenty miles to breakfast marched; and had to
    fight instead.
The morning smiled on arms up-piled, and weary
    wayworn men,
But soon the Assembly sounded, and they sprang
    to arms again;
The heaviest heart up-leaping light, as flames
    that tread on air.
The Rebel line bore down as they had caught us
    unaware;
But Maude dashed forward with his Guns, across
    the sandy mire,
And little did they relish our bright rain of rifle
    fire:
Quickly the onward way was ploughed, with
    heaps on either hand;
They broke the foe, then broke their fast, that
    dauntless little band.

"Again they felt our withering fire, by Pandoo
    Nuddee stream;
Again they feared the crashing charge, and fled
    the vengeful gleam:
Small loss was his in battle when the Conqueror
    looked round;
But many fell from weariness, and died without
    a wound.

Soft, whispering flowery secrets, came a low
    wind of the west
That eve, like breath made balmy with the sweet
    love in the breast ;
Breathing its freshness through the groves of
    Mango and of Palm ;
But the sweetest thing that wind could bring
    was slumber's holy balm,
To bless them for the morrow, and give strength
    for them to cope
With those ten thousand men that stood betwixt
    them and their hope.

" It must have been a glorious sight to see them
    as they went,
With veteran valour steady ; sure of proud
    accomplishment.
When Havelock bade his line advance, the
    Highlanders swept on ;
Each one at heart a thousand ; a thousand men
    as one ;
Linked in their beautiful proud line across the
    broken lands,
Straight on ! they never paused to lift the
    weapon in their hands ;
Silent, compact and resolute, charged as a
    thundercloud
That burst, and wrapped the dead and living in
    one smoky shroud ;
One volley of Defiance ! one wild cheer ! and
    through the smoke
They flashed ! and all the battle into flying
    fragments broke.

"When night came down they lay there, gashed
    all over, side by side,
The gray old warrior and the youth, his Mother's
    darling pride!
Rolled with the rebel in the dust, and grim in
    bloody death;
And over all the mist arose, dank as the grave-
    yard's breath.
But light of heart we took the hill, and very
    proud that night
Was Havelock of his noble men, and Cawnpore
    was in sight.
The men had neither food nor tent, but the red
    road was won:
And very proud were they to hear their General's
    ' *Well done* ';
Not knowing how their shout of triumph rang
    a fatal knell;
Nor what that wretch had wrought who has no
    match this side of Hell.

CAWNPORE.

"Cawnpore was ghastly silent, as into it they
    stepped;
There stood the blackened Ruin that the brave
    old Soldier kept!
Where strained each ear for the English cheer,
    and stretched the wan wide eyes,
Through all that awful night to see the signal-
    rocket rise;

No tramp, no cheer of Brothers near; no distant
       Cannon's boom;
Nothing but death goes to and fro betwixt the
       glare and gloom.
The living remnant try to hold their bit of blood-
       stained ground;
Dark gaps continual in their midst; the dead
       all lying round;
And saddest corpses still are those that die, and
       do not die :
With just a little glimmering light of life to
       show them by.

" Each drop of water cost a wound to fetch it from
       the well;
The father heard his crying child and went, but
       surely fell.
They had drunk all their tears, and now dry
       agony drank their blood;
The sand was killing in their souls; the wind a
       fiery flood;
Oh, for one waft of heather-breath from off a
       Scottish wold !
One shower that makes our English leaves smile
       greener for its gold !
Then life drops inward from the eyes; turns
       upward with last prayer,
To look for its deliverance; the only way lies
       there :
And then triumphant Treachery made leap each
       trusting heart,
Like some poor Bird called from the nest, up-
       poising for the dart.

"'*Come, let us pray,*' their Chaplain said. No
    other boon was craved :
No pleading word for mercy sued ; no face the
    white flag waved ;
But all grasped hands and prayed, till peace
    their souls serenely filled ;
Then like our noble Martyrs, there they stood
    up, and were killed.
Only One saved !
    He led our soldiers to the House of Blood ;
An eager, panting, cursing crew ! but stricken
    dumb they stood
In silence that was breathlessness of vengeance
    infinite ;
A-many wept like women who were fiercest in
    the fight :
There grew a look in human eyes as though a
    wild beast came
Up in them at that scent of blood and glared
    devouring flame.

"All the Babes and Women butchered ! all the
    dear ones dead ;
The story of their martyrdom in lines of awful
    red !
The blood-black floor, the clotted gore, fair
    tresses, deep sword-dints ;
Last message-scrawl upon the wall, and tiny
    finger-prints :
Gathered in one were all strange sights of horror
    and despair,
That make the vision blood-shot, freeze the life,
    or lift the hair.

Faces to faces flashed hell-fire ! Oh, but they
    felt 'twould take
The very cup of God's own wrath, that gasping
    thirst to slake :
For many a day ' *Cawnpore* ' was hissed, and, at
    its word of guilt,
The slaying sword went merciless, right ruddy
    to the hilt.

"There came a time we caught them, with a vast
    o'erwhelming wave,
And of their grand Secunder Bagh we made a
    trophied grave.
Once more the Highlanders pressed on with
    stern avenging tread,
And Peel was there with his big guns, and
    Campbell at their head :
A spring of daring madness ! and they leapt
    upon their prey
With hungry hearts on fury fed, for many and
    many a day.
For hours and hours they slew, and slew, the
    devils in their den :
' *Ye wreaked your will on Women weak, now try
    it with strong men.*'
The blood that cried to heaven long in vapours
    from our slain,
Fell hot and fast upon their heads in showers
    of ruddy rain.

"That day they saw their delicate white marbles
    glow and swim ;
There rose a cry like hell from out a slaughter
    great and grim :

And as they clasped their hands and sued for
    mercy where they fell,
One last sure thrust was given for that red and
    writhing Well.
And there was joy in every heart, and light in
    every eye,
To see the Traitor hordes that fled, make one last
    stand to die !
While from the big wide wounds, like snakes,
    the runlets crawled along
And stole away ; the reptiles who had done the
    cruel wrong !
A terrible reprisal for each precious drop they
    spilled.
Seventeen hundred cowardly killers there were
    bravely killed.

THE RELIEF OF LUCKNOW.

" England's unseen, dead Sorrow doth a visible
    Angel rise ;
The sword of Justice in her hand ; Revenge looks
    through her eyes :
Stern with the purpose in her soul right onward
    hastens she,
Like one that bears the doom of worlds, with
    vengeful majesty ;
Sombre, superb, and terrible, before them still
    she goes !
And though they lessen day by day, they deal
    such echoing blows,

That still dilating with success, still grows that
　　little band,
Till in the place of hundreds, ten thousand seem
　　to stand.
With arms that weary not at work, they bear
　　our victor flag,
To plant it high on hills of dead, a torn and
　　bloody rag.

"Proud Lucknow lies before them,—all its page-
　　antry unrolled;
Against the smiling sapphire gleam her tops of
　　lighted gold.
Each royal wall is fretted all with frostwork
　　and with fire,
A glory of colour jewel-rich, that makes a
　　splendour-pyre,
As wave on wave the wonder breaks, the pointed
　　flames burn higher,
On dome of Mosque and Minaret, on pinnacle
　　and spire;
Fairy Creations, seen mid-air, that in their plea-
　　saunce wait,
Like wingèd creatures sitting just outside their
　　heaven-gate.
The City in its beauty lies, with flowers about
　　her feet;
Green fields, and goodly gardens, make so foul
　　a thing seem sweet.

"The Bugle rings out for the march, and, with
　　its fiercest thrill,
Goes to the heart of Havelock's men, and works
　　its lordly will,

Making their spirits thrill as leaves are thrilled
          in some wild wind;
Hunger and heartache, weariness and wounds,
          all left behind.
Their sufferings all forgotten now, as in the
          ranks they form;
And every soul in stature rose to wrestle with
          the storm.
All silent! what was hid at heart could not be
          said in words:
With faces set for Lucknow, ground to sharp-
          ness, keen as swords.
A tightening twitch all over! a grim glistening
          in the eye,
' *Forward!*' and on their way they strode to
          dare, and do, and die.

"Hope whispers at the ear of some, that they
          shall meet again,
And clasp their long-lost darlings, after all the
          toil and pain;
A-many know that they will sleep to-night
          among the slain;
And many a cheek will bloom no more for all
          the tearful rain:
And some have only vengeance; but to-day 'tis
          bitter sweet;
And there goes Havelock! his the aim too lofty
          for defeat;
With steady tramp the column treads, true as
          the firm heart's-beat:
Strung for its headlong murderous march through
          that long fatal street.

All ready to win a soldier's grave, or do the
    daring deed!
But not a man that fears to die for England in
    her need.

"The masked artillery raked the road, and
    ploughed them front and flank;
Some gallant fellow every step was stricken
    from the rank;
But, as he staggered, in his place another sternly
    stepped;
And, firing fast as they could load, their onward
    way they kept.
Now, give them the good bayonet! with Eng-
    land's sternest foes,
Strong arm, cold steel has done it, in the wildest,
    bloodiest close:
And now their Bayonets flash in forks of
    Lightning up the ridge,
And with a cheer they take the guns, another,
    clear the bridge.
One good home-thrust! and surely, as the dead
    in doom are sure,
They send them where that British cheer can
    trouble them no more.

"The fire is biting bitterly; onward the battle
    rolls;
Grim Death is glaring at them, from ten thou-
    sand hiding-holes;
Death stretches up from earth to heaven, spread-
    ing his darkness round;
Death piles the heaps of helplessness face down-
    ward to the ground;

Death flames from sudden Ambuscades, where
　　all was still and dark ;
Death swiftly speeds on whizzing wings the
　　bullets to their mark ;
Death from the doors and windows, all around
　　and overhead,　　　　　　　　．
Darts, with his cloven fiery tongues, incessant,
　　quick, and red :
Death everywhere, Death in all sounds, and,
　　through its smoke of breath,
Victory beckons at the end of long dark lanes
　　of death.

" Another charge, another cheer, another Battery
　　won !
And in a whirlwind of fierce fire the fight went
　　roaring on
Into the very heart of hell : with Comrades fall-
　　ing fast,
Through all that tempest terrible, the glorious
　　remnant passed.
No time to help a dear old friend : but where
　　the wounded fell,
They knew it was all over, and they looked a last
　　farewell.
And dying eyes, slow-setting in a cold and stony
　　stare,
Turned upward, saw a map of murder scribbled
　　on the air
With crossing flames ; and others read their
　　fiery fearful fate,
In dark, swart faces waiting for them, whitening
　　with their hate.

" But, proudly men will march to death, when
    Havelock leads them on :
Through all the storm he sat his horse as he
    were cut in stone !
But now his look grows dark ; his eye gleams
    with uneasy flash :
' *On, for the Residency, we must make a last brave
    dash.*'
And on dashed Highlander and Sikh through a
    sea of fire and steel,
On, with the lion of their strength, our first in
    glory, Niel !
It seemed the face of heaven grew black, so
    close it held its breath,
Through all the glorious agony of that long
    march of death.
The round shot tears, the bullets rain ; dear
    God, outspread Thy shield !
Put forth Thy red right arm, for them, Thy
    sword of sharpness wield !

" One wave breaks forward on the shore, and one
    falls helpless back :
Again they club their wasted strength, and fight
    like ' *Hell-fire Jack.*' [1]
And ever as fainter grows the fire of that
    intrepid band,
Again they grasp the bayonet as 'twere Salva-
    tion's hand.
They leap the broad, deep trenches, rush through
    archways streaming fire ;
Every step some brave heart bursts, heaving
    deliverance nigher :

     [1] Sobriquet of Captain Olpherts.

‘ *I'm hit,*’ cries one, ‘ *you'll take me on your back,*
old Comrade, I
Should like to see their dear white faces once before
I die ;
My body may save you from the shot.’
His Comrade bore him on :
But, ere they reached the Bailie Guard, the
hurrying soul was gone.

“ And now the Gateway arched in sight ; the last
grim tussle came.
One moment makes immortal ! dead or living,
endless fame !
They heard the voice of fiery Niel, that for the
last time thrilled ;
‘ *Push on, my men, 'tis getting dark*’ : he sat
where he was killed.
Another frantic surge of life, and plunging o'er
the bar,
Right into harbour hurling goes their whirling
wave of war,
And breaks in mighty thunders of reverberating
cheers,
Then dances on in frolic foam of kisses, blessings,
tears.
Stabbed by mistake, one native cries with the
last breath he draws,
‘ *Welcome, My Friends, never you mind, it's all for*
the good cause.’

“ How they had leaned and listened, as the battle
sounded nigher ;
How they had strained their eyes to see them
coming crowned with fire !

Till in the flashing street below they heard them
    pant for breath,
And then the friendly faces smiled clear from
    the cloud of death ;
And iron grasp met tender clasp ; wan weeping
    women fold
Their dear Deliverers, down whose long brown
    beards the big tears rolled.
Another such a meeting will not be on this side
    heaven !
The little wine they have hoarded, to the last
    drop shall be given
To those who, in their mortal need, fought on
    through fearful odds,
Bled for them, reached them, saved them, less
    like men than glorious gods.

DEATH OF HAVELOCK.

" The Warrior may be ripe for rest, and laurelled
    with great deeds,
But till their work be done, no rest for those
    whom God yet needs :
Whether in rivers of ruin their onward way
    they tear,
Or healing waters trembling with the beauty
    that they bear ;
Blasting or blessing they must on : on, on, for
    ever on !
Divine unrest is in their breast, until their work
    is done.

Nor is it all a pleasant path the sacred band
    must tread,
With life a summer holiday, and death a downy
    bed !
They wear away with noble use, they drink the
    tearful cup ;
And they must bear the Cross who are bidden
    with the Christ to sup.

" Each day his face grew thinner, and sweeter,
    saintlier grew
The smiling soul that every day was burning
    keenlier through.
And higher, each day higher, did the life-flame
    heavenward climb,
Like sad sweet sunshine up the wall, that for
    the sunset time
Seems watching till the signal that shall call it
    hence is given ;
Even so his spirit kept the watch, till beckoned
    home to heaven.
His work was done, his eyes with peace were
    soft and satisfied ;
War-worn and wasted, in the arms of Victory
    he died.
' *Havelock's dead,*' and darkness fell on every up-
    turned face ;
The shadow of an Angel passing from its earthly
    place.

" In the red pass of peril, with a fame shall never
    dim,
Died Havelock, the Good Soldier : who would
    not die like him ?

In grandest strength he fell, full-length; and
      now our hero climbs
To those who stood up in their day and spoke
      with after times:
There on the battlements of Heaven, they watch
      us, looking back
To see the blessing flow for those who follow in
      their track.
He smileth from his heaven now; the Martyr
      with his palm;
The weary warrior's tired life is crowned with
      starry calm.
On many sailing through the storm another star
      shall shine,
And they shall look up through the night and
      conquer at the sign.

" They laid it low, the old gray head, not only
      gray with years;
It had been bowed in Sorrow's lap and silvered
      with her tears;
Our England may not crown it, with her heart
      too full for speech;
The hand that draws into the dark, hath borne
      it beyond reach.
The eyes of far-away heaven-blue, with such
      keen lustre lit,
As they could pierce the dark of death, and,
      star-like, fathom it,
They may not swim with sweetness as the happy
      Children run
To welcome home the Reaper, when the weary
      day is done!

How would the tremulous radiance round the
    old man's mouth have smiled;
Our good gray-headed hero, with the heart of a
    little child.

"Honour to Henry Havelock! though not of
    kingly blood,
He wore the double royalty of being great and
    good.
He rose and reached the topmost height; our
    Hero lowly born:
So from the lowly grass hath grown the proud
    embattled Corn!
He rose up in our cruel need, and towering on
    he trod;
Baring his brow to battle bold, as humbly to his
    God.
He did his work, nor thought of nations ringing
    with his name,
He walked with God, and talked with God, nor
    cared if following Fame
Should find him toiling in the field, or sleeping
    underground;
Nor did he mind what resting-place, with heaven
    embracing round.

"When swarming hell had broken bounds, he
    showed us how to stand
With rootage like the Palm amidst the maddest
    whirl of sand;
Undaunted while the swarthy storm around him
    swirled and swirled,
A winding-sheet of all white life! a wild Sahara
    world!

The drowning waves closed over him, lost to all
    human view,
And, like an arrow straight from God, he cleft
    their Twelve Hosts through.
No swerving as he walked along the rearing
    earthquake-ridge ;
He made a way for Victory, his body was her
    bridge.
Grand in the mouths of men his fame along the
    Centuries runs ;
Women shall read of his great deed and bear
    heroic sons.

" He leant a trusting hand on heaven, a gentle
    heart on home ;
In secret he grew ready, ere the Judgment hour
    was come.
War blew away the ashes gray, and kindled at
    the core
Live sparkles of the Ironside fire that glowed on
    Marston Moor.
Some Angel-Mute had led him blindfold through
    his thorny ways,
Till, on a sudden, lo, he stood, full in the glory's
    blaze.
Aloud, for all the world to hear, God called His
    servant's name,
And led him forth, where all might see, upon
    the heights of fame.
His arch of life, suspended as it sprang, in heaven
    appears,
Our bow of promise o'er the storm, seen through
    rejoicing tears.

"Joy to old England! she has stuff for storm-sail
    and for stay,
While she can breed such heroes, in her quiet,
    homely way:
Such martial souls that go with grim, war-figured
    brows pulled down,
As men that are resolved to bear Death's heavy,
    iron crown.
So long as she has sons like these, no foe shall
    make her bow,
While Ocean washes her white feet; Heaven
    kisses her fair brow.
If India's fate had rested on each single saviour
    soul,
They would have kept their grasp of it till we
    regained the whole.
The Lightnings of that bursting Cloud, which
    were to blast our might,
But served to show its majesty clear in the
    sterner light.

"Our England towers up beautiful with her dilat-
    ing form,
To greater stature in the strife, and glory in the
    storm;
Her wrath's great wine-press trodden on so
    many vintage fields,
With crush and strain, and press of pain, a
    ripened spirit yields,
To warm us in our winter, when the times are
    coward and cold,
And work divinely in young veins: wake boy-
    hood in the old.

Behold her flame from field to field on Victory's
  chariot wheels,
Till to its den, bleeding to death, Rebellion back-
  wards reels.
Her Martyrs are avenged ! ye may search that
  Indian land,
And scarcely find a single soul of all the traitor
  band.

" We've many a nameless Hero lying in his un-
    known grave,
  Their life's gold fragment glinting but a sun-
    fleck on the wave.
  But rest, you unknown, noble dead ! our Living
    are one hand
  Of England's power ; but, with her Dead she
    grasps into the land.
  The flower of our Race shall make that Indian
    desert bud,
  Its shifting sands drench firm, and fertilize with
    English blood.
  In many a country they sleep crowned, our con-
    quering, faithful Dead :
  They pave our path where shines her sun of
    empire overhead ;
  They circle in a glorious ring, with which the
    world is wed,
  And where their blood has turned to bloom, our
    England's Rose is red.

" Your brother Willie, Boy, was one of Havelock's
    little band ;
  My Son ! my beautiful brave Son, lies in that
    Indian Land.

They buried him by the wayside where he bowed
    him down to die,
While Homeward in its Eastern pomp the
    Triumph passed him by.
And even yet mine eyes are wet, but 'tis with
    that proud tear
A lofty feeling in its front doth like a jewel
    wear.
I see him! on his forehead shines the conqueror's
    radiant crest,
And God's own Cross of Victory is on his martial
    breast.
I should have liked to have felt him near, when
    these old eyes grow dim,
But gave him to our England in her greater
    need of him."

ONLY A DREAM.

As proper mode of quenching legal lust,
  A Roué takes unto Himself a Wife :
'Tis Cheaper when the bones begin to rust,
And there's no other Woman you can trust ;
But, mind you, in return, Law says you must
  Provide her with the physical means of life :
And then the blindest beast may wallow and roll ;
The twain are One flesh, never mind the Soul :
You may not cruelly beat her, but are free
To violate the life in sanctuary ;
In virgin soil renew old seeds of Crime
To blast eternity as well as time :
    She must show black and blue, or no divorce
    Is granted by the Law of Physical Force.

ONLY A DREAM.

Soft as a snow of light in a silent world
The veil of sleep dropped tremulously down
And gently covered up the face of life.
The nurse-like Spirit laid my body to rest,
And went to meet her Bridegroom in the night,
Who comes like music o'er the star-shored sea,
And clasps her at the portal with a kiss.
When lo, a hand reached through the dark, and
    drew
Me gliding wraith-like on, and looking up
The unfeatured gloom grew into Charmian's
    face ;
The stately Charmian with her lofty mien
Like a Greek Goddess Statue that had raised
The Veil of being in some diviner dawn,
When yearning Love did woo her into Woman,—
The warm heart glowing her white Silence
    through—
Who rose up in her crown the Queen of Smiles
With all the old majesty unweeting of
The old worship, conscious hearts must newly
    pay,—
Our English Vesture cannot mask her mould !

I read her look, and we two wandered forth
In the cool glory of the glimmering night:
The Earth lay faint with love at the feet of
        Heaven;
Her breath of incense went up through the
        leaves
In a low sough of bliss.   Above us burned
The golden legends on Night's prophet-brow;
The Moon rose o'er the city, a glory of gold;
All round us Life rehearsed Death's mystery.

And Charmian wore her June-like loveliness
As in a stole of sorrow; by day she moved
In some serene Elysium; queenly sweet,
And gracious; breathing beauty; a heaven of
        dreams
In her large lotus eyes, darkly divine:
Love-kindling Ardours curved her parted lips.
But now her blooming Life's luxuriant flower
Seemed withered into ashen spirit-fruit,
And like a Spirit's flashed her white, lit face!
Portentous things which hid themselves by day,
Sweet-shadowed 'neath her sunning beauty-bloom,
Came peering through the dim and sorrowy night.
Her lips, red-ripe to crush their fire-strong wine,
Pouting persuasive in perpetual kiss,
Were thin with anguish, bitter-pale with pain.

And from the windows whence young Beauty
        laughed,
As Age went by, a life of suffering looked,
And perished visions flashed their phantom-light.
White waves of sea-like soul had climbed, and
        dashed

The red light from its heaven of her cheek :
Her bounteous breast that breathed magnifi-
    cence,
And billowed with proud blood, sighed meekly
    now :
The flowers her Spartan spirit crowned her with
For the life-battle, dropped about her dead.
Diaphanous in the moonlight grew her life
With all its written agony visible ;
Down the dark deep of her great grief I stared,
And saw the Wreck with all its dead around.
And my heart melted in its mournfulness ;
She moaned, as hers were breaking in its pain ;
And then her voice vibrated piteous as
A Spirit wailing in a world of tears,
But stifled half its pathos not to hurt.

" *Earth sleeps, and wears the moonlight's mystic*
    grace,
The breath of blessings round her ; and all heaven
Is passing through her dream ; it trembles near ;
She feels the kiss of comfort on her face ;
But she will wake at morn in tears to find
The glory gone—all was a dream o' the night.
And thus my young Life slumbered, dreamed, and
    woke !

" *It ran in shadow like the woodland brook,*
Feeling its way, with yearnings for the light,
Until it flashes silver in the sun,
And takes a crown of radiance on its head.
Even so I found Him whom my soul had sought,
And fled into his breast with a cry of triumph,
Who lit up all things beautiful for me.
And through my happy tears there looked in mine

A spirit sweet as morning violets,
A face alight with love ineffable,
The starry heart-hid wonder trembling through :
And o'er me leaned,—as Spring-heaven over earth,
Dropping its love down in a rain of flowers,—
To feed me with all flowers of delight,
And crown me as his Queen of all delight.
Light hung a garland-grace about his brow ;
His voice, like footprints in the yielding snow,
Sank deepest with its softest fall of words.
He gave the casket of his happiness
Rich with Love's jewel for my hands to keep.
Around his stalwart strength my life entwined,
In golden oneness, and in proud repose ;
And like a God he clasped me with his strength !
And like a God he held me in his heaven ;
And all the air was golden with my God.

" Alas, that Woman's life divorced from Man's,
And seeking to be one again in love,
So often flies back through the grim wide wound !
Alas, that Time should crown with fruit of pain,
That seed from heaven whose fair flower is love !
They tore me from my Love ! they thrust him
        forth,
Spurned his rich love, and scorned his poverty ;
Rent all the twining tendrils of my life
To shrink back bleeding in their desolate home.
My life was shattered like the charmèd cup
That, breaking, brings the Hall in ruins round ;
And every fragment mirrored the great wrong !

" And while my mind yet wandered dark and dumb,
They sold me to a Worldling wrinkled, rich

And rotten, who bought Love's dear name for gold.
They dressed me in Bride flowers who should have
     worn
The white and wimpled weeds of widowhood,
And led me forth, a jewelled mockery!
'Twas like a wedding with the sheeted dead,
In silent hurry, and white ghastliness.
No bosoms beat Love's cymbals music-matched;
No blisses blushed, no bridal-kisses burned.
The ring was on my hand, few saw the chain
By which the owner drew me to his home,
And many envied me my happiness.
That night as we sat alone I felt his eyes
Burningly brand me to the core, his Slave.

" We dwelt amid a wildering world of wealth,
Which flamed a glistering glory, bloomed a warmth
Without, within was cold as a fireless hearth.
The Image of Nuptial Love to which they led
A maiden sacrifice i' the Sanctuary,
That should have raised me, smiled my tears
     away,
And into quickness all my coldness kissed,
And fed with precious oil the lamp of love
That in my heart, as in a tomb, burned on,
Was a gaunt Skeleton whose grave-like grasp
Clutched me for ever to a loveless breast.

" He was a cruel Tyrant, just too mean
To murder, although pitiless as the grave;
A human ink-fish spreading clouds around
When eyes of tender ruth would come too near.
He had a thin-lipped lust of power which looked
On torture in no rage of fiery blood,

But with infernal light of gloating eyes.
And yet I strove to love him.   O my God !
While reaching from the heights of blessedness,
How had I stretched my arms too eagerly,
And fall'n into a chasm that caught me and closed
Its dark inevitable arms, and crushed
Me, bruised and blind !   I struck, and struck,
    and beat
With bleeding strength, in vain.   A hundred
    hands
Fought in the gloom with mine as water weak.
At every step there stirred some loathly snake.
I felt as one that's bound, and buried alive ;
The black, dank death-mould stamped down over-
    head ;
I cried, and cried, and cried, but no help came.

" I heard the sounds above me far away ;
The feet of hurrying Life, and loitering Love ;
Rich bursts of music, hum of low, sweet talk ;
The dance of Pleasure dancing in her heaven,
And rustling rain of a thousand dear delights.
I knew the pictured world was lighted up,
And bloomed, like bridal chambers, soft and warm :
How sang the merry, merry birds of bliss ;
How Beauty's flower-guests stood crowned and
    drank
The health of Heaven with its dew for wine.
But not a crumb of all the glad life-feast,
Nor drop of all the wanton wealth for me,
And if I stretched weak arms to clasp my world,
A wormy mouth to my wild warmth was pressed ;
And if I turned to lift a prayer to God,
Above me burned two eyes like bottomless pits

> In which a brood of devils lurk and leer.
> And down my night there stooped no smiling
>   heaven,
>   With golden chances of a starry throne,
>   And beckoning looks that bid us come be crowned.

> " Around me rose the phantoms of the dark,
>   The Grave's Somnambules troubled in their dream,
>   Who walk and wander in the sleep of Death,
>   And cannot rest, they were so wronged in life.
>   The crownless Martyrs of the marriage-ring !
>   Meek sufferers who walked in living hell,
>   And died a life of spiritual Suttee.
>   They came to claim their kin in misery,
>   And show me, lifting up the mourning-pall,
>   Their symbols of unutterable woe ;
>   Scarred loves that bore the rack and told no tale ;
>   Tear-drownèd hearts and stifled agonies ;
>   The bleeding lips struck dumb by brutal hands ;
>   Slow murders of the curtained bridal-bed ;
>   The silent tortures and the shrouded deaths.

> " I wandered with them in the pitiless night
>   Who seek the jewel fallen from Life's crown ;
>   Oft stumbling, bled upon the cruel thorns,
>   But rose, and staggered on.   I strained mine eyes
>   Upon the dark, and raised mine empty cup ;
>   Surely with one gold drop of honey-dew,
>   Somewhere the heavens ran o'er t' enrich my
>   life ?

> " Then came to me a thing most sweet and strange,
>   As though an angel kissed me in the night,
>   Or Magic Rose flushed open in the gloom.

*A loosening charm wrought in my brain; the
    weight*
That ached to be dashed out in utter death,
Was thawing like a wintry clod in flowers.
In love's dead ashes burst a spark. I cried,
'O sweet light-bringer, in a bloom of dawn
Rise, let me see what treasure I have found !
My rich, warm jewel, crimson with sweet life,
Come shine where now I cross but empty palms,
And clasp the new love-raiment radiant round.
My little Bird shall hurry out the night,
Till all my world is touched with rosy gold :
My little Bird of God shall sit and sing
The dear day long, the dearer for the dark !

" ' If you rise beautiful from Sorrow's sea,
As Venice, Sorrow's Child, is Beauty's Queen,
Perchance thy little smiles, my Babe, may bring
Some human softness in his face, and I
Shall press the hand that hurts, for thy dear sake.
And I shall walk with thee, my Child, with thee,
Beneath new heavens, on an enchanted earth.
When I enfold thee in my arms, sweet Babe,
My heart will scarcely breathe lest it should wake
The sleeping wings of its new-nestling bliss.
When thou art born, my Child, all will be well ;
For surely love but vanished in the dark
To come back in the morning with my Babe ;
And all the sweetness liveth on when all
The bitterness is past ; and eyes that yearned
Wet through the gloom are glorified at last.
Soft baby-fingers feeling round my heart
Shall melt its frost ; and baby-lips shall turn
My tears to milk, and suck my sorrows dry.

All hell may wrestle in one human heart;
All heaven will nestle in my drop of dew.'

" *It came, my dazzling dawn's re-orient hope,*
My tiny babe, with its sweet mournful eyes!
And the pale innocent but fanned his hate
To frenzy; for, in many a desolate day,
And midnight, lying with my heart awake,
I had turned tearfully to look upon
A precious picture worn by Memory,
And in its beauteous image grew my Babe:
It had his likeness, was his Spirit-child.
Its luminous look had gathered all the light
That lost beloved Presence left with me.

My Tyrant poured his poison in the glass
My babe-joy-bearer lifted to my lips,
And dashe l the new love-vintage in the dust.
I ran the gauntlet of his hell for years,
And fell down on the threshold mad.   My Child!
They took my Babe from me, my pleading Babe;
And when the pretty one pined for me, and
     strained
His dim eyes for me till my darling died,
They called the Mother in to see her child
That lay there in the little shroud with all
Its beauty folded up for God in heaven:
Dead! dead! its dear eyes closed by stranger
     hands.

" *Much misery hath not made my spirit meek:*
Mine agony rends the bridal-veil: I cry,
Come see what ghastly wounds bleed hidden here!
Behold where all the Tortures of the Past

Are stored by Law, and sanctified for use.
I drag my burthen to a Nation's throne,
And pray deliverance from this despot's power.
Pity me, all good people, as ye sit
Within the happy circle of sweet marriage,
Loving and loved, glorying and glorified;
Whose love makes life so dear, that when ye die
And sit on heavenlier heights, your eyes will search
To find the garden where Love's fruitage grew;
The nest from whence your pretty nurslings flew;
Our old World smiling through its cloudy fold,
And love it for the marriage-love of old."

She ceased, and from afar methought there came
Across the night an echo sad and low,
Love answering love, heart crying unto heart.

———

" In the merry spring-tide when green buds start;
Wings break from the husk of care;
The dead beauty blossoms again in my heart
As I dream of the Springs that were:
The buried Past lifteth a radiant brow;
A phantom-bark toucheth life's shore;
And it floateth me far from the sorrowful Now,
Into Love's happy Nevermore.

" She rises before me, that Darling of mine,
Whom I lost in the world so wide;
O come to me, come to me, let thine arms twine
About me, my life! my Bride!
Ah me! I am breaking my heart to see
But her Image enshrined at its core;
Yet Memory's sighs bring a balm to me,
Out of Love's happy Nevermore.

" *Lovely she was as the lily is white,*
　　When the pride of the morning it wears :
Pure she was as the perfect light
　　That haloeth happy tears.
Hearts straightway rose from the shadow and
　　　　cloud,
　　Where the light of her presence kissed ;
Yet over the might of the proudest she rode,
　　Like Music, as she list.

" *Love, rosy-clear, in her cheek's faint dyes,*
　　Its first sweet bloom just took ;
Love came trembling up in her eyes,
　　As the stars in a happy brook :
Dear eyes ! they were dreams of heaven, with a
　　　　dance
　　Of light in their deep rich gloom ;
Whence the smiling heart looked like the golden
　　　　glance
　　From the pansy's purple bloom.

" *How I poured all my life in a beaker of bliss*
　　For her ! how I held the cup,
As the leaves, though the troubling winds will kiss,
　　Their tremulous dews hold up !
And my mind it walked in a raiment white,
　　Where starry thoughts reared a dome ;
And the feast was spread, and the chamber alight
　　For the Guest that never came home.

" *O Darling of mine ! does she ever think*
　　Of the old-time thoughts and things ?
O Darling of mine ! does she come to drink
　　At these wormwood spirit-springs ?

For I sometimes dream as I bend above,
  That the touch of her lip clings there,
And the fading balm of her breath of love
  Is eloquent in the air.

" *If we met unaware, just to ease her heart's pain,*
    Would she fall on my bosom and sob ?
Or would old memories glide through her brain
    With never an added throb ?
Is her pillow e'er wet in the dead night-hours ?
    When the heat of the day is o'er,
Does she turn, like me, for a handful of flowers,
    Into Love's happy Nevermore ?

" *O there is no heart that loves on earth*
    But may live to be loved again :
Some other heart hath the same dear birth,
    And aches with the same sweet pain.
And Love may yet come with a golden ray
    Shall lighten my life's despair :
But Love hath no second shaft can slay
    The first love nestling there.

" *In the merry spring-tide when green buds start ;*
    Wings break from the husk of care ;
The dead beauty blossoms again in my heart,
    As I dream of the Springs that were :
The buried Past lifteth a radiant brow,
    A phantom-bark toucheth life's shore :
And I am borne far from the sorrowful Now,
    Into Love's happy Nevermore.

All this was but the imagery of dream ;
For when the Morn in restless radiance rose,
Her breath of beauty palpitating light,
With clouds of colour smiling from the ground ;
A sparkling ecstasy in the blue air ;
And I with marvelling eyes had broke the seal
Of slumber, read the letter of my Dream,
Lo, Charmian in her summer-sumptuous beauty!
And oft the dimple gleamed upon her cheek,
To vanish like a dew-drop in a rose ;
And oft her laugh with reckless richness rung,
And shook a shower of music-pearls around.
I peered into the luminous dark of her eyes,
As one might come by light of day to look
Adown the glade where he had seen the dance
Of weird Elves in the night, but finds no trace.
Queen of the Sister-Graces ! who could know
Hers was the face that writhèd in my dream?

But still, as in my Dream, I see her stand,
Too living for a picture in romance,
Telling the wild stern story of her wrongs,
Holding the great Curse up to heaven for ever,
To call God's lightning down, although it kill
Her with her wedded Curse. And in my Dream
The kings and queens of prospering love go by,
And little heed this Martyr by the way ;
This poor weak woman trembling 'neath her load ;
This life fast fettered to a festering corse ;
This love that bleeds to death at many wounds :
This passing Tragedy of Soul within
Our five acts of the Sense, that breaks its way
Through human hearts i' the Theatre of a world.

Keir, 1856.

AN ORPHAN FAMILY'S CHRISTMAS.

AN ORPHAN FAMILY'S CHRISTMAS.

I.

A BLITHE old Carle is Christmas;
　You cannot find his fellow;
Match me the hale red rose in his cheek,
　Or the heart so mild and mellow;
The glitter of glory in his eyes,
　While the Wassail-cup he quaffs,
Or the humour that twinkles out of his wrinkles
　As helplessly he laughs.

Of all High-Tides 'tis Christmas
　Most richly crowns the year;
Right through the land there ripples and runs
　Its flood of merry good cheer.
Troops of friends come sailing down,
　Making a pleasant din;
Fling open doors! set wide your hearts!
　'Tis Christmas coming in.

A glorious time is Christmas,
　We gather all at home,
And like the Christmas fairies,
　With their pranks, our darlings come;
And gentle Sylvan Spirits hid
　In holly-boughs they bring,
To grow into good Angels,
　And bless our fairy-ring!

A jolly time is Christmas,
  For Plenty's horn is poured ;
Then flows the honey of the Sun,
  Our fruits all summer hoard !
Merry men tall march up the hall :
  They bear the meats and drinks ;
And Wine, with all his hundred eyes,
  Your hearty welcome winks.

And O the Fire of Christmas,
  That like some Norse God old,
Mounts his log up-chimney, and roars
  Defiance to the cold !
He challenges all out-of-doors :
  He wags his beard of flame ;
It warms your very heart to see
  Him glory in the game.

A happy time is Christmas ;
  Young hearts will slip the tether ;
Lips moist and merry, all under the berry,
  Close thrillingly together.
A gracious time ! the poorest Poor
  Will make some little show,
And ailing infants, seeing the fun,
  Will do their best to crow !

II.

But there are nooks in Poverty's dim world,
Where the high tide of bounty never runs.
No drop of all its wealth for some who sit
And hear the river of riches brimming by.

They see the Christmas shows of wealth and
        warmth,
At window, whilst shut out at every door!
The Plenty only flouts their poverty;
The music mocks them with its merriment;
They look into each passing face and find
No likeness of their own deep misery.

In one of these dark nooks, at Christmas time,
An Orphan family, with little fire,
And only light enough to see the gloom,
Together sat; two Sisters and one Brother;
The youngest six years old; the eldest twelve;
An old Grandfather lying ill a-bed.
They knew that Christmas came, but not for them.
Thus had they often sat o' winter nights,
Shivering within, as darkness shuddered without,
And creeping close together for heart-warmth;
Poor unfledged nurslings with the Mother gone!
Feeling a Presence brooding over them,
In whose chill shadow they were pall'd and hooded;
So mournfully it kept the Mother's place!
Till flesh would creep as though about to leave
The spirit naked—bare to the cold breath
That whispers of the grave—all lidless eye
To that appalling sight the helpless Dead
Lie looking on, in their amazement, dumb,
And petrified to marble! So they sat;
The Shadow in the house and on the heart;
The old Clock ticking through the lonely room,
With sounds that make the silence solemner,
And weird hands pointing to far other times;
Talking of merry Christmas coming in;
Of visionary futures, and old days,

With thoughts so far beyond their years !   The
    life
In their young eyes gleamed preternaturally,
Betwixt the fire-shine, and the dim night-shadows,
As their old inmates of the heart stole forth
To people the old ways they walked once more.
And so, like those lorn pretty Babes i' the Wood,
That Robins buried when the talk was done,
They told each other stories ; sang their Hymns ;
By way of bribing the gaunt Solitude,
Not to look down upon them quite so grim !
Poor darlings, with no Father, and no Mother.

III.

Ay me, dear Sister, gentle Brother,
    How soft the thought of a Mother lies
    At heart ; how sweet in sound 'twill rise ;
And these poor Children had no Mother !

No Mother-arms in secret nook
    To fold the sufferer to her breast,
    With love that never breaks its rest,
And Heartsease in her very look.

No Mother-wings to brood above
    The winter nest and keep them warm ;
    And shield them from the pitiless storm,
With the large shelter of her love.

No Mother's tender touch that brings
    A music from the harp of life,
    Like hovering heaven above the strife
And precious trembling of the strings.

No Mother with her lap of love
　　Each night for heads that bow in prayer ;
　　Dear hands that stroke the smiling hair,
And heart that pleads their cause above.

No Mother whose quick, wistful eye
　　Will see the shadow of Danger near,
　　And face, with love that casts out fear,
The blow that darkly hurtles by.

No Mother's smile ineffable,
　　To stir the Angel in the bud,
　　Till, into perfect womanhood,
The Flower blushes at the full.

No Mother ! when the Darling One
　　Bends with a grief that breaks the flower,
　　To loose the sorrow in a shower,
And lift the sweet face to the sun.

No Mother's kiss of comfort near
　　The River that Death overshades ;
　　Or voice that, when the dim face fades,
Sounds on with words of solemn cheer.

Ay me, dear Sister, gentle Brother,
　　How soft the thought of a Mother lies
　　At heart ; how sweet in sound 'twill rise ;
And these poor Children had no Mother.

IV.

Yet, God is kind ; His ways are Fatherly.
Affliction's hand, it seem'd, had, at a touch,
Awoke the Mother in the young Child-heart
Of little Martha, who had now become

A wee old woman at twelve years of age,
With many Motherly ways.   Yea, God is kind.

The tiny Snowdrop braves the wintry blast;
He tenderly protects its confidence
That lifts the venturous head, safe in His hand:
And Martha, in her loneliness of earth,
And such a dearth of human fellowship,
And such companionship with solitude,
Had found a way of looking up to Heaven:
And oft I think that God in heaven smiled;
Holding His hand about her little life,
As one that shields a candle from the wind.
She had the faith to feel Him nearest, when
The world is farthest off; and, in this faith,
Her spirit went on wings, or, hand-in-hand
With Love that digs below the deepest grave,
And Hope that builds above the highest stars.

In the old days before their sorrow came,
And vast Eternity oped twice to them,
And each time, following the lightning-flash,
They groped in darkness for a Parent gone,
She was the merriest of merry souls;
The gay heart laughing in her loving eyes;
The peeping rose-bud crimsoning her cheek;
There was as quick a spirit in her feet,
As now had passed into her toiling fingers,
That match the Mother's heart with Father's
      hands
In their unwearied working for the rest.
In those old days the Father made a song
About his little maid, and sang it to her.

V.

" It is a merry Maiden,
With spirits light as air;
While others go heart-laden,
And make the most of care,
She trips along with laughter:
Old Care may hobble after.

" A sunbeam straight from heaven,
She dances in my room;
The gladdest thing e'er given
To cheer a heart or home:
My stream of life may darkle,
She makes the brighter sparkle.

" Her smile it is the Morning
That turns the mist to pearls;
All thought of sadness scorning,
She shakes her sunny curls;
And, with her merry glancing,
She sets all hearts a-dancing."

VI.

But now the Maid was changed, for she had been
With Sorrow in its chilly sanctuary;
Her look was paler, for it had been touched
With that white stillness of the winding-sheet,
That smile forlornly sweet upon the face
When left forever widowed of the soul.
Henceforth her life went softly all its days
As if she felt the Grave-turf underfoot.

Her beauty was more spiritual ; not aged
Or worn ; less colour, but more light.
It was a brier-rose beauty, tremulous
With tenderest dew-drop purity of soul.

I've often seen how well their favour wears
Whose sufferings are for others, not for Self ;
How long they keep a fair unfurrowed face,
Whose tears are luminous with healing love,—
The pearly cars that bring good spirits down
To water and enrich their special flowers,—
And do not come from cares that kill the heart ;
These sere no bloom ; they leave no snaky trail.
So Martha kept her face, and might have been
The younger sister of that lily Maid,
The lovable Elaine of Astolat.

VII.

We write the tale of Heroes in the blood
They shed when dying where they nobly stood ;
And the red letters gloriously bloom
To light the warrior to a loftier doom.
But there are battles where no cheers arise,
And no flags wave before the fading eyes ;
Heroes of whom the wide world never hears ;
Their story only writ in Woman's tears.
Yet that invisible ink shall surely shine
Brightest in Heaven, and verily divine.
And when God closes our world's blotted book,
To cast it in the fire with awful look,
It was so badly written, leaf on leaf
   Thus lived might touch the Father's heart with
     grief.

P

And this Child-Mother's life may yield one story
That shall be told among the first in glory.

Her busy love and thoughtful care are such,
The others do not miss the Mother much.
From dawn to dark her presence lights the place
With many a gleam of reliquary grace.
Their few poor things in seemly order stand,
Bright as with last touch of the Parent's hand.
The clothes are mended, and the house is kept
Clean as of old ; bravely hath Martha stepped
In Mother's footprints ; her wee feet have tried
Their best to track the Parent's larger stride.
With household work her little hands are hard,
Her arms are chilled, her knees with kneeling
          scarred :
Dusty her hair that might have richly rolled
With warm Venetian glow of Titian's gold.
Great-hearted little woman ; she toils still,
Though the Grandfather, lying old and ill,
To her twin troubles adds a heavier third,
She works on without one complaining word.

VIII.

And once a year she has her Holiday ;
One day of airy life in fairyland,
When young leaves open large their palms to
    catch
The gold and silver of the sun and shower ;
Shy Beauty pusheth back her glittering hood,
To peep with her flower face ; the Silver Birk
Shakes out her hair full-length against the blue ;

The Fir puts forth her timid finger-tips,
Like shrinking damsel trying a cold stream
In which she comes to bathe.
                                    In merry green woods
She rambles where the blue wild hyacinths
Smile with their soft dream-haze in tender shade :
The lightsome dance of gladsome green above ;
The whispering sweetness of the wood below ;
Birds singing, as for love of her, all round :
Or, by the Brook that turns some stray sunbeam
To a crooked scimitar of wavy gold,
Then to itself laughs at the elvish work !
With her large eyes, and eager leaping looks,
She pores o'er Nature's living picture-page,
And gets some colour in her own pale life.
Then home, with kindled cheek, when Eve's one
        Star
Stands, waiting on the threshold of the night,
In lively expectation of all heaven.

IX.

Home when the happy day is done,
    Home comes my little Maid ;
Her pleasure—golden in the sun—
    Now dewy in the shade.
Thoughts of the day will hover and bless
Her sleep with sacred balminess.

Through shutting eve the stars will peep,
    But still there comes no night ;
'Tis but the Day hath fallen asleep
    And smiles in dreams of light.

And Martha feels the heart of Love
Beat on in silent stars above.

X.

To-night they sit with sadder, lonelier thought
Than ever; closer comes the Wolf of Want,
And darklier falls the shadow of Orphanhood.
For now the old man keeps his bed, and seems
Death-stricken, with his face of ghastly gray;
His life all crowded in cold glittering eyes
Watching the least light movement that is made.
The Boy, a blithe and sunny godsend, gay
As singing fountain springing in their midst,
With loving spirit leaping to the light,
Is low at heart to night, and sad and still.
While Dora, in whose purple-lighted eyes
There seems the shadow of a rain-cloud near,
With but a faint shine of the cheery soul;
She longs to fly away and be at rest,
And give her wishes wings in measured words
That win strange pathos from her sweet young
      voice.

" Come to the Better Land, that Angels know;
They walk in glory, shining as they go !
The King in all His beauty takes the least
To sit beside Him at the eternal feast."
Thus sings the voice that calls me night and day.
    " This is a weary world,
          Come, come, come away !
      Ah, 'tis a dreary world,
          Come, come away."

" *From old heart-ache, and weariness, and pain—*
Sorrows that sigh, and hopes that soar in vain—
Come to the Loved and Lost who are now the Blest ;
They dwell in regions of Eternal rest."
Thus sings the voice that calls me night and day.
     " *This is a weary world,*
          Come, come, come away !
     Ah, 'tis a dreary world,
          Come, come away."

" *Here all things change ; the warmest hearts grow*
          cold ;
The young head droops and dims its glorious gold ;
Where Love his pillow hath made on Beauty's breast,
The creatures of the Grave will make their nest."
Thus sings the voice that calls me night and day.
     " *This is a weary world,*
          Come, come, come away !
     Ah, 'tis a dreary world,
          Come, come away."

" *The dear eyes where each morning rose our light,*
Soon darken with their last eternal night ;
The heart that beat for us, the hallowed brow
That bowed to bless, are cold and silent now."
Thus sings the voice that calls me night and day.
     " *This is a weary world,*
          Come, come, come away !
     Ah, 'tis a dreary world,
          Come, come away."

" *Nor fear the Grave, that door of Heaven on Earth ;*
All changed and beautiful ye shall come forth,
As from the cold dark cloud the winter showers
Go underground to dress, and come forth Flowers."

Thus sings the voice that calls me night and day.
     " This is a weary world,
        Come, come, come away !
     Ah, 'tis a dreary world,
        Come, come away."

" Come to the Better Land, that angels know ;
They walk in glory, shining as they go !
The King in all His beauty takes the least
To sit beside Him at the eternal feast."
Thus sings the voice that calls me night and day.
     " This is a weary world,
        Come, come, come away !
     Ah, 'tis a dreary world,
        Come, come away."

XI.

" NAY, Sister," says the cheery Martha, " though
Our lot be sad, your strain's too sorrowful !
We cannot spare you yet.   Nor must we stoop
To make our burthen heavier ; hear me, love.

    " A little Flower so lowly grew,
      So lonely was it left,
    That Heaven looked an eye of blue
      Down in its rocky cleft.

    " What could the little Flower do
      In such a darksome place,
    But try to reach that eye of blue,
      And climb to kiss Heaven's face ?

"And there's no life so lone and low
But strength may still be given
From narrowest lot on earth to grow
The straighter up to Heaven."

Again she sang, and set them singing too.

" Here we are poorest of God's Poor,
Toiling for bread from day to day,
But laid up in Heaven a treasure is sure,
While Money is round and rolls away.
And though there's room for all the rest,
I think God loves the Little Ones best.

" Little hearts make merry, and sing
How His love to Children warms!
Little voices ripple and ring—
How He takes them in His arms!
And though there's room for all the rest,
I think God loves the Little Ones best."

XII.

THEN, silent Fabyan lifted up his look,
Bright as a Daisy when the dews have dried;
A sudden thought struck all the sun in his face.
" Martha and Dora, I know what I'll do!
I'll write a Letter to the good Lord Jesus,
Who helps us if we put our trust in Him."
The sisters smiled upon him through their tears.

This was the Letter little Fabyan wrote.

" *Dear, beautiful Lord Jesus,*
  Christmas is drawing near ;
Its many shining sights we see,
  Its merry sounds we hear :
With presents for good Children,
  I know Thou art going now,
From house to house with Christmas trees,
  And lights on every bough.

" *I pray thee, good Lord Jesus,*
  To bring one tree to us,
All aglow with fruits of gold,
  And leaves all luminous.
We have no Mother, and, where we live,
  No Christmas gifts are given ;
We have no Friends on earth, but Thou
  Art our good Friend in Heaven.

" *My Sisters, gentle Jesus,*
  They hide the worst from me ;
But I have ears that sometimes hear,
  And eyes that often see.
Poor Martha's cloak is worn threadbare,
  Poor Dora's boots are old ;
And neither of them strong like me,
  To stand the wintry cold.

" *But most of all, Lord Jesus,*
  Grandfather is so ill ;
'Tis very sad to hear him moan,
  And startling when he's still.
Ah ! well I know, Lord Jesus,
  If Thou would'st only come,
He'd look, and rise, and leave his bed,
  As Lazarus left his tomb.

" Forget us not, Lord Jesus,
*   I and my sisters dear;*
We love Thee! when Thou wert a Child
*   Had we been only near,*
And seen Thee lying, bonny babe,
*   In manger or in stall,*
Thou should'st have had a home with us;
*   We would have given Thee all."*

XIII.

THE Letter signed and sealed, their prayers are said,
And Martha lights the younger Bairns to bed.
With all a Mother's heart she bends above
Their rest, her eyes filled with a Mother's love.
For soon their voices cease; life fades away
Into its quiet nest, till morrow-day:
As the lake-lilies shut their leaves of light
When down the gloom descends the hush of night,
In fear of what is passing, bow the head
Beneath the water, they shrink down in bed.
But soon the Angel Sleep doth smile all fear
Away with wooing whispers at the ear;
And they will ope at morn eyes bathed in bliss;
Their faces fresh from their good Angel's kiss.
But Martha sleeps not yet; now they are gone,
Brave little woman, she must still work on,
And watch, to-night, for Grandfather is worse,
She thinks, with no one near, save her for nurse.

XIV.

'TIS very sad to hear a man so old,
Talk of *his* mother who, beneath the mould.

Has lain an age, and see his childish tears,
That have to pierce the crust of eighty years.
He turns and turns, incapable of rest,
Tossed on the billow that heaves in brain and
    breast ;
A life that beats with all too weak a wave
To land him on the other side the Grave !
The old man mutters in his broken dream.
   " Last night I wander'd in a world of moan ;
    I saw a white Soul going all alone,
     Over the white snows of eternity ;
     I followed far, and followed fast to see
    The face, and lo, it was my own."

And now he muses by some weird sea-side.

   " The tide is a-making its bonny Death-bed ;
   The white sea-maidens rise ready to wed ;
   Nearer and nearer, unveiling their charms,
   They toss for their lovers, long, shadowy arms !
    Dancing with other-world music and motion ;
    Brides of dead Sailors ; the Beauties of Ocean.

   " Wave after wave my worn, old Bark has tossed ;
   One moment saved, another it seemed lost
   For ever, still it righted from each blow ;
   But the great wave is coming on me now !
   I see it towering high above the rest ;
   A world of eyes in its white glittering crest ;
   See how it climbs, calm in its might, and curls
   Ready to clasp me in the wildering whirls,
   And when it bursts, in darkness, for last breath,
   I shall be fighting, grappled fast with Death."

He sees an image of Martha now, with dim
Wet eyes; it moves in brightness far from him.

> *" I am like the hoary Mountain,*
> *Gray with years, and very old;*
> *And your life, a sprightly fountain,*
> *Springs, and leaves me lone and cold;*
> *Dancing, glancing on its way,*
> *Down the valleys warm and gay.*
>
> *" There you go, Dear, singing, sparkling,*
> *I can see your dawn begin;*
> *While the night, around me darkling,*
> *With its death-dews, shuts me in—*
> *Hear you singing on your way*
> *To the full and perfect day."*

The suffering passes into weariness;
The weariness fades into kind content:
Faintly the tired heart flutters into stillness,
And he has done with Age, and Want, and Illness.
Gently he passed; the little Maiden wept;
Sank down, o'erwearied, by the dead, and slept,
With such a heavenly lustre on her face,
You might have fancied Angels in the place:
Companions through the day of our delight,
That watch as wingèd Sentries all the night.

XV.

NEXT day a group of serious silent men
Found a *Dead Letter* with strange life in it;
It was addressed to *Jesus Christ in Heaven.*
It called up their old hearts into their eyes,

For lofty meeting in a touch of tears.
At length it reached the Lady Marian,
And the Boy's letter had not missed its mark.

XVI.

THIS is my Lady Marian :
She walks our world, a Shining one !
A Woman with an Angel-face,
Sweet gravity, and tender grace ;
And where she treads this earth of ours,
Heaven blossoms into smiling flowers.
    This is the Lady Marian.

One of the spirits that walk in white !
Many dumb hearts that sit in night,
Her presence know, just as the Birds
Know Morning, murmuring cheerful words.
Where Life is darkest, she doth move
With influence as of visible Love.
    This is the Lady Marian.

Her coming all your being fills
With a balm-breath from heaven's hills :
And in her face the light is mild
As though the heart within her smiled,
And in her bosom sat to sing
The spirit of immortal Spring.
    This is the Lady Marian.

  " *We shall not mend the world ; we try,*
    And lo, our work is vain !" they cry.
  With her pathetic look, she hears ;
  You see the wounded soul bleed tears ;

Against the dark she sets her face,
And calmly keeps her onward pace.
    This is the Lady Marian.

One of God's treasurers for the Poor!
She keepeth open heart and door.
That heart a holy well of wealth,
Brimming life-waters, rich with health;
That door an opening you look through,
To find God our side of Heaven's blue.
    This is the Lady Marian.

XVII.

FROM out the darkness that took shape in Her,
The Lady Marian came on Christmas day,
Quick with maternal tenderness of soul,
Her starry smile so radiant through their night,
Her hands brimful of help, as was her heart
With yearnings to arise and go when first
She read the letter little Fabyan sent
In his confiding simpleness of faith,—
One of those representatives of God
Who help to make the Poor believe in Him
Because He hath some living like on Earth.
And Martha knows that their worst days are done;
In Dora's rich sad eyes a merry light
Soon dances! Lady Marian will prove
A Mother, sent of God, to all the three.
A trembling prayer had shook the Tree of Life,
And, golden, out of heaven the fruitage falls
Into their midst they think direct from God.

THE BRIDEGROOM OF BEAUTY.

" *Who wears the Singing-Robe is richly dight,*"
Said Mabel—" *He is greater than a King,*"—
Mabel, the saintly-sweet and fairily fine
As Maiden rising from Enchanted Mere ;
A queenly creature with her quiet grace,
And dazzling white hand veined cerulean :
Her eyes of violet-gray were coloured rich
With shade of tender thought, and mirrored large
Within them starry futures swam and shone :
Ah ! what a smile to fill a life with light,
And make the waking heart to sing in sleep !—
" *I would I were a Poet,*" Mabel said,
" Up like a Lark i' the morning of the times,
To carol o'er the human harvesters ;
Drop fancies, dainty-sweet, to cheer their toil,
And hurry out a ripe luxuriance
Of life in song, as though my heart would break ;
To sing them sweet and precious memories,
And golden promises, and throbbing hopes ;
Hymn the great Future with its mystery,
That startles us from out the dark of time
With secrets numerous as a night of stars :

" Those days hung round with loftier heavens, where
      move
The larger souls with their God-liker pace :
Or send wronged Races to the battle-field
With eyes that weep and burn—stir as with fire
The grand wild beast of Valour, till it leapt
The red Arena fiery for the fight :
Then bind with flowers, or plume the Patriot's brow.
Anon I would sing songs so sweetly pure,
That they might pillow a budding Maiden's cheek,
Like spirit-hands, and catch her tender tears ;
Or nestle next her heart lapt up in love :—
Songs that in far lands, under alien skies,
Should spring from English hearts like flowers cf
      home ;
Strive to bring down a light from heaven to read
The records writ on Poverty's prison walls ;
The signs of greatness limned in martyr blood,
And make worn faces glow with warmth of love
Into the lineaments of heavenly beauty.

" Who wears a singing-robe is richly dight :
The Poet, he is greater than a King.
He plucks the veil from hidden loveliness :
His gusts of music stir the shadowing boughs,
To let in sunshine on the darkened soul.
Upon the hills of light he plants his feet
To lure the people up with harp and voice ;
At humblest human hearths drops dew divine
To feed the violet virtues nestling there.
His hands adorn the poorest house of life
With rare abiding shapes of loveliness.
All things obey his soul's creative eye ;
For him earth ripens fruit-like in the light ;

" Green April comes to him with smiling tears,
Like some sweet Maiden who transfigured stands
In dewy light of first love's rosy dawn,
And yields all secret preciousness, his Bride.
He reaps the Autumn without scythe or sickle ;
And in the sweet low singing of the corn,
Hears coming Plenty hush the pining Poor.

" The shows of things are but a robe o' the day,
His life down-deepens to the living heart,
And Sorrow shows him her wise mysteries.
He knows this Life is but a longer year,
And it will blossom bright in other springs.
The soul of all things is invisible,
And nearest to that soul the Poet sings ;
A sweet, shy Bird in darkling privacy.
He beckons not the Pleasures as they pass,
And lets the money-grubbing world go by.
He hath a towering life, but cannot climb
Out of the reach of sad calamity :
A many carking cares pluck at his skirts ;
Wild, wandering words are hissing at his ear ;
He runs the gauntlet of his woes to reach
The inner sanctuary of better life.
But though the seas of sorrow flood his heart,
Some silent spring of flowers blossoms there.
His spirit-wounds a precious balsam bleed.
The loveliest ministrants that visit him,
Rise veiled when his heart-fountains spring in
     tears.
And when this misty life hath rolled away
The turmoil hushed ; all foolish voices still ;
The bonds that crushed his great heart shattered
     down,

And all his nature shines sublimely bare;
Death whitens many a stain of strife and
    toil,
And careful hands shall pluck away each weed
Around the spring that wells melodious life."

———

Many are called, Aurelia replied,
But few are crowned.   I knew a Poet once;
One of the world's most marvellous Might-have-
    beens;
A strange wild harper upon human heart-strings.
Life's morning-splendour round him prophesied
That he should win his garland in the game.
But he was lost for lack of that sweet thing,
A Wife, to live his love's dear dream of beauty,
And wandered darkling in his dazzling dream.
Life's waters—troubled till that Angel comes—
Never grew calm above the jewel he sought,
Till in Death's harbour all their surges slept.

He was betrothed to Beauty ere his birth—
That silent Spirit of the universe,
Which seeks interpreters of her dumb shows,
'Mong human lovers whom she may not wed.
This Spirit arose from many things, as soars
The soul of Harmony from many sounds.
Out of the by-way of his lonely life,
She beckoned him for her Evangelist,
And straightway he arose and followed her,
And in the shadow of her loveliness,
Or in her wake of glory, walked our world.

Q

That shining Shape, in her sweet mystery, seemed
Some beauteous miracle of eternal love.
Through smiles, and tears, he saw his visioned Bride,
With gorgeous grace, and twinkling limbs of light,
Aye dancing on in her delightsomeness.
His love-dream glided silent through his life,
Like rosy-handed Day 'twixt Earth and Night,
And came betwixt his mind and all its glooms;
Her sandals wet and fragrant with Heaven's dew.
She set the barren thorns in jewelled glow,
And sowed the furrows of his life with flowers.
He followed with wild looks and heart a-fire,
And that rich mist of feeling in the eyes,
Whose alchemy half-creates the thing we see.

She rose at dawn in sparkling clouds of dew,
And kept the Morning's ruddy-golden gates;
Stood high in sunrise on the mountain-top;
Or in her bower of the ambient air
Sat, shedding her rich beauty on the sea,
Which of her likeness took some trembly tints;
Voyaged like Venus in her car of cloud
About the sapphire heaven's lake of love,
Or danced on sunset streams to harp of gold:
Then twilight mists would robe more dainty-rare
Her dim, delicious, dreamy loveliness.

The buds that startle at the voice of May
And open merry eyes, had been with her;
Their subtle smile said what they could reveal.
She nestled glancing at him from the flower
He plucked, and only caught her passing breath;
Even as he grasped her vesture she was gone.
Among the boughs that burgeon into bloom;

The coloured clouds that kindle and richly rise
From out the bosom of Earth's emerald sea;
Hedge-roses set in dewy radiance green;
The lush Laburnums, all a rain of gold;
She seemed to have fled and left her robe afloat.
An Ariel now, she murmured in the Pines;
He heard, but had no magic word or wand.
A wavy Naiad, she rippled the cool brooks
That round her dallied, babbling in their dreams.
The fragrant feeling of the languorous air
Was as the soft endearment of her arms,
That wound him in a tremulous caress.

Not by appointment do we meet Delight
And Joy; they heed not our expectancy;
But round some corner in the streets of life,
They, on a sudden, clasp us with a smile.
So on him rose his visitant divine,
From many a magic mirror of the mind;
With elfin evanescence came and went.

When, thronged with life, the Year in beauty
        burst,
Lifted her lids, and blossomed from the trees,
She glanced from all the gateways of the spring.
In burnished bark swam down the summer-tide
That floods the valleys, breaks o'er all the hills,
In sparkling spray of flowers, and leafy life.
She roofed the Autumn forests with the wealth
Of melted rainbows, caught from summer heaven.
And winter trees stretched fingers weird to win
The perfect-pearl of her white purity.
Where'er she went Earth looked up and was glad.

Through Music's maze she glode at hide-and-seek ;
Played with the Storm, then in her Iris-shape
Laughed from the purple skirts of Heaven, as laughs
Some radiant Child from Mother's hiding robe.
Adown dim forest-windings he would peer ;
Surprise his Beautiful at her woodland bath,
And in a solemn hush of heart stand still
Like fixèd flame ! for lo, how softly glowed
Her dainty limbs in depths of dissolved pearl !
Then swift as runs a wind-wave over grass,
He saw her garments gleam in leafy light.
Were those love-whisperings among the leaves,
Or elvish laughters twitting through the trees ?
Sometimes the boughs let in her haunting face ;
But the old Forest kept the secret still,
And hushed it round with grave unconscious look.

In vernal nights so tender, calm, and cool,
When eerie Darkness lays its shadowy hands
On Earth, and reads her sins with searching eyes,
Like a Confessor o'er a kneeling Nun ;
He stood in God's wide whispering-gallery,
And breathed his worship : down from visible
    heaven
Her influence fell, and thrilled in music through
The silences of space, and soothed his soul,
Till life was folded up brimful of beauty,
As the flower clasps its pearl and droops to dream.

At times, from out the curtains of the dark,
Her face would meet him through the glowing
    gloom.
Sometimes she passed ; her rippling raiment
    touched

His sense, and sphered him with diviner air,
Like honeysuckles brushed at dewy dusk.
The fragrance of her breath made old earth
          young.
From mystery to mystery, like a Bride,
The dainty-waisted darling led him on,
And dropped love-tokens in his pilgrim path.
The red Rose peering from its cool green leaves
Like warm Love lifting half its hiding veil,
Symbolled her soft red mouth held up to him.
A virgin whiteness in a dream of bloom,
Gave to her tender cheeks their taking tint.
Her eyes were orbs of thought that on him burned
Fervent as Hesper in the brow of night.
He walked as in a clime of golden eves.
The vineyard of his life reeled lusty-ripe;
He ached to press the wine upon her lips,
But aye she melted from his love's embrace,
To float him far away in faëry lands.
The wooing wind would murmur of her fairness,
And round him breathe in many whispers sweet;
Bring dews of healing as from Hermon hill;
Creep to his burning heart with drink of life,
And cool him with her kisses.   Oft he hushed,
As one who pauses on a midnight heath,
To catch the footfall felt by Fancy's ear.

When he awoke in Dreamland, 'twas to find
He had been floated through some starry dark
Far from earth's shore, on an enchanted sea:
And he lay pillowed 'twixt her white warm breasts,
In glowing arms of glorifying love:
A light of love-dreams on her features shone,
And she had laid her daylight mask aside;

All the sweet soul of things bare to him, as lies
The mirrored moon in silver sleeping seas.

A shimmering splendour from the By-gone broke,
As the Ship leaves a luminous wake behind ;
And, looking back, his Childhood's world she ringed
With rich auroral hues of summer dawns.
When weird, dark shapes of sorrow hunted nigh
With their slow solemn eyes, and silent aim,
She dropped the gold cloud of her tresses round
    him.
When o'er him hung the night of adverse fate,
She was a light along his perilous path,
And through the darkness of his soul there broke
A heaven of worlds all tenderness and peace.

At times he walked with glad and dauntless
    step,
As inner wings to heroic music moved ;
And men who read his lighted look might deem
His life a summer story told in flowers.
But often he would falter weeping-weak,
With claspèd hands, and very lowly heart.
Then she rose radiant in a finer light,
Seen through the altar-smoke and mist of tears.
So his life grew to beauty silently,
And shaped his soul into an orb of song.
He sang of Her his beautiful Unknown !
And to his music she would coyly come ;
He ceased—to look on her—and she was gone.
He sang of Her his beautiful Unknown,
Heart-wild, as some glad bird that tells of spring,
He would have made the world her worshipper,
And all Earth's voices ring a rich refrain.

One day our passionate pilgrim sat him down
By the wayside of life, and thus he prayed—

    "O thou Belovèd!   O thou Beautiful!
    On our perfection throned for pedestal :
    O Spirit as the lightning wild and bright,
    Come from thy palace of the purple light !
    Come down to mortal arms a living form,
    With heavenly height of brow, and bosom warm.
    Glow human from the mist, thou Shape of Grace ;
    Thou tender wonder, fold me face to face.
    Art thou not mine, thou delicate Delight ?
    Hast thou not visited me noon and night ?
    Freighted with my dead Hopes I follow thee,
    Like some Norse Sea-king flaming out to sea.
    Say, are the pleasant bowers far away,
    Decked by thy dear hands for our Marriage-day,
    Where we the gardens of delight shall roam
    In endless love ?   Now wilt thou lead me home,
    To find our bliss in heaven's honied heart ;
    Live secret soul to soul, never to part ?

    "O awful Glory, felt, but nowhere found,
    I have but seen thy Shadow on life's ground.
    I know thee now, Immortal ! show the way
    To thine Elysium, I would die to-day.
    Break into wings this chrysalis of my life,
    That I may soar to thee my spirit-wife.
    Thy dark bower-door, the Grave, gives me no fear ;
    When I emerge beyond, thou wilt be near."

O'er all his face a light of glory smiled,
His soul had rent the veil 'twixt life and life.
Slowly the shining vapours orb a Star,
By fine degrees before his fixèd eyes.

The Spirit he had sought through all the world,—
Had sought without but only found within,—
Turned full upon him face to face at last.
She laid her hand upon his throbbing harp;
She pressed her lips upon his passionate life;
And both stood still.　In death he had found his
　　Bride.

POEMS FOR CHRISTIE.

A WINTER'S TALE FOR THE LITTLE ONES.

A MERRY sound of clapping hands,
   A call to see the sight ;
And lo ! the first soft snow-flakes fall,
So exquisitely virginal :
'Tis my wee Nell at window stands,
   And the world is all in white.

Her eyes, where dawns my bluest Day,
   Dance with the dancing snow !
I see delicious shivers thrill
Her through and through. She feels the chill
Of Earth so white, and skies so gray
   Enrich our fireside glow.

" *No Winters now, my little Maid,*
   Like those that used to come,
Making our Christmas sparkle, bright
As crystallized plum-cake at night,
And Frost his Puck-like trickeries played,
   With fancies frolicsome.

" *He fixed your breath in flowers, the Trees*
   To Chandeliers would turn :
He pinched your toes, he nipped your nose,
He made your cheek a wrinkled Rose :
Perhaps at night you heard him sneeze,
   And the Jug was cracked at morn !

" *The Snow-Storms were magnificent !*
    And in the clear, still weather
Against the bitter wintry blue
And Sunset's orange-tawny hue
You saw the smoke straight upward went,
    For weeks and weeks together.

" *At night the Waits mixed with our dream*
    Their music sweet and low :
We children knew not as we heard,
Each, listening, nestled like a Bird,
Whether from Heaven the music came,
    Or only over the snow !

" *No winters now-a-days like those.*"
    And then my darling tries
To coax me for a " *tale that's true :*
A story that is new — quite new."
And up the arch of wonder goes,
    Above the frank, blue eyes !

" *Once on a time* "—" *Do tell me when,*
    And where ? " says my wee Nell—
" *When Christmas came on Thursday—now,*
Some five-and-thirty years ago !
Superbly we were snowed-up then,
    Who lived in Ingle Dell.

" *His icy Drawbridge Winter dropped ;*
    The running springs he froze ;
The Roads were lost ; the hedges crossed ;
All field-work ceased through the ' Long Frost.'
But there was one thing never stopped—
    That was Grandmother's nose !

" *The snow might fall by day, by night,*
    The weather wax more rough,
And up to our bedroom windows heap
The drift, and smother men like sheep,
And wrap the world in a shroud of white—
    Old Gran must have her snuff!

" *So Uncle Willie, then a lad*
    Not more than nine years old,
Upon the Christmas morn must go
And fetch her snuff, and face the Snow,
Which surely had gone dancing mad,
    And wrestle with the cold.

" *Wrapped in his crimson Comforter,*
    His basket on his arm,
He started. Mother followed him
With her proud eyes so dewy-dim;
While kisses from the heart of her
    Within his heart were warm.

" *How gentle is the gracious Snow,*
    When first you watch her dance;
Her feathery flutter, winding whorls;
Her finish perfect as the pearl's;
She looks you in the face as though
    'Twere unveiled Innocence.

" *But now, 'tis wild upon the waste,*
    And winged upon the wind:
You see, just passing out of sight,
The Ghost of things in a swirl of white!—
The Storm unwinkingly he faced,
    Though it snowed enough to blind.

" *Fire-pointed, stinging, strikes and burns*
    To the bone, each icy dart.
He stumbles—falls—is up again,
And onward for the Town a-strain;
Backward our Willie never turns,
    And never loses heart.

" *He looks a weird and wintry Elf*
    With face in ruddy glow;
And all his curls are straightened out,
Hanging in Icicles about
A sparkling statue of himself,
    Shaped out of frozen snow.

" *He still fought on, for though the Storm*
    Might bend him, he was tough;
And when the Blast would take his breath,
With kisses like the kiss of death,
One thought still kept his courage warm—
    It was Grandmother's Snuff!

" *At length with many a danger passed,*
    Unboding worse to come,
He has got the Snuff.   Far more than food,
Or wine, 'twill warm her poor old blood.
He has it safe at last, at last!
    And sets his face for Home.

" *He has the Snuff; but it were well*
    If Granny had it too!
For early closes such a day,
And wild and dreary is the way;
If dark before he reach the Dell,
    What can poor Willie do?

" *Within the Town the blast is hushed;*
　　The snow-flakes from you melt:
But out upon the pathless moor,
The storm grows madder than before;
And at him all its furies rushed,
　　Till he faint and fainter felt.

" *His thoughts are whirling with the Snow:*
　　His eyes get dizzy and dim!
And on the path, 'twixt him and night,
Now dancing left, now dancing right,
It seems a white Witch-Woman doth go,
　　With white hand beckoning him!

" *To the last stile he clung—maybe*
　　A furlong from our door;
Then missed his footing on the plank,
And deep into the snow-drift sank.
O, my belovèd Willie, we
　　Shall never see you more!

" *Ah, they looked long and wistfully*
　　Who waiting sat at home:
At every sound they leaned to hark;
They strained their eyes through the deepening
　　　dark,
And wondered where could Willie be,
　　And when would Willie come?

" *Through all that night of wild affright*
　　They searched the road to Town;
They called him high, they called him low,
They mocked each other through the snow,
And all the night, by lanthorn light,
　　They wandered up and down.

" *They sought him where the waters plash*
   Darkly by Deadman's Cave !
They sought him at the Rag-Pit, near
The Mill, and by the awesome Weir ;
At the Cross-Roads where ' Harry's Ash '
   Grows from the Suicide's Grave.

" *In Ingle Dell they locked no door,*
   Put out no light.   At such
A time you cling to a little thing
That's done for neighbourly comforting !
Old Gran thought she would snuff no more,
   And she took thrice as much.

" *All night the Snow with fingers soft*
   Kept pointing to the ground.
Only too well they knew 'twas there ;
But had no hint to guide them where !
And he so near.   They passed him oft,
   Close by his white grave-mound.

" *And did he die ? "* cries little Nell.
   " *No, he was nestled warm.*
The Snow's white arm that round him curled
Had caught him into another world :
What other world he could not tell,
   But, out of all the storm.

" *And all was changed too suddenly*
   For him to know the place.
He swooned awhile, and when he woke
A lightning from his darkness broke ;
Alone with the Eternal he
   Seemed standing face to face !

" There in his grave alive, he knew
　　He stood, or sat upright!
With burning brain, and freezing feet:
And he so young, and life so sweet;
And, bitter thought! what would Gran do
　　Without her snuff that night?

" A long, long night of sixty hours
　　Did Willie pass.　I know
Not how he lived.　But Heaven can hold
A life as safe as Earth can fold
Her hidden life of fruit and flowers,
　　Through her long trance of snow.

"'Tis Sabbath day.　How quietly gleams
　　That snow-drift o'er him driven!
The winds are softly laid asleep,
In their white snow-bed covered deep.
The white Clouds all so still! it seems
　　Like Sunday up in Heaven!

" The Country-folk are passing near
　　His tomb—no tale it tells—
Old Ploughmen in their white smockfrocks,
Old Women in long scarlet cloaks,
And Lad and Lass,—when on his ear
　　There faints a sound of Bells!

" And, looking up, a tiny hole
　　Was melted with his breath;
Where-through a bit of God's blue sky
Was smiling on him like an Eye;
A living eye with a loving soul
　　Shone in that face of death!

" O joy !   He shouted from his grave,
*   And finding room to stir,*
He tooth and nail began to climb ;
He clutched the top o' the bank this time ;
Thrust his hand through the snow to wave
*   His good old Comforter !*

" ' I'm here !' ' It's me !'   His flag they see,
*   And know lost Willie's voice ;*
They quickly answer shout for shout,
And with their hands they dig him out,
And carry him home.   Oh ! didn't we
*   In Ingle Dell rejoice ?*

" There be some tears that smile, and such
*   Were wept by Woman and Man.*
But while they glistened in each eye,
He pulled the snuff out sound and dry ;
Snow might cover him, cold might clutch,
*   The Snuff was safe for Gran."*

FOR CHRISTIE'S SAKE.

UPON us falls the shadow of night,
    And darkened is our day !
My Love will greet the morning light
    Four hundred miles away.
God love her ! torn so swift and far
    From hearts so like to break !
And God love all who are good to her ;
    For Christie's sake.

I know whatever spot of ground
   In any land we tread—
I know the eternal arms are round;
   That heaven is overhead,
And faith the mourning heart will heal;
   But many fears will make
Our spirits faint, our fond hearts kneel,
     For Christie's sake.

Good-bye, Dear! be they kind to you
   As though you were their ain!
My Daisy opens to the dew,
   But shuts against the rain!
Never will New Moon glad our eyes
   But offerings we shall make
To old God Wish! and prayers will rise
     For Christie's sake.

Four years ago we struck our tent;
   O'er homeless Babes we yearned;
Our all—three darlings—with us went,
   But only two returned!
While life yet bleeds into Her grave
   Love ventures one more stake;
Hush, hush, poor Hearts! if big, be brave,
     For Christie's sake.

Like Crown to most ambitious brows
   Was Christie to us given;
To make our Home a holy house,
   And nursery of heaven!
O softer was her bed of rest,
   Than lily's on the lake;
Peace filled so deep each billowy breast,
     For Christie's sake.

To music played by Harps and Hands
    Invisible, were we drawn
O'er charmèd seas, through faëry lands,
    Under a rosier dawn !
We entered our new world of love
    With blessings in our wake,
While prospering Heavens smiled above
        For Christie's sake.

We gazed with proud eyes luminous
    On such a gift of grace—
All heaven narrowed down to us
    In one dear little face !
And many a pang we felt, dear Wife,
    With hurt of heart and ache,
All shut within like clasping knife,
        For Christie's sake.

I would no tears might e'er run down
    Her patient face, beside
Such happy pearls of heart as crown
    Young Mother—new-made Bride !
For 'tis a face that, looking up
    To passing Heaven, might make
An Angel stop, a blessing drop,
        For Christie's sake.

If Love in that child's heart of hers
    Should breathe and break its calm
With trouble sweet as that which stirs
    The brooding buds of balm,—
Listening at ear of peeping pearl
    Glistening in eyes that shake
Their sweet dew down ! God bless our Girl ;
        For Christie's sake.

But, Father ! if our Babe must mourn,
　Be merciful and kind ;
And if our gentle Lamb be shorn,
　Attemper Thou the wind !
Across the Deluge guide our Dove,
　And to Thy bosom take
With arm of love, and shield above,
　　For Christie's sake.

We have had sorrows many and strange.
　Dear Christie ! when I'm gone,
Some of my words will weirdly change
　If she read sadly on !
Lightnings, from what was dark of old,
　With meanings strange will break
Of troubles hid or dimly told
　　For Christie's sake.

Wife ! we should still try hard to win
　The best for our dear Child ;
And keep a resting-place within,
　When all without grows wild.
As on the winter graves the snow
　Falls softly flake by flake,
Our love should whitely clothe our woe,
　　For Christie's sake.

For one will wake at midnight drear
　From out a dream of death,
And find no dear head pillowed near ;
　No sound of peaceful breath !
May no weak wailing words arise,
　No bitter thoughts awake
To see the tears in Memory's eyes :
　　For Christie's sake.

And *There!* where many crownless kings
  Of earth a crown shall wear,—
The Martyrs who have borne the pangs
  Their palm at last shall bear,
When, with our lily pure of sin,
  Our homeward way we take ;—
There, may we walk with welcome in ;
  For Christie's sake.

CHRISTIE'S PORTRAIT.

Your tiny picture makes me yearn ;
  We are so far apart !
My Darling, I can only turn
  And kiss you in my heart.
A thousand tender thoughts a-wing
  Swarm in a summer clime,
And hover round it murmuring
  Like bees at honey-time.

Upon a little girl I look
  Whose pureness makes me sad ;
I read as in a holy book,
  I grow in secret glad !
It seems my darling comes to me
  With something I have lost
Over life's tossed and troubled sea,
  On some celestial coast.

I think of her when spirit-bowed ;
  A glory fills the place !
Like sudden light on swords, the proud
  Smile flashes in my face ;

And others see, in passing by,
  But cannot understand
The vision shining in mine eye,
  My strength of heart and hand.

That grave content and touching grace
  Bring tears into mine eyes;
She makes my heart a holy place
  Where hymns and incense rise!
Such calm her gentle spirit brings
  As—smiling overhead—
White statued saints with peaceful wings
  Shadow the sleeping dead.

Our Christie is no rosy Grace
  With beauty all may see;
But I have never felt a face
  Grow half so dear to me.
No curling hair about her brows,
  Like many merry girls;
Well, straighter to my heart it goes,
  And round it curls and curls.

Meek as the wood-anemone glints
  To see if skies are blue,
Is my pale flower with her tints
  Of heaven shining through!
She will be poor and never fret,
  Sleep sound and lowly lie;
Will live her quiet life, and let
  The great world-storm go by!

Dear love! God keep her in His grasp,
  Meek maiden, or brave wife,
Till His good Angels softly clasp
  Her closèd book of life;

And this true picture of the Sun,
  With birthday blessings given,
Shall fade before a glorious one
  Taken of her in heaven.

THE TWO HEAVENS.

THERE are two Heavens for natures clear
  And calm as thine, my gentle Love!
One Heaven but reflected here;
  One Heaven that waits above:

As yonder Lake, in Evening's red,
  Lies smiling with the smile of Rest;
One Heaven glowing overhead;
  One mirrored in its breast.

SLEEP-WALKING.

OFT in the night I am with you, Dear!
I lean and listen your breathing to hear;
Little you dream of any one near.

No one knoweth that I am gone;
Curtains closely about me drawn,
When dreams dissolve at a touch of Dawn!

Nobody meets me under the sky,
Only the staring Owl goes by
Softly as though the night should sigh.

Under the moonlight, over the moss!
I need no bridge the river to cross,
Though winds awake and waters toss.

O sweet, so sweet the Nightingale's strain!
Is it her pleasure that works us pain,
Or her pain that with pleasure pierces the
        brain?

Window or door I pass not through :
The way I never could show to you
By day.   I enter as spirits do!

There you are ! lying cheek-on-palm,
Drinking of slumber's dewiest calm,
Brimming your life with the rosiest balm.

The little wee bird that beats in the breast,
Hath folded its wings in a wee white nest,
Breathing the fulness of innermost rest.

But the other night—see my blushes bloom—
Somehow I missed my way in the gloom,
And, thinking myself quite safe in your room,

I nestled my face, as I thought, in your bed
To kiss you, and—now let me hide my head—
I kissed—I kissed—your Teacher instead.

CHRISTIE'S POOR OLD GRAN.

No green age, beautiful to see,
    Hath Poor Old Gran!
No ripe life mellowed goldenly
    Hath Poor Old Gran!
One by one we have left her fold,
Her lonely hearth is growing cold,
Faint is her smile as the primrose gold,
    Our Poor Old Gran!

Ah! whitened face, and withered form,
    Of Poor Old Gran!
Beaten and blanched in many a storm:
    Poor Old Gran!
She hath wept the bitter tears that sow
The dark grave-violets in the snow
Where once the red young rose did glow!
    Poor Old Gran!

There's few have lived a harder lot,
    Poor Old Gran!
But she toiled on and murmured not;
    Poor Old Gran!
For us she toiled on starvingly,
And fought the wolf of poverty;
Upon her heart's blood suckled me,
    Our Poor Old Gran!

Her river of life hath roughly rolled;
    Poor Old Gran!
A Wreck lies dark, its tale untold,
    Poor Old Gran!

Yet shall her old heart laugh with ye,
My Bird's-nest in the mouldering tree!
And soft in heaven the bed shall be
　　For poor Old Gran!

The grip of Poverty is grim;
　　Poor Old Gran!
Lustres of lip and eye will dim;
　　Poor Old Gran!
But through the frailty of her face
There gleams a light of tender grace,
Or else I see through a tearful haze
　　Poor Old Gran!

You came in all our sorrowings,
　　Poor Old Gran!
How your weakness hurried on wings,
　　Poor Old Gran!
You stood at Bridal, Birth, and Bier:
Our darlings dead and gone seem near
When you are near, and make more dear
　　Our Poor Old Gran!

So come to our Cottage up the lane,
　　Poor Old Gran!
Follow our fortune's harvest-wain,
　　Poor Old Gran!
We'll shelter you from wind and rain,
Hunger you shall not know again,
Plenty shall smile away your pain,
　　Poor Old Gran!

And little laughing Stars shall rise
　　On Poor Old Gran!
In the clear heaven of Childhood's eyes,
　　For Poor Old Gran!

Wee fingers, stroking her gray hair,
Shall almost melt the hoarfrost there,
Wee lips shall kiss away the care
    From Poor Old Gran!

So come and sit beside our hearth,
    Poor Old Gran!
Come from the darkness and the dearth,
    Poor Old Gran!
And you shall be our fireside guest,
And weary heart and head will rest;
And your last days shall be your best,
    Our Poor Old Gran.

NEWS OF CHRISTIE.

WE read your Letters! no word lost;
    All, all is rememberèd;
And often when there comes no Post,
    Once more are the old ones read.

Of all she did we love to hear,
    And how the days have sped;
But to our listening hearts most dear
    Is something "*Christie said.*"

LITTLE WILLIE.

Poor little Willie,
  With his many pretty wiles;
Worlds of wisdom in his look
  And quaint, quiet smiles;
Hair of amber, touched with
  Gold of heaven so brave;
All lying darkly hid
  In a Workhouse Grave!

In the day we wandered foodless,
  Little Willie cried for bread!
In the night we wandered homeless,
  Little Willie cried for bed.
Parted at the Workhouse door,
  Not a word we said:
Ah, so tired was poor Willie,
  And so sweetly sleep the dead.

You remember little Willie;
  Such a funny fellow! he
Sprang like a lily
  From the dirt of poverty.
Poor little Willie!
  Not a friend was nigh,
When, from the cold world,
  He crouched down to die.

'Twas in the dead of winter
  We laid him in the earth;
The world brought in the New Year,
  Mocking us with mirth:

But, for lost little Willie,
  Not a tear we crave;
Cold and Hunger cannot wake him,
  In his Workhouse Grave.

We thought him beautiful,
  Felt it hard to part;
We to him were dutiful;
  Down, down, poor heart!
The storms they may beat;
  The winter winds may rave;
Little Willie feels not
  In his Workhouse Grave.

No room for little Willie;
  In the world he had no part;
On him stared the Gorgon-eye,
  Through which looks no heart.
Come to me, said Heaven;
  And, if Heaven will save,
We will grieve not, though the door
  Was a Workhouse Grave.

WHEN CHRISTIE COMES AGAIN.

When the merry spring-tide
  Floods all the land;
Nature hath a Mother's heart,
  Gives with open hand;
Flowers running up the lane
  Tell us May is near:
Christie will be coming then!
  Christie will be here!

O the merry spring-tide !
  We'll be glad in sun or rain,
In the merry, merry, merry days
  When Christie comes again.

Pure is her meek nature,
  Clear as morning dew,
We can see the Angel
  Almost shining through.
To Earth's sweetest blessing
  She the best from Heaven did bring ;
Good Genius of our Love-lamp ;
  Fine Spirit of the Ring !
O the merry spring-tide !
  We'll be glad in sun or rain,
In the merry, merry, merry days
  When Christie comes again.

All our joys we'll tell her,
  But for her dear sake,
Not a word of sorrow,
  Lest her little heart should ache.
She shall dance and swing and sing,
  Do as she likes best ;
Only I must have her hand
  In ramble or in rest.
O the merry spring-tide !
  We'll be glad in sun or rain,
In the merry, merry, merry days
  When Christie comes again.

We'll romp in jewelled meadows,
  Hunt in dingles cool with leaves,
Where all night the Nightingale
  Melodiously grieves.

In her cheek so tender
  The shy and dainty rose
Shall colour, and come for kisses,
  To every wind that blows.
O the merry spring-tide !
  We'll be glad in sun or rain,
In the merry, merry, merry days
  When Christie comes again.

Hope will lay so many eggs   .
  In her little nest;
Doesn't your heart run over,
  Christie, in your breast ?
Thinking how we'll greet you
  Safe once more at home,
Ours will run to meet you,
  Often ere you come.
O the merry spring-tide !
  We'll be glad in sun or rain,
In the merry, merry, merry days
  When Christie comes again.

O the joy in our house,
  Hearts dancing wild !
Christie will be coming soon,
  She's our darling child.
Holy dew of heaven
  In each eyelid starts,
Feeling all her dearness,
  Darling of all hearts.
O the merry spring-tide !
  We'll be glad in sun or rain,
In the merry, merry, merry days
  When Christie comes again.

Dreary was our winter;
   Come! and all the place
Shall breathe a summer sweetness,
   And wear a happy face;
There will be a sun-smile
   On stern, old Calaby,
Tender as the spring-gold
   On our old Oak-Tree!
O the merry spring-tide!
   We'll be glad in sun or rain,
In the merry, merry, merry days
   When Christie comes again.

Jack, the Dog, will run before,
   First to reach the Rail;
Jack, the Pony, whisk you home,
   With long trotting tail!
We have had our struggles, dear,
   But couldn't part with Jack :
We shall all be waiting there,
   To welcome Christie back!
O the merry spring-tide!
   We'll be glad in sun or rain,
In the merry, merry, merry days
   When Christie comes again.

Then blow you Winds, and shake up
   The sleeping flower-beds!
Make the Violets wake up,
   The Daisies lift their heads;
The Lilacs float in fragrance,
   Dim-purple, saintly-white!
And bring the bonny bairn to us,
   The flower of our delight.

O the merry spring-tide!
We'll be glad in sun or rain,
In the merry, merry, merry days
When Christie comes again,

———

CHILDREN AT PLAY.

"*Open your mouth and shut your eyes*,"
Three little Maidens were saying,—
"*And see what God sends you!*" little they
thought
Who listened while they were playing!
So little we guess that a light light word
At times may be more than praying.

"*I*," said Kate with the merry blue eyes,
"*Would have lots of frolic and folly;*"
"*I*," said Ciss with the bonnie brown hair,
"*Would have life always smiling and jolly;*"
"*And I would have just what our Father may
send,*"
Said lovable little pale Polly.

Life came for the Two, with sweetnesses new
Each morning in gloss and in glister:
But the Father above, in a longing of love,
Caught up little Polly and kissed her.
And the Churchyard nestled another wee
grave;
The Angels another wee Sister.

LITTLE LILYBELL.

WHEN unseen fingers part the leaves,
  To show us beauty's face;
And Earth her breast of glory heaves,
  And glows from Spring's embrace:
Flowers Fairy-like on coloured wings
  Float up,—Life's sea doth swell
And flush a world of vernal things,
  Came little Lilybell.

And like a blessed Bird of calm
  Our love's sweet want she stilled;
Made Passion's fiery wine run balm,—
  Life's glory half fulfilled!
From dappled dawn to twinkling dark,
  Our witching Ariel
Moves through our heaven!   O, like a lark
  Sings little Lilybell!

And she is fair—ay, very fair!
  With eyes so like the dove;
And lightly leans her world of care
  Upon our arms of love!
It cannot be that ye will break
  The promise-tale ye tell;
Ye will not make such fond hearts ache,
  Our little Lilybell!

As on Life's stream her leaflets spread,
  And tremble in its flow,
We shudder lest the awful Dead
  Pluck at her from below!

Breathe faint and low, ye winds that start;
  O stream, but softly swell;
Your every motion smites the heart
  For little Lilybell!

We tremble lest the Angel Death,
  Who comes to gather flowers
For Paradise, at her sweet breath
  Should fall in love with ours!
O, many a year will come and go,
  Ere from Life's mystic well
Such stream shall flow, such flower shall blow,
  As little Lilybell!

Ah, when her dear heart fills with fears,
  And aches with Love's sweet pain,
And pale cheeks burn through happy tears,
  Like red rose in the rain!
I marvel, Sweet, if we shall see
  The sight, and say 'tis well,
When the Beloved calls for thee,
  Our dainty Lilybell!

How rich Love made the lowly sod,
  Where such a flower hath blown!
O Love, we love, and think that God
  Is such a love full-grown!
Dear God! that gave the blessed trust,
  Be near, that all be well;
And morn and eve bedew our dust,
  For love of Lilybell!

OUR WHITE DOVE.

A WHITE Dove out of glory flew,
　White as the whitest shape of Grace
　That nestles in the soft embrace
Of heaven when skies are summer blue!

It came with dew-drop purity,
　On glad wings of the morning light,
　And sank into our life, so white
A VISION! sweetly, secretly!

Silently nestled our WHITE DOVE:
　Balmily made our bosoms swim
　With still delight, and overbrim;
The air it breathed was breath of love.

Our Dove had eyes of baby-blue,
　Soft as the speedwell's by the way,
　That looked up to us as they would say,
" *Who kissed me while I slept, did you?* "

God love it! but we took our Bird,
　And loved it well, and merry made;
　We sang and danced around, or prayed
In silence, wherein hearts are heard.

It seemed to come from far green fields
　To meet us over life's rough sea,
　With leaf of promise from the tree
In which a dearer nest it builds.

As fondling Mother-birds will pull
　The softest feathers from their breast,
　We gave our best to line the nest
And make it warm and beautiful!

We held it as the leaves of life
   In hidden silent service fold
   About a Rose's heart of gold,
So jealous of all outer strife!

When holy sleep in soothing palms
   Pillowed the darling little head,
   How lightly moved we round the bed,
And felt the silence fall in balms!

But all we did or tried to do,
   Our flood of joy it never felt;
   Only into our hearts would melt
Still deeper those dove-eyes of blue.

Quick with the spirit of field and wood,
   All other Birds would chirrup and sing
   Till hearts did ripple and homes did ring:
Our white Dove only cooed and cooed—

With every day some sweetness new,
   And night and day and day and night
   It was the voice of our delight,
That gentle, low, endearing coo!

God! if we were to lose our child!
   O, we must die, poor hearts would cry:
   She looked on us so hushingly;
So mournfully to herself she smiled.

One day she pined up in our face
   With a low cry we could not still,
   A moaning we might never heal,
For sleep in some more quiet place.

We could not help and yet must see
  The little head droop wearily,
  The little eyes shine eerily,
My Dove ! what have they done to thee ?

The look grew pleading in her eyes,
  And mournful as the lonesome light
  That in a window burns all night,
Asking for stillness, while one dies.

The hand of Death so coldly clings,
  So strongly draws the weak life-wave
  Into his dark, vast, silent cave ;
Our little Dove must use its wings !

And so it sought the dearer nest ;
  A little way across the sea
  It kept us wingèd company,
Then fled into its leafier rest,

And suddenly left us long to feel
  A sadness in the sweetest words,
  A broken heartstring 'mid the chords ;
A tone more tremulous when we kneel.

But, dear my Christie, do not cry,
  Our White Dove gave for you and me
  Such blessed promise as must be
Perfected in the heavens high.

Our Bird of God but soars and sings :
  Oft when life's heaving wave's at rest,
  She makes her mirror in my breast,
I feel a winnowing of wings,

And meekly doth she minister
  Glad thoughts of comfort, thrills of pride;
  She makes me feel that if I died
This moment I should go to her.

Be good! and you shall find her where
  No wind can shake the wee bird's nest;
  No dreams can break the wee bird's rest;
No night, no pain, no parting there!

No echoes of old storms gone by!
  Earth's sorrows slumber peacefully;
  The weary are at rest, and He
Shall wipe the tears from every eye.

POOR ELLEN.

'Tis hard to die in Spring-time,
  When, to mock our bitter need,
All life around runs over
  In its fulness without heed:
New life for tiniest twig on tree,
New worlds of honey for the bee,
And not one drop of dew for me
  Who perish as I plead.

'Tis hard to die in Spring-time,
  When it stirs the poorest clod;
The wee Wren lifts its little heart
  In lusty songs to God;
And Summer comes with conquering march;
Her banners waving 'neath the arch
Of heaven, where I lie and parch—
  Left dying by the road.

'Tis hard to die in Spring-time,
  When the long blue days unfold,
And cow-lip-coloured sunsets
  Grow, like Heaven's own heart, pure gold !
Each breath of balm brings wave on wave
Of new life that would lift and lave
My Life, whose feel is of the grave,
  And mingling with the mould.

But sweet to die in Spring-time,
  When these lustres of the sward,
And all the breaks of beauty
  Wherewith Earth is daily starr'd,
For me are but the outside show,
All leading to the inner glow
Of that strange world to which I go—
  For ever with the Lord.

O sweet to die in Spring-time,
  When I reach the promised Rest,
And feel His arm is round me—
  Know I sink back on His breast :
His kisses close these poor dim eyes;
Soon I shall hear Him say "*Arise*,"
And, springing up with glad surprise,
  Shall know Him and be blessed.

'Tis sweet to die in Spring-time,
  For I feel my golden year
Of summer-time eternal
  Is beginning even here !
" *Poor Ellen !* " now you say and sigh,
" *Poor Ellen !* " and to-morrow I
Shall say " *Poor Mother !* " and, from the sky,
  Watch *you*, and wait you there.

THE NABOB'S DOUBLE.

Has Man a spirit that's more than breath,
A spirit that walks in sleep or in death ;
Shakes off at will its dust of the earth,
And, waking by night, goes wandering forth
To work its wish with a noiseless tread,
While the body lies bound full-length in bed ?

This is the fact, as sure as fate,
For Burglar Bill, and his midnight mate,
That frightened until it converted him,
To join the "Salvation Army " with Jim.

Many a " *crib* " had the couple " *cracked* " ;
Large was their luck with the swag they sacked.
Many a time thought Burglar Bill,
" *Old Nabob's looks very lone on the hill !* "
But, there was the Dog whose infernal bark
Could be heard through a mile of solid dark.

One day it was rumoured that " Keeper" was
    dead.
To himself Bill knowingly nodded his head,
" *To-night or never,*" he cunningly said.

That night up-hill the couple crept,
To rifle his store as the rich man slept.
All heaven mirrored, with stars agleam,
The dazzle of diamonds in their dream !

They entered their treasury—struck a light—
A tiny light—but it showed a sight
To make the Burglar's heart turn white !
The Nabob sitting alone in his chair,

Facing them there with his long white hair,
And his eyes wide open with corpse-like stare.
And close by his side, keeping watch and ward,
The statue as 'twere of a dog on guard,
With mouth agape, but never a bark;
The dog that was dead and stiff and stark;
Threatening them as if in life!

Jim rushed at the old man with his knife,
And drove it right through—an empty chair,
Instead of the figure sitting there.
For the Nabob vanished, dog and all,—
And the burglars vanished without their haul.

Meanwhile, at the moment he felt the stroke,
Upstairs in bed the Nabob woke.
" Oh wife! are you here ? Am I dead ? is it night ?
Oh wife! I have suffered an unked fright!
I dreamed I was dozing below in my chair,
When suddenly, helplessly, I was aware,
In the dead of the night there was life in the
  gloom ;
Then a light—and two masked men in the room:
One of them dealt me a murderous blow,
And—I woke from my dream in the room below.
But this, O my God! was the strangest thing,
' Keeper ' was with me ; I saw him spring:
Swift as the flash of the falling knife
He flew at the Thief as he would in life !"

Only a dream ! but they went down-stair,
And there were the burglar's tools, and there
Was the knife stuck fast in its stab of the chair!

———

THE DIAKKA.

You are the Merry men, dwarfs of soul,
Who can get your hand through the tiniest hole,
And make your bells jingle outside of the show;
Prove there's life beyond, and on that we go!
'Tis trying to find that we ARE more near
To you than to those we have held more dear,
But I think they are backing you all the while;
And down on our efforts benignly may smile
To see how we strive and are ever unable
To meet and shake hands with the leg of a table.
> So holloa, boys, ring the bells, let them see how
> You can wake up the world with YOUR row-de-dow.

Folk say you are Devils : then act as such !
Give them a touch of the devil's clutch.
In times like ours 'tis a comfort to know
For certain there *may* be a devil or so !
We need them to prove how the lusts of old
For women or wine, for gore or gold,
Are not to be quenched with their burning breath
By the waters of Winter that drown us in death,
But still live on, all a-crave to be fed
In the earth-life lived by the homeless dead.
> Holloa, boys, ring the bells, let us see how
> You can wake up the world with YOUR row-de-dow.

Many a fathom deep under the ground
Souls like toads in the rock lie bound,
Awaiting the resurrection sound
Of the Crack of doom, for them to be found !

Nothing short of an earthquake-kick
Will send them heavenward, make them quick.
Spirits far off, invisible, mute,
Can no more reach to the buried root,
Than we upon earth to the moon can shoot,
Or open oysters by playing a flute!
　　Holloa, boys, ring the bells, show them how
　　You can wake up the world with YOUR
　　　row-de-dow.

"THEY SANG A NEW SONG."

GATHER round the Table,
　When the day is done;
Lay the Electric Cable
　That weds two Worlds in one.
We have found the passage
　Past the frozen pole;
We have had the Message
　Answering, soul to soul.

Gather round the Table
　In a fervent band :
Learn the Lost are able
　To join us hand in hand
With ties no longer riven :
　Empty in the Past
Stretched our hands toward Heaven—
　They are filled at last.

Gather round the Table :
　The silent and the meek,
So long belied, are able
　For themselves to speak,

Open but a portal :
  Every Spirit saith,
Man is born immortal,
  And there is no death.

Gather round the Table :
  By knowledge faith is fed !
Ours the fact they fable ;
  Presence is the Bread.
Come with cleanliest carriage,
  Whitely-pure be dressed :
For this Heavenly Marriage,
  Earth should wear its best.

———

FLOWER AND FRUIT.

THE flower you placed within my button-hole
Has faded ; but there lives within my soul
Another rose, unfolding hour by hour—
Your beauty's self in its immortal flower.

So living-warm this dainty blossom blows,
As if a sunbeam blushed into a Rose,
To make me rich with its ungathered wealth,
And happy in the glory of its health ;

With fragrance like a waft from heaven afar,
And look as lustrous as the morning-star.
I do not come to crown your beauty, Sweet !
Nor thank you for it, kneeling at your feet ;

But pray that on Love's bosom it may rest,
As thornless as its likeness in my breast ;
And ask Him who such promise here hath given
To let me see the Flower fulfilled in heaven.

PEGASUS IN HARNESS.

They pity Pegasus because
The Matrimonial Car he draws
   Along the ruts of life :
And hot and dusty is the road,
And heavy is the living load
   Of leaning weans and wife.

Poor Pegasus ! to turn the Mill,
And grind, and pull the plough until
   The work his withers wrings !
Why not ? 'tis he should do it best,
And tread his measure easiest,
   Or where's the use of wings ?

LOVE AND DEATH.

This butterfly of human breath,
Is followed far and fast by Death ;
Some flower of life it settled on
He clasps and crushes, but—'tis gone.

ORPHANS.

Who would not wish the Dead were near,
If we can dry the mourners' tear ?
Who would not pray the Dead may sleep,
When starving Orphans wake to weep ?

ONE OF SHAKSPEARE'S WOMEN.

I sometimes think that Shakspeare has revealed
To me that very self so long concealed :
But if his soul my soul has lightened through,
I sometimes think it was to gaze on you,
   To find, with loving wonder in his looks,
   One of his Women living out of his Books !

IMPERFECTION.

Ah, never is the Almighty Artist's plan
Crowned and completed in the life of man.
At best a broken fragment we up-rear
Above the tomb, that like a visible prayer
Pleads on and ever with the Infinite,
For other lives to come and finish it,
And for the eternal temple make it fit.

SO IT GOES.

The tender green that laughs out in the light,
   And drinks the freshness of the dew and rain,
Must take the cloud of dust that turns it white
   And burnish every tiny blade again !
The river into which heaven cometh down,
   It is so exquisitely pure and still,
Must also soil itself to cleanse the town,
   And with hard labour tread and turn the mill.

GROWING OLD.

THE stream of Life that brimmed its banks of old,
We drain to gather Wisdom's grains of gold;
And often as we count the riches o'er,
Half wish our wealth were drowned in it once more !

A GREEK REPLY.

"So many are your foes, their arrows shroud
The very Sun with an eclipsing cloud."
"We'll fight them in the dark then ! and the horde
Illumine with the lightning of the Sword."

MAN AND HIS TWO MASTERS.

"*You cannot serve two Masters,*" saith the Word.
　But Satan nudges us and whispers, "*Gammon !*
You lend your Womenkind to love the Lord,
　And give Yourselves to serve and worship
　　Mammon."

WOMANKIND.

DEAR things ! we would not have you learn too
　　much—
Your Ignorance is so charming ! We've a notion
That greater knowledge might not lend you such
　　Sure aid to blind obedience and devotion.

A VERY EARLY RISER.

At the Last Day while all the rest
Are soundly sleeping underground,
He will be up clean-shaved and dressed
An hour before the Trumpets sound.

A PECULIAR PERSON.

You perfect, pure, original,
Writ in a tongue unknown to all;
Translated, in some other sphere,
You may be read; but will not here.

DELIA BACON.

The Delian diver wrecked her life to grasp
A pearl she saw by Visionary gleams,
And died with empty hand that could not clasp
The treasure only Real in her dreams.

A PAINTED SPRAY OF APPLE-BLOSSOM.

Throughout the year and year by year will bloom
This blush of Spring arrested in my room,
Whilst Nature's self to rival it must bring
Her breathing buds renewed each passing Spring.

T

AN ANGEL IN THE HOUSE.

You have your Angel in the House! but look
On this, her likeness, mirrored in a book,
If but to learn how shadowy the Ideal
In presence of the living, loving Real.

SOULS OF ANIMALS.

Such look of an immortal likeness springs,
At times into the eyes of dear dumb things,
As if Hereafter we must recognize
The Unknown Life that knew us in their eyes.

TRUE POETS.

True Poets conquer Glory—do not woo
  It; do not beg their way to Fame;
Nor at her skirts in private bend and sue,
  Nor sow the public broadcast with their name:
They are the great High Priests of Heaven who
  Hold sacred as they feed their Altar-flame
Within the Temple: No man hears their cry
For recognition to the passers-by!

They toil on like old Noah with his Boat;
  "EL" hath forespoken it, and it shall be
Ready, although the need may seem remote:
  No sign that it will ever get to sea!

They fight the Deluge—keep the soul afloat—
   And still work on, and leave the issue free
With Him whose flood shall fall, or high-tide
    climb,
To launch the Vessel in His own good time.

Alone, in silence, secretly, they grow
   Invisibly, where no voice is raised to bless :
Creating in the dark like Hills below
   The ocean, shaped by Nature's strong caress :
Wave after wave sweeps over them ; they know
   How many failures go to make success.
Their victory's in their work, not in the word
That waits to praise, as servant waits his Lord.

At last they mount from out the Lethean flood
   Beyond the cloud that covers and conceals
The present time, to join the Brotherhood
   Of minds that rise up lofty as the hills :
Heaven crowns them in majestic solitude ;
   The world, that saw not once, in wonder kneels !
The less they wooed it all the more it heeds,
And still they mount the more their Age recedes.

HYMNS.

THE LIFE BEYOND.

Although its features fade in light of unimagined
    bliss,
We have shadowy revealings of the Better World
    in this.

A little glimpse, when Spring unveils her face
    and opes her eyes,
Of the Sleeping Beauty in the soul that wakes in
    Paradise.

A little drop of Heaven in each diamond of the
    shower,
A breath of the Eternal in the fragrance of each
    flower!

A little low vibration in the warble of Night's
    bird,
Of the praises and the music that shall be here-
    after heard!

A little whisper in the leaves that clap their
    hands and try
To glad the heart of man, and lift to Heaven his
    grateful eye!

A little semblance mirrored in old Ocean's smile
    or frown
Of His vast glory who doth bow the Heavens and
    come down !

A little symbol shining through the worlds that
    move at rest
On invisible foundations of the broad Almighty
    breast !

A little hint that stirs and thrills the wings we
    fold within,
And tells of that full heaven yonder which must
    here begin !

A little springlet welling from the fountain-head
    above,
That takes its earthly way to find the ocean of all
    love !

A little silver shiver in the ripple of the river
Caught from the light that knows no night for
    ever and for ever !

A little hidden likeness, often faded or defiled,
Of the great, the good All-father, in His poorest
    human child !

Although the best be lost in light of unimagined
    bliss,
We have shadowy revealings of the Better World
    in this.

————

THE DIVINE LIKENESS.

Spirit Divine, we yearn and strive
Within our souls to keep alive
    Some likeness of Thy love !
But 'tis at best a glimpse, a gleam,
Uncertain as a troubled stream
    Reflects the heavens above.

The more we strive, the more we seem
To mar the vision ; break the beam
    Of glory that we chase.
A breath disturbs Thy still design ;
We try to mirror the Divine,
    And blur what we embrace.

Spirit Divine, brood down and fill
Us with Thy calm and make us still ;
    All sighing cares to cease.
Our restless longings cannot hold
The face of heaven unless it fold
    Us round and whisper " *Peace.*"

THE HIDDEN LIFE.

We are not only where we seem
To live, but in some Astral gleam
Dwell also in a world of dream !

Some heavenward window opes above
The shut-up soul, to lean out of,
Or let in waiting wings of love.

And thence we pass from out our night
A little nearer to the light,
Transfigured in the eternal sight!

And oft when darkness fills the place
We thrill with Dawn upon the face,
And feel the Infinite embrace.

Beyond the clouds 'tis golden day;
Soft airs of heaven about us play,
That waft all weariness away.

Dear friends we see no longer here
Are with us: We can feel them near;
To comfort us and heal and cheer.

And thus in secret life is fed,
Till full in flower it lifts the head
With all its leaves to heaven outspread.

And by the peace within the breast,
All stormy passions rocked to rest,
We know that God hath been our guest.

JERUSALEM THE GOLDEN.

JERUSALEM the Golden!
  I weary for one Gleam
Of all thy glory folden
  In distance and in dream!
My thoughts, like Palms in Exile,
  Climb up to look and pray
For a glimpse of thy dear Country
  That lies so far away!

Jerusalem the Golden!
  Methinks each flower that blows,
And every bird a-singing,
  Of thee some secret knows;
I know not what the Flowers
  Can feel, or Singers see,
But all these summer raptures
  Seem prophecies of thee.

Jerusalem the Golden!
  When Sunset's in the West,
It seems thy gate of glory,
  Thou City of the Blest!
And Midnight's starry torches
  Through intermediate gloom,
Are waving with our welcome
  To thy Eternal Home!

Jerusalem the Golden!
  Where loftily they sing,
O'er pain and sorrows olden
  For ever triumphing :
Lowly may be the portal
  And dark may be the door,
The Mansion is Immortal—
  God's palace for His Poor!

Jerusalem the Golden!
  There all our Birds that flew,—
Our Flowers but half-unfolden,
  Our Pearls that turned to dew,—
And all the glad life-music,
  Now heard no longer here,
Shall come again to greet us
  As we are drawing near.

Jerusalem the Golden !
  1 toil on day by day ;
Heart-sore each night with longing,
  I stretch my hands and pray,
That 'mid thy leaves of Healing
  My soul may find a nest ;
Where the troubles are all over,—
  The Weary are at rest !

POOR MAN'S SUNDAY.

We thank Thee, Lord, for one day
  To look Heaven in the face !
The Poor have only Sunday ;
  The sweeter is the grace.
'Tis then they make the music
  That sings their week away :
O, there's a sweetness infinite
  In the Poor Man's holiday !

'Tis here the weary Pilgrim
  Doth reach his House of Ease !
That blessèd House, called " Beautiful,"
  And that soft Chamber, " Peace."
The River of Life runs through his dream
  And the leaves of Heaven are at play ;
He sees the Golden City gleam,
  This grateful holiday.

'Tis as a burst of sunshine,
  A tender fall of rain,
That set the barest life a-bloom ;
  Make old hearts young again.

The dry and dusty roadside
  With smiling flowers is gay :
'Tis open Heaven one day in seven,
  The Poor Man's holiday !

AT EVENTIDE.

FATHER in Heaven, we seek Thy face
When darkness is our dwelling-place.
Our foolish hearts, that daily roam,
Would nightly nestle with Thee at Home.
Be with us Here, and grant that we
Hereafter, Lord, may be with Thee !

Father ! our inmost parts lie bare
To Thine own purifying air ;
We spread our stains out in Thy sight ;
O, Sun of Pureness, turn them white :
And make our spirits clear as dew
For Thine own Self to lighten through.

Send down the Comforter, we plead,
For all who are in bitter need ;
May homeless Hagars find, we pray,
Some well of succour by the way—
The Angel of Thy Presence bless
All wanderers in the wilderness.

God keep our darlings safe this night,
Though scattered, *one* still in Thy sight !
Lead on, by many ways, and past
All perils, till we join at last :
With us the broken links ! with Thee
The circle perfect endlessly.

Now take us, Father, to Thy breast,
And still our troubled thoughts to rest;
Thy watch and ward about us keep,
That tired souls may smile asleep,
And, having been with heaven awhile,
May wake to-morrow in Thy smile!

GONE BEFORE.

ONE of God's own Darlings was my bosom's nest
　　ling Dove,
　With her looks of love and sunshine, and her
　　voice so rich and low:
How it trembled through my life, like an Immor-
　　tal's kiss of love!
　How its music yearns through all my memory
　　now!
How her beauty rainbows round me, and her sweet
　　smile, silverly
　As a song, fills all the silence of the Midnight's
　　charmèd hours;
And I know from out her grave she'll send her
　　love in death to me,
　By the Spring in smiling utterance of Flowers.

O my Love, too good for Earth, has gone into the
　　land of light;
　It was hard, she said, to leave me, but the Lord
　　had need of her;
And she walks the heavens in glory like a Star i'
　　the crown of Night,

With the Beautiful and Blessed mingling
    there.—
Gone before me, to be clothèd in a bridal robe of
    white,
    Where Love's blossom comes to fruit, and all
        its suffering's glorified!
May my love but make me meet and worthy of
    her presence bright,
    That in heaven I may claim her as my Bride.

A CRY IN THE NIGHT.

Dark, dark the night, and tearfully I grope,
    Lost in the Shadows, feeling for the way,
But cannot find it.   Here's no help, no hope,
    And God is very far off with His day.

Hush, hush, faint heart! why this may be thy
    chance,
    When all is at the worst, to prove thy faith;
Be still, and see His great Deliverance,
    And trust Him at the darkest unto Death.

Often upon the last grim ridge of war
    God takes His stand to aid us in the fight;
He watches while we roll the tide afar,
    And, beaten back, is near us with His might.

We hear the Arrows in the dark go by:
    The cowering soul no longer soars or sings,
Or it might know His presence then most nigh,
    Our darkness being the Shadow of His wings.

No need of faith if all were visibly clear!
  'Tis for the trial-time its help was given;
Though clouds be thick, the Sun is just as near
  That shines within and makes the heart its
      heaven.

Amidst our wildest night of saddest woes,
  When Earth is desolate—Heaven dark with
      doom,
There is a fire-flash of the soul that shows
  The face of the Eternal through the gloom.

HIS BANNER OVER ME.

SURROUNDED by unnumbered Foes,
Against my soul the battle goes!
Yet though I weary, sore-distressed,
I know that I shall reach my Rest:
    I lift my tearful eyes above,—
    His Banner over me is Love.

Its Sword my spirit will not yield,
Though flesh may faint upon the field;
He waves before my fading sight
The branch of palm—the crown of light;
    I lift my brightening eyes above,—
    His Banner over me is Love.

My cloud of battle-dust may dim;
His veil of splendour curtain Him!
And in the midnight of my fear
I may not feel Him standing near:
    But, as I lift mine eyes above,
    His Banner over me is Love.

REST.

Slow step by step, day after day,
I journey on my homeward way;
And darkly dream the Land of Light
Is drawing near, night after night;
  Where I shall reach my Rest at last,
  And smile at all the troubles past.

Sometimes I sing; sometimes I sigh;
Sometimes I lift the longing eye;
Sometimes my heart laughs 'neath its load,
To think of that august abode,
  Where I shall reach my Rest at last,
  And smile at all the trials past.

She will be near, my Star of Hope,
When at the gloomy gate I grope,
And take my hand and ope for me
The door of Immortality!
  And I shall know my Rest at last,
  And triumph in the perils past.

AT LAST.

A few more Meetings on the Deep,
  And partings on the shore;
And then in Heaven at last we keep
  Our tryst for evermore.

A little further we must bear
  The load, and do our best;
Then take immortal solace where
  The wretched are at rest.

Our Pilgrimage will soon be past,
  Our worst afflictions borne ;
Some weary night, 'twill be the last,
  And then Eternal Morn.

HYMN OF THE PRESENT.

Not only in old days He bowed
  The heavens and came down ;
We, too, were shadowed by the cloud,
  We saw the glory shown !
The nations that seemed dead have felt
  His coming through them thrill :
Beneath His tread the mountains melt :
  Our God is living still !

He who in secret hears the sigh,
  Interprets every tear,
Hath lightened on us from on high,
  Made known His presence near !
The Word takes flesh, the Spirit form,
  His purpose to fulfil ;
He comes in person of the Storm—
  Our God who governs still !

We saw—all of us saw—how He
  Drew sword and struck the blow,
And up and free through their Red Sea
  He bade the Captives go :
Yea, we have seen Him, clearly seen
  Him work the miracle :
We know, whate'er may intervene,
  Our God is with us still !

The veil of Time a moment falls
  From off the Eternal's face:
Recede the old horizon-walls
  To give fresh breathing-space:
And all who lift their eyes may learn
  It is our Father's will,
This world to Him shall freely turn,
  A world of freedom still!

FAITH AND FACT.

THERE is no gleam of glory gone,
  For those who read in Nature's Book;
  No lack of triumph in their look
Who stand in Her Eternal Dawn.

Friends of a failing Faith! while your
  Lighthouses of eternal life
  Hold tremulous lamps across the strife,
That die and darken hour by hour;

And higher climb the waves that drench,
  And on the rocks the breakers roar;
  While Light for you opes no new door;
And higher climb the waves that quench,—

While Heaven-scalers in the dust
  Sit, with their hopes dead or discrowned;
  Their splendid dreams all shivered round,
And broken every reed of trust,—

While timid souls that sail the sea
  Of Time are fearful lest yon band
  Of Cloud should not be solid Land,
To step on for Eternity,—

U

And faint hearts flutter 'twixt a nest
    That is not sealed to wind and wet,
    And one that is not ready yet,
With wandering wings, and find no rest.—

There is no gleam of glory gone
    For those who read in Nature's Book ;
    No lack of triumph in their look,
Who live in her Eternal Dawn !

THE HAUNTED HURST.

THE HAUNTED HURST,

A TALE OF ETERNITY.

As One who, in a strange and far Country,
In presence of his future Bride may be,
That keeps the secret of her face concealed,
Until, as Wife, the Maiden stands revealed :
And who doth make blind guesses at the face ;
Its wealth of nature and its gifts of grace :
Much marvelling if the form beneath the folds
Be like the picture that at heart he holds !
And who, as chance befall, may furtively
Feel the hid features that he cannot see—
Trying to gather, with a Lover's touch,
The least of all he longs to know so much :
Even thus, before the Next World's face I stand,
And o'er its clouded features pass my hand ;
Groping to get, where mortal sight doth fail,
Some likeness of the face behind the Veil !
It is the voice of Vision in the night ;
I learned in darkness what I speak in light :
Perchance such ne'er attains the perfect True,
And yet may utter meaning for the few,
As sandiest Desert wastes reflect afar
Light from our Sun to some benighted Star !

PART I.

Night after night I wakened with a start
That tore the curtain-cloud of Sleep apart,
As though I had been fettered fast by Death,
Who imaged Sleep to take away my breath.
The silence looked so ominous, the gloom
Just losing shape and feature in the room:
Had I but wakened sooner, without doubt,
I should have found some dreadful secret out!
Nothing to grapple with; nothing to see:
Yet something fearful there must somewhere be;
Some shadow of the Unapparent stole
Over me, with a shiver of the soul:
Dim horrors loomed from out each hiding-nook;
A strange life lurked in the familiar look
Of innocent things, as though upon the eve
Of issuing, terrible as its prey perceive
The *Mantis* in the likeness of a leaf,
Changed in a moment to a Murderous Thief.
I peered out of the window,—nothing there
But the vast heavens with all their loneness
      bare—
The phantom presence of Immensity
That from behind its dumb mask whispered me.

At times a noise, as though a dungeon door
Had grated, with set teeth, against the floor:
A ring of iron on the stones; a sound
As if of granite into powder ground;
A mattock and a spade at work! sad sighs
As of a wave that sobs and faints and dies.

And then a shudder of the house; a scrawl
As though a knife scored letters in the wall.
About the room a gush and gurgle went,
As if the water-pipe got sudden vent;
Drop after drop, I heard it plop, and ping,
Into some vessel, with metallic ring.
Yet, on these very nights there was no rain;
And then, betwixt the ear's suspense and strain,
A faint voice crying in the air or brain.

The wind would rise and wail most humanly
With a low scream of stifled agony
Over the birth of life about to be.
Through all the house its coldest wave hath
    rushed,
Although a moment since the night was hushed.
And ere the hurried gust had ceased to moan,
The dreaming dog would answer with its groan.

At times I seemed to waken at a call,
And rose up listening for the next footfall
Which never came, as though it could not keep
The step with that my spirit caught in sleep;
For I, in waking, must have crossed the line
Bounding the range of spirit-life from mine.
I felt the Presence on that other side
Grope where some secret door might open wide.
I knew the brain might strike the electric spark
Which should make live this phantom of the
    Dark.
Once as I woke I could have sworn I saw
A white face from the window-pane withdraw!
But, softly in its place the curtain slid,
Even in the unlifting of the swift eyelid.

Sometimes I woke with lashes wet and bright
With a strange glory of delicious light,
As though an Angel had shone my shut eyes
    through
And filled my soul with heaven, as Dawn with
    dew :
A fragrance from afar with me would stay,
And at my work my heart sang all next day.

I am no Coward ; never did believe
That spirits can their hell or heaven leave
To walk by night in the old human ways.
For forty years this was my creed o' days.
Somehow the dark another tale doth tell :
We are so fearful of the Unfathomable !
The Infinite is full of whisperings ;
With mortal tug the wildered spirit clings
To its known shore of firm reality,
Yet feels drawn outward—like the ebbing
    sea
That hugs its beach so closely and in vain—
In this vast ebb of Being to its main.

And it is eerie in the night to lie
Lonesome, all naked to the awful sky—
This secret spawning-time of hell on earth,
When mist and midnight give the toadstools
    birth,
And worlds of shy leaf-shadowed life steal forth,—
What time the Powers of Darkness have their
    day ;
Our world asleep and Heaven so far away :
When in the shroud-like stillness there may be
Shapes moving round us that we do not see !

Our little sphere of life is darkly rimmed
In the wide universe of Being brimmed
With life perhaps inimical to us!
Nor could we live if all were luminous.
But is it certain we have lost the sight
They had of old in watches of the night,
Who heard the voices, saw the shape that stood
Before them in the Soul's similitude?
They saw with eyes of spirit—Heaven keep
The veil of flesh about me dark and deep!

What does the Darkness mutter?   Is it Death
That makes the light burn bluer with his breath?
Was that a creaking of the stair? a Rat
Nibbling the wainscot? did a flittering Bat
Flap at the window? Floors will crack for sure,
But may not unseen feet be on the floor?
Spirits stand rapping at Life's outer gate,
And, if we dare not open, will they wait?
Was that the Death-Watch ticking in the wall?
One's hair with reptile-life begins to crawl.
Is there some Whispering Gallery of the ear,
In which the other world we overhear?
The very Mirror is a doorway, through
Whose dark another face may look at you!

Who knows with what those ghostly gleams are
        rife
In spectral semblance of our sunlit life?
What Night hath shielded from pursuing Day
In sanctuary darkness, hid away,
As Paramour of hers in some foul play?
What viewless horrors in the wind may lurk,
That fill the mind with Shadows grim and murk?
What demons may be audibly at work?

Maybe the voices of a sunless world
That in the eclipse of night is doomward hurled :
What groping outcasts of ignoble soul
Are working through the darkness, like the
    mole,
Crouching in dreams to steal on sleeping Men :
Red-handed spirits that flung life back again
To Him who gave, and hide their murder-mark
In any secret corner of the dark :
Eaves-droppers leaning listening with a grin,
To think how some small keyhole-creeping sin
Will ope the door and let the Tempter in.

What wappened wantons lurking 'twixt the
    lights,
May lie in wait for wanderers o' nights :
What phantom shapes forlorn may meet and
    march
In long procession under Night's dark arch,
Stretching their arms to us, worm-fretted, all
Hueless and featureless and weirdly tall :
What rootless strays of life are ever blown
About like floating ghosts of thistle-down,
That seek a foothold and are whirled away—
Dead leaves a-dancing—vanishing sea-spray ;
Homeless, as drifted clouds are hurried past
Their heaven for ever, by the driving blast.

And now we come to think, may we not hold
Ghost-hands in ours, that turn them icy cold ?
A ghostly presence whitens in the cheek,
And makes the blood run water,—wan and weak
The swooning life from out us faintly fleets,
And turns to drops at the chill touch it meets.

The walls of flesh are waxing all too thin
To keep the world of spirits from crowding in.
We wrap the clothes about us; but, still bare
In soul, we feel a wave of chillier air,
Like that which brings the dawn, but that's a
    breath
Of sweet new life, this hath the feel of death!
The spirit-spiracles all open wide,
And life seems drowning in the flooding tide;
We cannot cry, the Unseen world doth strive
To seal the mouth and bury the soul alive.
I must believe in Ghosts, lying awake
With them o' nights, when flesh will creep and
    quake,
And lustily one pulls the Bell of Prayer,
From this thick snow of Spirits to clear the air.

No marvel that the Birds salute the Dawn,
For all the dangers of the dark withdrawn;
Break into singing with their first free breath,
That they have swum the dim, vast sea of death,
And hymn the resurrection of the Light,
In praise to Him who kept them through the
    night
And cared for His least little feathered things,
Encompassed with the safety of His Wings;
While those that cannot warble, twittering tell
Of darkness passed once more, and all is well.

With what a thankful heart I often heard
The blessed cry of Morning's earliest Bird!
How eagerly watched the weird and waning
    Night
Turn deathly pale and pass away in light.

Yet, I believe that God is master still.
He reigneth ; He whose lightest breath can
　　thrill
The universe of worlds like drops of dew,
And if the Spirit-world hath broken through
It cannot be unknown, unseen by Him ;
It must be with His will, not their mere whim.
And if our world of breath be set aflood,
Swimming in supra-normal neighbourhood,
There is a soul within will not be drowned,
Even though a sea of spirits surges round :
An inner infinite with power to reach
The level of its outer ocean-beach !
Therefore I trust Him ; shut mine eyes and say
" *Lead on, O Thou, who only know'st the way !*
Father in Heaven, take my hand in Thine ;
Be at my heart, and in my countenance shine.
Then, all unfearing, shall I face the gate
At which the powers of Darkness lie in wait."

PART II.

ONCE on a time, the ancient story saith,
Some foolish Mummers danced a masque of
　　Death.
They bore his emblems, trying, every one,
To out-parody the bony Skeleton ;
And, as the merriment grew, there glided in
Grim Death Himself, mocking with ghastly grin
At their poor make-believe ; as who should say,
" *This is the real thing and no mere play.*"

" *Talk of the Devil*," say we, " *and he's here,*"
Sudden as thunder-claps, when skies are clear.

'Twas thus all fears and phantoms of the past,
Shaped into something palpable at last.

One night, as I lay musing on my bed,
The veil was rent that shows the Dead not dead.

Upon a Picture I had fixed mine eyes,
Till slowly it began to magnetize.
So the Ecstatics on their symbol stare,
Until the Cross fades and the Christ is there!
Thus, while I mused upon the picture's face,
A veil of white mist wavered in its place;
And to a lulling motion I sank deep,
With spirit awake and senses fallen asleep,
Down through an air that palpitatingly
Breathed with a breath of life unknown to me;
And when the motion ceased, against the gloom,
There lived another Form within the room,
As if the Dark had suddenly made a face
I saw the haunting Presence of the Place
Embodied, strange and horrible, as rise
The Torturers that stare in dying eyes:
Or, as the Serpent—ere a leaf be stirred—
Looks through the dark on some bewildered
    bird:
A face in which the life had burned away
To cinders of the soul and ashes gray:
The forehead furrowed with a sombre frown
That seemed the image, in shadow, of Death's
    crown;
His look a map of misery that told
How all the under-world in blackness rolled.
A human face in hideous eclipse;
No lustre on the hair, nor life i' the lips;

The faintest gleam of corpse-light, lurid, wan,
Showed me the lying likeness of a Man!
The old soiled lining of some mortal dress:
A Spirit sorely stained with earthiness.

But, almost ere I could have time to fear,
I saw what seemed an Angel standing near,
And on Her face a smile for my relief:
A dream of glory in my night of grief,
Shedding an influent mildness through the
        awe,
Pleasant to feel, as was the smile I saw:
Indeed, methought she breathed a fragrance
        faint,
That overcame some rotting charnel-taint.
She wore a purple vesture thin as mist,
The Breath of Dawn, upon the plum dew-kissed.
No flame-hued, flame-shaped, Golden-Holly tree
Ere kindled at the sun so splendidly
As that self-radiant head, with lifted hair
A-wave in many a fiery scimitar.
The purple shine of Violets wet with dew
Was in her eyes that looked me through and
        through.
We think of Shades as native to the night;
We photograph the other world in white,
That will not paint its tints upon our sight.
But there are Colours of the Eternal Light,
And these were of them; pulsing such live
        glows
As never reddened blood or ripened rose:
No Mist from the past life as some have deemed
The Dead to be; no pallid shadow dreamed
By Greeks of old, but Life itself this seemed.

And such a light was in the Angel's face,
It made a glory round about the place
To see by : as you mark in the gold ray
The Motes that dance invisibly in the gray.
But, deep in shadow of his inner night,
The Dark Shape stood and sinned against the
     Light.

As men have felt, when earth rocked underfoot,
Their trust in it was wrenched up by the root ;
The firm foundations of all things had given,
And any instant they might be in heaven :
As one midway across a wide, white road,
In winter, when all night the skies have snowed,
Learns 'tis not earth but frozen stream beneath,
And he is leaning on the arms of Death :
So did I feel to find our earthy bound
Of Substance was no longer safe or sound ;
That spirit-springs make quicksand of firm
     ground ;
That spirit-hands withdraw our curtains round ;
That spirit between particles can pass
Surely and visibly, as light through glass ;
With power to come and go, stand upright,
     loom
Dense to the eye, outlined against the gloom.

The Dark Shape on me turned its eyes of guile,
Sullen yet fierce.   I read the wicked smile
That sneered—"*Behold the cause of all your fear!
You need not shudder though while She is near.*"
And then he spoke, or seemed to speak, in words,
Although I saw his thoughts like murderous
     swords,

Or toothèd wheels, go whirling round within
The fearsome face so shadowy and thin,
And did not always need the speech to know
What dreadful thing it was he had to show.

" Lo ! I am one of those doomed souls who dwell
In Heaven's vast Shadow which the Good call Hell.
Lo ! I am he, most miserable, who did
His deed of darkness, fancying all was hid ;
The Awful eyes being on me all the while,
And demons pointing at me with their smile ;
Who carry such a hell within my breast,
That all about me throbs with my unrest,
As though the heavens were shaken, or the earth
Were overtaken in the throes of birth :
Doors tremble open, walls disintegrate,
And world to world flings wide its secret gate.
With such a pulse of power my pangs awake
At midnight, that from sleep they sometimes shake
You ! Matter, with Mind's thrillings, doth so
    quake,
That atoms from their fellow atoms start,
As though each felt the heave of some live heart."

Then seeing the questioning wonder in my look,
He answered, as my turn of thought he took,

" Yes, it is true, all true, the thing you dreamed ;
Most real is the life that only seemed.
Soul's no mere shadow that gross substance throws ;
Our passions are not pageantary shows,
Exhaled from Matter, like the cloud from cape,
They are the life's own lasting final shape.
This scheme of things with all the sights you see,
Are only pictures of the things that be.

What you call Matter is but as the sheath,
Shaped, even as bubbles are, by spirit-breath.
The mountains are but firmer clouds of earth,
Still changing to the breath that gave them birth.
Spirit aye shapeth Matter into view,
As Music wears the forms it passes through.
Spirit is lord of substance, Matter's sole
First cause, formative power and final goal."

"And who is this," I asked, "that in Her face
Doth image humanly celestial grace:
That calms my soul as when the Moon looks
     forth,
Whose smile in heaven makes stillness on the
     earth?"

" One of those Ministers who are sent below
To walk the earth, patrolling to and fro,
As sentinels on guard, night after night,
That in the darkness make a watch-fire light,
Lest sleeping souls be helplessly surprised
By the wild beasts of worlds not realized."

I looked, the shining face serenely smiled
Away all terror like a thing beguiled.

" One of the dreadful Angels of the Lord,
Who are His fiery-flaming two-edged sword,
Which at each door and window waves and burns
Until the Angel of the Dawn returns.
They are with you, watching through the murkest
*   hour,*
And seen, or unseen, hold us in their power,
That when the devil rages in us, lo!
We strike and strike, and yet there falls no blow.

x

They maze and daze us standing there behind,
And, as in dreams, we struggle bound and blind.
The sharpest tortures that I have to bear
Are when I feel Her presence hovering near.
A ray from heaven turns to a sword in hell;
The flash is maddening, we so darkly dwell!
The heat of heaven is like the blazing ring
Of fire that makes the Scorpion try to sting
Itself to death; an air of Heaven's breath
Is poison; hell is spiritual death:
And this awakes us, with its stir and strife,
Like tinglings of the drowned recalled to life."

I glanced again: I saw the look arise
As of a drawn Sword in the Angel's eyes!

" We have met here for years.   She comes to see
Me digging nightly; grope for my lost key;
Her presence kindles round me such a light,
All heaven can see me prowling through the night;
All hell make merry at the gruesome sight.

" I never told my secret in your world,
I kept it at the heart too closely curled;
There, at my life-springs, did I nestle and nurse
The hidden snake, my bosom's clinging curse;
My worm of torment biting bitterly,
And fed it fat for all eternity.
And no eye saw it writhe in my white face,
Or heard it hiss in its dark hiding-place,
When any voice of secret murders told,
And in its might it wantoned and grew bold.
It gnawed my heart as with hell-fire for years.
Drink would not drown it, nor a sea of tears

Quench it, nor all the waters of the land
Whiten my soul, or wash my red right hand!
Whate'er I did, my heart with hell-fire burned ;
Mine eyes with redness swam where'er I turned.
I fled and fled, and could not leave behind
The still, unwinking Bloodhounds of the mind.
I dared not slumber soundly, lest asleep
The unsleeping secret from my lips should leap
In dreams, and I on waking might have found
Myself had turned Informer, and was bound
In handcuffs, with the accusing faces round.

" And so, at last, I pricked the bubble of breath,
I plunged to hide me from Myself in death :
I found the hell-hole in the wild whirlpool ;
Plucked the cold hand down on my brain to cool :
I grovelled out my own deep grave ; I fell
Right through it, into open arms of hell.

" I fancied, when I took the headlong leap,
That death would be an everlasting sleep ;
And the white Winding-sheet and green sod might
Shut out the world, and I have done with sight.
Cold water from my hand had sluiced the warm
And crimson carnage ; safe the little form
Lay underground : the tiny trembling waif
Of life hid from the light ; my secret safe.
In vain.   You cannot hide a deed like this,
With all the heavens one cloud of witnesses :
Useless to blot the blood out with the dust,
When it hath eaten with its ruddy rust
Into your spirit's hand, where, visibly
The murder-stain leers through eternity !
Look there ! "

X 2

I looked, and saw what seemed a hand,
Or gore-soaked shadow of one that, like a brand
When breathed on, kindled fiercely as he sighed;
And plucked it from his bosom, where he tried
To hide its guilty red.

      " *That gripped the knife*
That slew my child. This is its ruddy life,
Red-hot; on fire of hell! In burning rings,
The blood my fingers clutched, for ever clings,
And clamps them with relentless ache and smart
So closely that they will not pull apart.
Once only, while I wept and almost prayed,
They yielded just a little: then was played
A spectral trick upon me; all between,
They shone, thin-webbed with gore, and clearly seen
As through a window, through the web there
   smiled
Up in my face the face of my dead child.
Better to bear this fiery grip of pain,
Than they should open on that sight again.

" *The whirling world had flung my life from it,*
 And I felt falling through the Infinite,
 For weeks and months, and years on years of
   nights
Innumerable, from stupendous heights;
For, as a minute's slumber may be all
As one with that of a million years, my fall
So quickened being, that a minute's fears
Made instantaneous a million years.
No God to call upon, no Power to stay,
No hand to clutch at on my endless way!
When just as I was plunging in a cloud

That lightened with the laugh of Hell, and showed
It made of devilish faces, which grew glad
And kindled at my coming, and all had
A gap-toothed wicked grin, as though each one
Saw in my face the kindred of its own,—
All the dark host rejoicing as I came;
All making sure as Marksman of his aim,
When lo! a Hawk swoops from its height unheard,
And from before his gun bears off his Bird!—
So, while the gulf I gazed on grew and gaped,
The black cloud curled about me demon-shaped,
And all their claws for cruel welcome spread,
I was caught up; borne swiftening overhead,
By one on wings of light, with lightning shod,
And then I knew that I was going to God,—
That life but sets in life still more profound,
As sunset into sunrise the world round;
That all who enter by the gate of breath,
Must pass before the Awful eyes in death,
And stand all naked to the searching mien.
I could not shrivel nor slink away unseen!

" To me the vast and horrible Unknown
Was one dread face, and all the face one frown!
Pain, sternness, pity eternal in a look
That read my life, wide-open as a book.
Not that the leaves turned over one by one,
Revealing, page by page, all I had done,—
The Sense is as a scroll where manifold
Indelible things are day by day uprolled
And registered for Memory to recall;
Maps of the mental world hung on the wall:
But Life is more than Letter or than Law,
And deftly as the brain may take or draw

Its daily tallies, never can it keep
In fixèd figure all the fathomless Deep
Of Consciousness conceals, whose restless sea
Ripples on changing sands unceasingly.
Spirit is one.   It is the crystal book,
Clear through and through; read at a single look.
To all the thoughts that ever passed through us
In life, in death we grow diaphanous.
We do not think what we have been, we ARE
Past, present, future, without near or far.
A glimpse of this is lightened, when the blind
Is raised, in drowning, from the seeing Mind!
So the electric flash, thrown on the wheel
Revolving swift in darkness, will reveal
Each whirling spoke distinctly standing still.
In spirit-world at once you find the whole
Of life contemporary with the soul.

" There is strange writing of the passing guest
Featured upon the form it leaves at rest,
Which men in some dim wise may read, but here
Is the live Chronicler itself! the clear
Truth naked—brain and body were but dress—
Quickened by the Eternal consciousness.

" So, when before that face, I felt the frown,
There was no need of Hell to drag me down,
I could have welcomed wafts of burning flame
To clothe my nakedness of dead'y shame.
I lifted to my brow one shading hand,
But snatched it burning from the Murderer's
        brand.
The other to mine eyes I pressed; 'twas red
And wet and dripping with the blood I shed.

I tried to cover up my aching sight,
And found myself all eye to pitiless light.

" In olden times, it was the wont, they say,
To bring the Murderer where his victim lay,
And at his touch, as to his slaying knife,
The wound would flush: Death speak with lips of
    Life.

" So, from the frown, a little tiny Child
Looked out on me and innocently smiled !

" I shrieked my guiltiness at sight of it,
And downward plunged, for hiding in the Pit.

" ' Curse God and die,' the Tempter said of old.
I curse, and back the curses crowd tenfold.
Against the cold Heaven strikes my burning breath,
To fall in dews of wrath with second death.
And still I curse, and yet I cannot die ;
And still I watch for Death with pleading eye,
To find that he will nevermore draw nigh.
Would the Almighty One had spit on me,
And wiped the blot from His eternity !

PART III.

" My Temptress lives on still.
                    She is a Wife
And Mother ; lives an unsuspected life.
She hath grown fat and flourished on the ill,
The poison, that should naturally kill.
That cruel stain of Murder seemed to pass
From off her face of life as breath from glass.

I sometimes play the devil in her dream,
And plague her with a glimpse, one lurid gleam
Of all my torment ; her thick veil I tear,
And lay the unholy of unholies bare,
Else were her heart untroubled, deaf and blind.
Things out of sight with her are out of mind,
And should she hear a voice from the Unknown
She takes it for an echo of her own.

" Ah, Mistress, did you know we have to stand
Together yet, as equals, hand in hand,
Like Eve and Adam, shivering side by side,
Where not a leaf our nakedness can hide ;
Our secret blazoned, as a flag unfurled
High on the housetops of another world !

" She was a buxom beauty ! In her way
Imperious as the Thane's Wife in the Play.
A woman who upon the outside smiled,
Burnished like beetles, inwardly defiled ;
With hair that like a thunder-cloud, black-
      brightening,
Caught the sunlight, and flashed it back in
      lightning.
No Demon ever toyed with worthier folds,
About a comelier throat, to strangle souls ;
A face that dazzled you with life's white-heat,
Devouring, as it drew you off your feet,
With eyes that set the Beast o' the blood astir,
Leaping in heart and brain, alive for her ;
Melted the sword of soul within its sheath :
The knee-joints loos-ned, smitten by her breath,
Until you bowed, as the strong beast boweth,
When taken captive by the dark of death :

Lithe, amorous lips, cruel in curve and hue,
Which, greedy as the grave, my kisses drew
With hers, that to my mouth like live things clung
Long after, and in memory fiercely stung :
A dainty morsel of the Devil's meat
To roll beneath my tongue, as poison sweet !
Had not the Mother ate forbidden food,
This was the Daughter among Women who would

" But what avails to cast on her the blame ?
I will not : will not name her by her name.
The deed is done ; the sin is sinned ; the brand
Is on my brow ; the blood burns on my hand.

" I must have been a beast myself from birth.
We lived as Beasts in that old burrow of earth
They called a House ; the Cot where I was born ;
One of those dwellings Poets will adorn
Outside with Honeysuckle and climbing Rose,
But where, within, no flower of Heaven blows
With sweetening breath, for want of air and
  light,
And in the wild weeds crawl the things of night :
Where any life-warmth quickens the dark slime
Of hovelled sin to swarm in shame and crime.

" My Pastoral Home was one wherein are grown
Boys for the Hulks ; girls for the pitiless Town
That flaunts beneath the gaslights on the highway,
The full-blown flowers of many a filthy by-way !
Where Virtue has no safeguard, Vice no veil ;
The Devil sowed his seed, never to fail—
With such a soil—in growing harvest meet
For him, as sure as corn is grown to eat.

" *I should have been the beast that Nature binds*
  To beaten ways, and with her blinkers blinds,
  But, was a Beast with scope to work all ill;
  Treat Wife and dumb things cruelly—sin—kill—
  And go to Hell by freedom of the will.
  And yet I knew not—such the curse of sin!—
  Until the fall came, what was ripe within;
  What demon I had nursed past suckling-time,
  To find that it could go alone in crime.

" *She came to me, her great black eyes aglare*
  Like stars of bale, yet with the hunted stare
  Of wild things; such as made me stare to see
  What danger followed her and threatened me.
  I knew that Nemesis was drawing near,
  And in the beating of my heart could hear
  The footsteps that will shake strong men with fear.
  'What is it?' I asked. What need for her to tell?
  'Twas writ all over her.   I knew too well.
  And still I stared beyond, as if that way
  The blackness rose that blotted out my day.
  For days, and weeks, and months her secret lay
  Safe-nestled, unsuspected by her friends,
  But one day all disguise in sinning ends,
  And every way-side hiding-place is past.
  She had to leave her home and flee at last—
  Mad with the misery of a Mother's pain,
  She ran to me, through fire, and hail, and rain,
  And mire below, and thunder overhead;
  Ran lightning-dazed, and drenched, till nearly
      dead.

" *Well I remember that* LAST DAY.   *I see*
  It lightning-lit.   I feel it stamped in me,

As with the black seal of Eternity.
It was about mid-Spring, when suddenly
The rear of beaten Winter turned in ire,
And there was battle fierce of Frost and Fire.
The Birds stopped singing; all the golden flame
O' the Sun went out; the Cattle homeward came.
With a forerunning shiver rushed the breeze,
And, in the Woods, the hushed and listening trees,
That had been standing deathly-dark and still,
Wind-whitened sprang, with every leaf athrill.
I watched the tortured clouds go hurrying by,
Racked with the rending spirit of prophecy:
Like Pythonesses in the pangs, they tossed
And writhed in shadowy semblance of the Lost:
They met, they darted death, they reared, they
    roared,
And down the torrent of the tempest poured!
Through heaven's windows the blue lightnings
    gleamed,
And like a fractured pane the sky was seamed:
Hailstones made winter on the whitened ground,
And for two hours the thunder warrayed round.
And then I heard the Thrush begin again,
With his more liquid warble after rain.

" Tearing through all the fearful storm she came;
Worse storm within, and in her eyes hell-flame
Had broken loose to kindle, past control,
In huge dare-devilry of reckless soul.
As springs a Madman, dancing upon deck,
Who hath doomed the Ship, and glories in the
    wreck;
As at a Prison-window one may stand
Who fired the house, and waves the lighted brand,

Her spirit sprang at mine.   Her looks were wild.
She had come to me, she said, to bring the child,
For no one had a greater right to it !
This was God's truth, not merely meant for wit.
She swore that she had come there and would stay
Till it was born, and safely put away.
And even while I cursed her pangs grew worse,
And stopped me with an everlasting curse.

"'Good God ! this is too bad,' *I thought; and
        laughed*
A laugh as bitter as the cup I quaffed.
I had been married just a month ! my Wife
Knew nothing of this dead love come to life.
As Fate would have it, she had gone from home :
I knew that any minute she might come.
With desperate voice the woman made me writhe ;
Harsh as the whetstone on the Mower's scythe
She rasped me all on edge ; the hell-sparks flew,
Till there seemed nothing that I dared not do.
'Kill it, you Coward !   Why not kill us both ?'
She taunted me ; and I felt little loth.
Then something whispered, 'Why not kill them
        both ?'
I said I would, and clenched it with an oath."
Now, while he spake, there came a frightful
    change
Upon him with transfiguration strange,
And slowly he assumed his mortal dress
With a last look of dying consciousness :
The eyes turned stony in a sightless stare,
And of all presence he grew unaware :
Clouded and lost within his dreadful dream
He went ; a Man once more, each pore a stream

Of inner agony ; his body shook,
And from his mazèd face did " MURDER " look.
It was as when in dreams you see a dumb
Mouth shaped to cry it, though no sound will
    come !
While in his hand he grasped a gleaming knife,
So keen, you saw it thirst for a drink of life :
And, as he passed into his haunted gloom,
His dreadful purpose drew him from the room.

So terrible the scene, I should have cried
For help in the death-eddies,—must have died
But for the strong calm Spirit at my side,
Who took me by the hand and turned on mine
Her cordial face with comfortable shine.
And then the darkness gave a sudden sigh,
And a wind rose that went lamenting by.
" *Listen*," She said.   I leaned, all ear, to hark ;
I felt the quake of footsteps through the dark,
Heavily hurrying down a distant stair,
And caught a piteous wail faint on the air.
The dog howled his lone cry, as he would fain
Give warning, knowing it was all in vain.
Then came the liquid gurgle and the ring
Metallic, with the heavy plop and ping,
Heavier than largest water-drops that fall
From melting icicles on house-eaves tall.
I knew them now ; this resurrection night
Sounds were translated into things of sight.
These were the innocent drops a father shed ;
They had the weight of blood, fell heavy as
    lead.
And now again I felt the grinding sound
O' the grating door ; the digging underground ;

The shudders of the house; the sighs and moans;
The ring of iron dropped upon the stones;
The cloudy presence prowling near; the quake
Of walls that vibrate with the parting shake;
Then the relief. As they who stoop with dread,
While the Simoon goes withering overhead
Like iron red-hot, look up and breathe at last,
So felt I when that thing of Night had passed.

'Tis but a dream, methought, and I shall wake
Ere long and from its dread embraces break.
And if I could but only wake, I knew
By light of day these things could not be true!
How many a dream before had wraith-like gone
To nothing at the sceptic smile of Dawn.
And still I could not wake, nor wake my Wife;
And still the dream went on, and like as life
There stood the Angel in it; overshone
The well-known room.
     And then Her voice went on.

" *The nether world hath opened at your feet,*
And you have seen ascending from the Pit
The torment-smoke, where furnace-fires of Crime
Have cracked the crust of this your world of Time.

" *It was an awful hour of storm and rain*
And starless gloom in which the Child was slain.
Wild, windily the Night went roaring by,
As if loud seas broke in the woodlands nigh,
Or all the blasts of Heaven at once were hurled
To stop the onward rolling of the world.
The firmament was all one flash, and fled:—
The lightning laughed, as Hell were overhead.

" *He had dug his grave amid this war of storm;*
He bore the murdered Babe upon his arm
For burial, where no eye should ever mark !
Just then Heaven opened at him with the bark
Of all the Hell-hounds loosed.   And in the dark
Out went the light, and down he dropped the key,
That was to lead to safety secretly.
He was alone with Death, and paces three
Beyond the door an open grave gaped, free
For all the daylight world to come and see ;
And he was fastened.
                    Like the luckless wight
Who wagered he would enter a Vault at night
In some old Graveyard, and, in proof he did,
Would leave his dagger stuck in a Coffin-lid.—
He ventured : bravely dashed the weapon down,
And turned to triumph, when, by the student-gown
He was held fast, as if the living Tomb
Had closed upon him ; clutched him in the gloom.
He had pinned his long robe to the coffin !   Fright
Came on him like a snow-fall !   Weirdly-white
His hair turned, and the youth was a forlorn,
Old, gray-faced, gibbering Idiot next morn.

" *The murderer did not madden thus, but he*
Was stamped as if for all Eternity.
He stooped with his dead child, he groped and
        found
The key, and got the Corse safe underground,
And out of sight had hid his murder-hole,
Ere Dawn looked ghostly on his guilty soul,
And on his hands no man could see the stain.
His madness went beyond the burning brain ;
His was the frenzy of a soul insane.

" *The hour came when he lost that key again.*
As the death-rattles thundered in his throat,
And earth was rushing past his soul afloat,
And pain had fiercely throbbed itself to rest,
And time stopped ticking in the brain and breast,
It g'eamed and vanished from his fading sight,
And snapped his eye-strings straining through the
      night.
Thenceforth it was his hottest hell to be
Living the moment when he lost his key :
Hell that is permanent insanity !

" *There was a man who died ages ago,*
And 'tis his madness still to wile his woe
At work for ever, perfecting the plan
That should have, must have shown his fellow-man
How innocent he was of that old crime
He died for justly—had he thought in time.

" *Even so this lost soul whirls and eddies round*
The grave-place where the lost key must be found,
If the mad motion would a moment cease,
And he could only get a moment's peace ;
He often sees it, but he cannot touch
It ; like a live thing it eludes his clutch—
Gone like that glitter from the eyes of Death
In the black river at night that slides beneath
The Bridges, tempting souls of Suicides
To find the promised rest it always hides.

" *For seven years it was his curse to come*
At midnight and fulfil his dreadful doom,
Looking for that lost key, lest it revealed
The secret he so carefully concealed ;

Feeling at times he could endure his hell
If in one world of torment he might dwell.
And still from world to world he had to go
Wandering with incommunicable woe;
Well knowing that, for every moment lost,
His soul would be in treble anguish tossed,
While every storm of wind and rain would beat
Down on him, kindle hell to tenfold heat,
And make him hurry to your upper air,
Lest it should blow and wash the bones all bare.
For often will a wind of God arise
At midnight, and the voice of Murder cries
From it, and bones of murdered babes are found;
Earth will no longer be their burial ground.
And so on stormy nights his pangs are worst;
More live the portent in the blackness hearsed:
More dread the gnashings of that soul accursed.

" For seven years he came, unseen, unheard.
'Twas but the other day the bones were stirred.
As men were delving heedless underground,
They broke in on them, scattered them around:
Not guessing they were human.
       Lower in hell
His spirit sank, like waters in a well
Before there springs the Earthquake. Tremblings
  sore
Shook him with vengeance never felt before.
He came; he found the murder had leaped out;
The grave was burst; the bones were strewn about
For all the world to find!
      It mattered not
To him that no one knew them; they might rot

To undistinguishable dust in peace ;
That Death had signed his order of release
From this world's law ; Death had no shadows
    dim
Enough to hide the blacker truth from him.
He was the Murderer still, who had to hide
The proofs of murder on the human side !
The Child was his ; these were its tender bones,
Blown with the dust and dashed against the stones.
And all his care, his self-enfolded pain
And midnight watchings lone, were all in vain.

" The worms that in the dead flesh riot and roll
Are poor faint types of those that gnawed his soul !
For ever beaten now ; though he should find
And grasp the key he lost when he went blind
In death : In vain he mounts upon a wind
Of torment ; tries to fan the dry dust over them
With endless toil ; no sooner does he cover them
Than there's an ominous muttering in the air,
And in an instant all the bones lie bare ;
While lurking devils grin through masks at him,
In likeness of his Child's head, gorily grim !

" It comes upon him, almost with a gleam
Of comfort, when he's rapt into the Dream
You saw him change in, and he passes through
His night of murder ; lives it all anew,
So vividly each sound is heard by you ;
Each particle of Matter set afloat
Upon a Mind-wave, tossing like a boat
The Spirit rides.
              For, as, upon his brain,
The sounds one midnight smote in a ruddy rain,

Till sense had dyed the spirit with their stain,
And Memory was branded deep as Cain,
So now his spirit echoes back again
The fixed ideas of a soul insane,
Till Matter taking impress of his pain,
Reverberates the sounds within your brain."

PART IV.

I MUSED and mused in great astonishment,
While on, and on, the growing wonder went
Within, without, on wings that widelier spread.
"*How many things,*" oft to myself I had said,
"*I have to ask, if one came from the dead.*"
And now I had my wish.   My thought could
    rise
No fleeter than the answer filled her eyes
And flashed electric utterance with the whole
Illumined figure of a living soul !

"*More Laws than Gravitation keep us down*
To the old place from whence the soul had flown.
Not every one in death can get adrift
Freely for life.   Some have no wings to lift
Their weary weight : the body of their sin
Which they so evilly have laboured in :
Others will touch as 'twere the window-sill
To flutter back upon the ground-floor still.
Others yet grovel like the least belogged
In the old ways, to which they are self-clogged.
Just as the Spirits of an earlier race
Of Man in dwarfhood, kept their dwelling-place

On earth, and revelling in the moon's pale rays,
Were seen as Wee Folk in old wondering days.

" A-many wander this side of the grave
To get the last glimpse they can ever have
Of those they loved, who will be lost in light,
While they go darkling and are lost in night.
They see them sometimes in the world of breath;
They part for ever at the second death.
Others would blot from out the book of Time
The published proofs of their long-secret crime
That glare so guiltily to spirit-sight.
Teachers who called Good evil; darkness light;
Who see more clearly in the unclouding day,
Strive to recall the souls they led astray,
And find the world, that once hung on their breath,
Goes by them now; heedless, and deaf as Death.
Some, who have done a wrong that, unperceived,
Ran to a sea of sin, are sorely grieved,
And ready to spend the next life shut from bliss,
Might they but right the wrong they did in this:
So clear, so awful, when the past is seen,
Grows the dark mystery of might-have-been.

" This happened under the broad shining day,
Right in the rush of life that makes its way
Through London streets.
                        Slowly, 'mid that swift throng,
A thoughtful man went mooningly along;
More lonely in that wilderness of men.
And at a corner where the Devil's den
Is palace-fronted now—all gilt and glass—
Illuminating nightly all who pass
By the broad way to He'l with gin and gas,

*And souls are sloughed, like city sewage, down
Dead-Sea-ward, through the sink-holes of the town,
He heard a pitiful voice that took strange hold
Of him; ran through his blood in lightnings cold;
Mournful, remote, and hollow, as if the tomb
Had buried a live spirit in its gloom,
Monotonously praying on below
A vast unutterable weight of woe;
A voice that its own speaker would not know!
As if unbreathing life were doomed to bear
Shut down on it the load of all the air.
He stopped.*

    *A woman clothed in rags he saw
With fixed beseeching eyes begin to draw
Him to her; left no power to say them nay.
With one stretched arm she begged; on the other
  lay,
Soft in a snow of gold, a Cherub Child!
So have you seen a Glowworm on the wild
Wide moorland; all the dusk a moment smiled.*

*" For the babe's sake he thrust a coin of gold
 Into her hand! but, it fell through, and rolled
 Ringing along the stones : he followed, found
 It, brought it back and looked around :
 There was no woman waiting with her hand
 Outstretched, no Child, where he had seen them
  stand.
 In vain he searched each by-way round about;
 Through life even, never made the mystery out.*

*" The truth is, he was one of those who see
 At times side-glimpses of eternity.*

The Beggar was a Spirit, doomed to plead
With hurrying way-farers, who took no heed,
But passed her by, indifferent as the dead,
Till one should hear her voice and turn the head;
Doomed to stand there and beg for bread, in tears,
To feed her child that had been dead for years!
This was the very spot where she had spent
Its life for drink, and this the punishment;
She felt she had let it slip into the grave,
And now would give eternal life to save:
Heartless and deaf and blind the world went by,
Until this Dreamer came, with seeing eye;
The good Samaritan of souls had given
And wrought the change that was to her as Heaven.

" It is not Crime alone brings Spirits back
To pull beside you in the wonted track.
Shadows of mortal care will cloud the brow
That should have shone as clear as sunlit snow:
And those who hindered here must help you now.
Not always can the soul forgive in heaven
Itself for deeds that have been long forgiven.

" A wedded couple, bedded, snug as birds
In nested peace, one night must needs have words
Of strife before they slept.   A foolish thing
Had on a sudden set them bickering;
Some wild-fire wisp had dropped a subtle spark
That kindled at a breath blown through the dark,
And all their passion burst in tongues of flame:
Their anger blinding both to personal blame.
She had been pillowed on his beating heart,
And in an instant they had sprung apart!

The arm that wound about her he withdrew,
And Night, with dark divorce, came 'twixt the
  two.

" *A little thing had plucked them palm from palm;*
A little thing had broke their happy calm;
A little thing fall'n in the pleasant path
Of their life-stream, that turned to bubbling wrath!
And little might have made them yield and cling
Repentant; yea, a very little thing.
A touch would have sufficed to make the stream
Flow calm once more; dream out its happy
  dream.
A kiss have fused them into one again,
And saved them many a year of piteous pain.
'Twas such a little thing they had to do;
Both yearned to make it up, and this each knew.
If one could but have said 'Good-night,' scared
  Love
Would have come down to brood like Holy Dove.
And, being done, all would have been so well.
Not being done, it left the rift for Hell
To break through, and another triumph win,—
Ever the worst of Traitors are within:
But neither spoke, though long upon the wing
Love waited lingeringly listening!

" *Waking, he heard her in her slumbers weep,*
And then he slept, and in the guise of Sleep
Death came for him, nor gave him time to say
'Good-night,' 'Good-bye,' and at his side she lay
A Widow! And upon that dark no day
Hath broke for her. For him, no hell nor heaven
Will open; praying still to be forgiven,

Night after night at her bedside he stands,
Wringing his soul as one may wring the hands;
By natural law of grieved love; not sent
By Vengeance for unnatural punishment.

" The unslain shadows of the Martyrs slain,
Rise on their fields of old heart-ache and pain,
To fight their battle over and over again.
Half-buried hands, still thrust up through the soil,
From fields of carnage, prayerfully to God,
Will grasp the weapons of immortal war.
Freed spirits make their conquering battle-car
Of human hearts: they do but hold their breath
To smite unheard in their dark cloud of death.
They work for Freedom still, though out of sight;
They are torch-bearers in your mortal night.
The Tyrants may destroy the body; drench
The life out with the blood, but cannot quench
It !　They may string the corses high in air,
But cannot keep the soul suspended there.

" Wide as the wings of Sleep by night are spread,
Are Freedom's Exiles scattered, and her dead
Have lain them wearily down beneath God's dome.
But every banished spirit hurries home,
Soon as the free, long-fettered life up-springs
Awave one day on mighty warrior-wings.
Each soul, let out, fights with the strength of seven,
Under God's shield, and on the side of Heaven.

" The other world is not cut off from this:
Forgetfulness is not the gate of bliss.
At times the buried dead within you rise
To look out on their old world through your eyes;

They touch you with the waving of their wing,
Lightly as airs of heaven the Æolian string.
At times as Comforters above you stoop,
To lift the burden from you when ye droop!
As parents on their little ones may peep
Ere going to rest, they bend to bless your sleep.
They show you Pictures which are faintly wrought
In shadows that take life in waking thought.
With fruit from our Lord's Garden dear ones
　　come
To bring you a foretaste: try to lure you home.

" With clap o' the shoulder, friends behind you steal
The old glad way which ye no longer feel:
They watch you as ye watch the darkened mind
Of some arrested spirit; try to unwind
A way to it; with drops of pity melt
The clod about it; have your fondness felt:
Even as ye turn your thoughts to them above,
Do they return to you; look back for love.

" They left you standing still at gaze upon
The cloud they entered, where the light last shone.
And while the wet eyes yearn and watch the track,
As if by that same way they might come back,
And through the dark ye stretch the ungrasped
　　hand,
There, at some window of the soul, they stand
All whitely clothed with immortality,
Closer to you than flesh and blood can be.
The cloud is lifted from the vapoury bourne;
Although you know them not, the dead return;
To dry the Mourner's tear and hush the wail,
There's nought between you but a Viewless veil!

" *Old loves are with you in your dreams ; but fear*
  Lest they should make their presence felt too near ;
  The face of Love in Heaven they dare not show,
  Lest with its glory they might set aglow
  Your earthly love, which leaps to embrace a bliss
  That lives and dies in a consuming kiss.
  So warm Laodamïa wooed her dead
  Dear Husband's Shade, as if they were new-wed !

" *And certain spirits are perplexed to find*
  How like their life to that they left behind
  In natural nearness to their darlings here,
  Who lose them just because they are so near
  In life that grows impenetrably clear !

" *Many who tossed together on the sea,*
  And parted in the storm ; lost utterly ;
  Find they were only wrecked to meet again,
  Safe on the same shore, after all the pain.
  God hath so many paths by which we come
  To Him ; through many doors He draws us Home.
  'Tis but His wilderness of secret ways
  That to our vision seems a trackless maze.

" *Others are horribly startled at the change*
  Revealed in death, all is so wondrous strange !
  So many weeds, your blind world flung aside,
  Are gathered up as flowers, thrice-glorified.
  So many Masters in the realms of breath
  Serve at the feet of those who are crowned in
        death.
  So many who ruled the world are set to rule
  Themselves for ages in a painful school.

The Invisible dawns!   The sleepers wake to find
Less death in dying than in living blind:
And now the eyes their earthly scales let fall,
They see that they have never lived at all.

" I knew a follower of the strictest faith,
Whose dead religion rested on a death,
And frequent praying in the market-place,
With proclamation of his private grace;
Who sat among the loftiest Self-Elect,
But had not learned through life to walk erect—
Strait-waistcoated in stony pieties—
And when Death came—the Iconoclast who frees—
He could not stand without their rigid stay:
The Maker's image had but stamped the clay.
As one may don the fashion of a day,
On earth he wore the mask of Man awhile,
But when the Searchers stripped him, with a
        smile,
The wizened spirit shrank from man's disguise:
It fled, and fell, and wriggled, reptile-wise.
Some had been hailed immortals upon Earth—
Immortals prematurely brought to birth.
' And are you happy in your Heaven,' they said,
' O Great One?'   But he sadly shook his head,
And with both clutching hands upheld his crown
That only kept on—toppling, tumbling down.
His earthly halo was a world too wide;
His glory of greatness shrank so when he died,
That blatant Fame evoked with her misfit
Derisive laughter from the Infinite.

" I have seen the foolish slaves of luxury,
Who loll at ease and live deliciously;

In Pleasure's poppy-garden drowse and press
With amorous arms my Lady Idleness;
Who, floating downward in voluptuous dream,
Just lean to catch the sparkles from Life's stream
That runs with Siren-sound and dizzying
    dance,
And hides its wrecks with winking radiance,—
Who, risen from life's feast, came reeling thence
Immortals, drunken with the fumes of Sense;
I've seen them in a pleasure-seeking group,
At Death's low door with mock politeness stoop,
And wantonly they went, nodding the head,
As though to lightsome music they were led:
Heedless the merry madcaps came before
The awful gate, as 'twere a Playhouse door;
It opened, and the darlings entered in
As to the secret Paradise of Sin!
But in a moment what a change there was.
In front of them there rose a mocking glass
In place of drop-scene—this was not a Play—
'In which they stared, and could not turn
    away,
But still stared on, in silence one and all,
To see their finery fade, their feathers fall;
In this grim moulting of the plumes of pride
They had to lay all ornaments aside;
And on the face of every Woman and Man,
Like wet paint on a mask, the colours ran;
The skin grew writhled, and within the head
Their eyes looked like gray ghosts of hopes long
    dead.

" The naked image of their own Selves they see,
Stripped in the Mirror of Eternity;

Worm-eaten through and through with thoughts
  that prey
On life itself, and eat the soul away.
Wine-cups await them; though well-kept for years
The wine, it had been made of human tears,
And tasted bitter! Fruit was given to eat,
The fruit of their own life; so smiling-sweet
It looked! like apples when the shining round
Is made of rose-leaf on a golden ground;
The crimson and the golden melting through,
Right to the core, in one delicious hue.
But these were Apples of the Dead-Sea shore;
Ashes without, and maggots at the core.
Saluting their fine nostrils Odours rise;
The scent of lifelong human sacrifice!
The brother's blood, that climbs to them and cries.
Then are they led where healing waters wait
To wash the soilèd soul; repristinate
The image of God so earthily concealed;
But while they lave find, more and more revealed,
Deeper disfigurement and deadlier stain,
As wetted marble shows the darker grain.

PART V.

" The dim world of the dead is all alive;
All busy as the bees in summer hive;
More living than of old; a life so deep,
To you its swifter motion looks like sleep.
Whether in bliss they breathe, in bale they burn,
His own eternal living each must earn.
We suck no honeycomb in drowsy peace,
Because ennobling natural cares all cease;

We live no life, as many dream, caressed
By some vast lazy sea of endless rest—
For there, as here, unbusy is unblest.

" *Man is the wrestling-place of Heaven and Hell,*
  Where, foot to foot, Angel and Devil dwell,
  With both attractions drawing him.   This gives
  The perfect poise in which his freedom lives.
  No one so near to heaven to lack for scope ;
  No one so near to hell to lose all hope.
  Whichever way he wills, to left or right,
  Lets in a flood of supernatural might.
  He flames out hellward, and all hell is free,
  Rejoicing in the gust of liberty,
  To rush in on him, work its devilry !
  In strength of faith, or feebleness of fear,
  He bows and bends the highest heavens near.
  The brightness upon Prayer's uplifted face
  Reflects some spirit-presence in the place.

" *Each impure nature hath its parasites,*
  That live and revel in unclean delights.
  Like moths around a flame they float and swarm ;
  Like flies about a horse, they ride the warm
  And reeking air which is their atmosphere,
  Their breath of life, the ranker the more dear.
  They glory in the grossness of the blood,
  For, reptile-like, they lay their eggs in mud.
  In every darksome corner of the mind
  They hang their webs, the wingèd life to bind ;
  Weaving the shadow of the Evil One
  To darken 'twixt the spirit and its sun.

" *If those blind Unbelievers did but know*
Through what a perilous Unknown they go
By light of day ; what furtive eyes do mark
Them fiercely from their ambush of the dark ;
What motes of spirit dance in every beam ;
What grim realities mix with their dream ;
What serpents try to pull down fallen souls,
As earth-worms drag the dead leaves through their
        holes ;
What cunning sowers scatter seed by night
That flames to fatal flower in broad daylight ;
And rub their hands at having danced it in
Ere the sun rise to ripen it in sin !
What foul birds drop their eggs in innocent nests,
To win their heat from warmth of innocent breasts :
What snaky thieves surmount each garden wall ;
On life's fresh leaves what caterpillars crawl ;
What cool green pleasaunces and brooding bowers
Are set with soul-snares hid among the flowers ;
What Tempters in the Chamber of Sleep will break,
And with insidious whisperings keep awake
The Soul !   How, toad-like, at the ear will lurk
The squatted Satan, wickedly at work :
What evil spirits hover in amorous hate
Round him who nibbles at the devil's bait,
Or him who dallies, fingering the sharp edge
Of peril, or sits with feet beyond the ledge,
By some dark water, with his face ash-wan,
Until they urge him over : a doomed Man !
What cruel demons try to break a way,
Through weak brains, back to their lost world of
        day,
Till from some little rift in nature yawns
A black abysm of madness, and Hell dawns :

What starvelings seek to drink Corruption's breath
From rosy life, more rich than rot of death;
What ghosts of drinkers old would quench their
        drouth
At the wine-bibber's dreaming stertorous mouth;
What Sirens seek to kindle at your fire
Of passion some live spark of dead desire—
They would be ready even to doubt God's power
To shield their little life from hour to hour,
And many would be going, with idiot-grin,
Out of their mind to let the marvel in.

" But do not think the Devil hath his will.
  Whate'er he doth he is God's servant still.
  And in the larger light of day divine
  The spark of his hell-fire shall cease to shine.
  God maketh use of him; what he intends
  For evil Heaven will turn to its own ends.
  With subtle wile he tries to circumvent
  The Lord, and works just what the Master meant.
  He hangs the dark cloud round this world of
          yours;
  God smileth, and a rain of good down-pours.
  He strove to found the Empire of the Slave,
  It crumbled in: he had but delved its grave.

" He stole upon a Nation, in disguise
  Of thieves that prowled by night; day-lurking
          spies;
  Plotters who privily set their eyes to mark
  Her weakness, and garrotted her i' the dark!
  The face of Freedom frightfully they scarred,
  That men might know her not, so sadly marred,
  And, seeing her in the dust, misjudge her stature;

And, finding she grew calm, mistake her nature!
They built about her; dreamed not she would
    stand
Up, terribly tall once more; and, in her hand—
Clenched, till the knuckles whiten with their
    grip—
And the blood blackens 'neath the nails that nip—
The sword set sharp as is her red-edged lip:
And in her eyes the lightnings that should break
In blinding, black, irreparable wreck:—
Rending their roof to heaven, their walls to earth,
(The sorer travail the more glorious birth!)
An Earthquake crash! the edifice is crowned,
And there's a heap of ruin on the ground!—
Arise, to sweep them from her onward path,
Stern as the Spectre of God's whitest wrath.
Even while they clutched the gains of their foul
    play
And parted them, I heard the Avengers say—
'They plant in dust a breath will blow away,
Although they wet it well with blood to-day.

" ' Ay, Traitor, mount your topmost pinnacle.
The merry-making Heavens would mark you well,
Where all the gazers of the world may see
You throned upon the peak of infamy!'
So crooned the implacable ministers of Fate,
Standing in shadow where they watch and wait.

" ' Well done. Now place the crown upon your
    brow,
With its brave glitter all eyes dazzle now:
Lost in its splendour is that frightful stain
Branded beneath; the murder-mark of Cain!'

z

So crooned the implacable ministers of Fate,
Standing in shadow where they watch and wait.

" ' Well done. Now fold the Imperial Purple round,
And let a Pope's Anointed, robed and crowned,
Thus glorify the blood so basely spilt ;
Thus image to all time the loftiest guilt.'
So crooned the implacable ministers of Fate,
Standing in shadow where they watch and wait.

" ' Well done, thou faithful servant. Hell shall
    rise
From half her thrones to offer you their prize,
And meet you coming ; greet you with a kiss
Of benison, for such a deed as this ! '
So crooned the implacable ministers of Fate,
Standing in shadow where they watch and wait."

" Was Satan sent from heaven to ruin earth ?"
I asked, " or what the story of his birth ?"

" *Both heaven and hell are from the human race,*
And every soul projects its future place :
Long shadows of ourselves are thrown before,
To wait our coming on the eternal shore.
These either clothe us with eclipse and night,
Or, as we enter them, are lost in light.

" *We look on Evil as the shadow dark*
Of the reflected bridge ; the nether Arc,
That makes some perfect circle of night and day,
Through which our river of life runs on its way
To that wide sea where, all Time-shadows past,
It shall but mirror one clear heaven at last.

There is no Devil such as Milton saw;
No fallen Angel's eyes divined the flaw
In God's work, whereby Man might be accursed.
The Devil was a murderer from the first,
Was said of old.   But it was softly nursed
Up from a babe in arms.   A little seed
Of sin was sown that grew with little heed.
By door or window little sins will win
A way that widens for the larger sin,
As tiniest lichens, climbing up the wall,
May lend a hand to help the Ivy crawl
That is to tower a conqueror over all
The house in ruin, crumbling to the fall.
Once life is set in motion there upspring
Infinite issues to the smallest thing.
A finger's breadth in swerving as we start
May land us in the end two worlds apart.

" Our parents were not tempted by a Tree
That hung out luscious fruitage, visibly
Held in God's hand, on purpose to beguile
Their simpleness with its suggesting smile.
Take this as symbol of a world within;
There was the serpent born, there bred the
        sin.
The trees that midmost in the Garden stood,
Took root in soul and blossomed in the blood.
Nor were they left without the inward light,
The starry presence shining through your night,
That shows the wrong while it reveals the
        right:
The magnet in the soul that points on through
All tempests and still trembles to be true.

Z 2

" *The still small voice within cried*

       'Do not this,
Or it will lead from me, and ye will miss
The innocent brightness of your morning bliss,
And long in a wild wilderness will stray,
Farther and farther from the primal way,
Until ye lose me, darkling in a cloud
Of your own making, winding like a shroud
About the life I gave; nor feel me near
When ye do call and think there's none to hear.'

" *And yet men dally with the thought of wrong*
Until they do it: looking down too long,
Like him who, on a perilous mountain ledge,
Gazes upon the gulf, dark o'er the edge,
Till he grows dizzy, and, with brain a-swim,
Forgetting to look up—drops!   Or, like him
Who stood and watched that Titan, face to face,
The vast Steam-Hammer, with its monster mace,
Until the blows of its recurrent sound
Snapped his last trembling hold of things around;
Mazed him and drew him nigher, slip by slip,
To thrust his hand into its crushing grip.

" *They dallied with wrong-doing, and it grew*
Too strong to wrestle with, and overthrew.
Eyes play with Pleasure!   Looking overmuch
Sets all the blood a-tingle for the touch!
How the fruit smiles, delicious to the eyes;
How quietly the Snake behind it lies,—
The Beast that in the man erect and crowned
Tends ever to go grovelling on the ground,—
With all his weight bending the branch down near;
The reptile music, sliding through the ear,

Winds round the soul, makes it a-tiptoe stand
With love-sick longing till it lifts the hand
To pluck, and feel, and smell, and taste just one
Ripe Apple, whose gold glistens so i' the sun!
But one step over the forbidden marge;
The sin so little, the delight so large!

" Thus is the Devil born: born every day,
Harmless at first as toothless whelps at play;
Is born in thoughts which are the quick live
    seeds
That will be striving to take shape in deeds;
So would be born could any race begin
Afresh; so form the protoplasm of Sin,
The pustule raised at just a prick of pin;
The nest-egg which the Devil is hatched in.
For Man, the outcome of Creation's past,
Is flower of all earth's life from first to last:
No lower life hath ever passed away
But left its larvæ in the human clay.
No reptile of the slime, no beast of prey,
But human passions personate to-day.
And these break loose to rend in deadly strife,
And will break loose, till, in the higher life,
The soul arisen to her immortal stature
Leads, Una-like, these grim necessities of Nature.

" To picture what I mean: see here, a Wife,
With bosom just a-brood o'er life-in-life,
Who in a fury-fit snatched up a knife
And hurled it at her husband. 'Twas a miss,
. Though near enough to hear Death's arrow hiss!
She had not dyed her hand in human blood,
But she had dipped her Unborn in a flood

Of wrath that surged and smoked and flashed
    hell-flame ;
Given her babe baptism in the Devil's name :
Stained the pure thing of heaven a lurid hue
With fume o' the pit, the white star reddened
    through.
And from that Mother-stricken life there grew
A Murderer whose own hand that Mother slew.

" The ghosts of our own crimes long-buried will
Live after us and haunt our children still.
Our vices, hid for generations past,
Break out and blab their secret tale at last.

PART VI.

" But Earth is not the Devil's merry-go-round.
The Angels of the Lord are ever found
Encamped about the soul that looks to Him :
These are an inner lamp when all is dim
Without, they light poor souls through horrors
    grim.
Even as a myriad sunbeams hour by hour
Melt to make rich one little summer flower ;
Or as a myriad souls of flowers fleet
Away to make a single summer sweet—
So many spirits make one smile of God
That feeds your life transfiguring from its clod.
There is no lack of Angel-carriers
When mortals post to heaven their fervent prayers !
And these are happy in their work, for still
They find their heaven in doing the Father's will.
The Blessèd do not leave some happy seat
When they draw near ye upon silent feet.

They have no need to thread their starry way
Through worlds of night, or wilderness of day.
Spirit to Spirit hath not far to run,
Because in God all souls are verily one
Throughout all worlds : there are no walls of
  Space
Where all eternity is dwelling-place.

" *Distance is nothing in the world of Thought ;*
So in the world of Spirit space is nought.
You hear of dying men whose souls have been
Present with distant friends ; most surely seen
Before the breathing ceased ; for they were there
In Thought so fixed, intense, that, on the air,
Their lineaments the utter yearning wrought,
In spiritual apparition of their thought,
Till they grew visible. This Murderer dwells
In Spirit where his Thought is—hottest Hell's
For him where his infernal deed was done !
The blood effaced so safely from the sun
Hath stained right through beyond this world of
  time,
Red to the other side, with his old crime.
He does not merely come and go ; he is
All presence to the proofs and witnesses.

" *Spirits may touch you, being, as you would say,*
A hundred thousand million miles away.
Those wires that wed the Old World with the
  New,
And do your bidding hidden out of view,
Are not the only links Mind lightens through !
The Angels, singing in their heaven above,
Feel when ye strike the unison of love.

The prayers of heaven fall in a blessèd rain
On souls that parch in purgatorial pain.
Desires uplift from earth with a sense of wings,
Poor souls that drift as helpless outcast things.

" A luminiferous motion of the soul
Pervades the universe, and makes the whole
Vast realm of Being one ;—all breathing breath
Of the same life that is fulfilled in death,
And human spirits, from their earthy bound,
Can thrill the Immortals, in their crystal round,
Like flames that leap to a point at some sweet
    sound,
As though they rose on tiptoe listening ;
And set the farthest heavens vibrating,
As air will dance close to a live harpstring.

" God, the Creator, doth not sit aloof,
As in a picture painted on the roof,
Occasionally looking down from thence.
He is all presence and all providence ;
Sentient in whatsoever life may draw
Breath from Him, and, beyond, He lives in law.
He doth not sit at one end of the chain
Of Being, thrilling it now and again ;
He who is Being and doth bound and bind
Its particles in the Eternal Mind.
Outside His providence we cannot stand.
His presence makes the smallest room expand
Wider than wings of Day and Night e'er fanned.
I who am here, His Messenger, to-night,
But bring that presence to a point in light.
We are the agencies, the living laws,
Whereby Creation is eternal Cause.

" This human life is no mere looking-glass,
    In which God sees His shadows as you pass.
    He did not start the pendulum of Time,
    To go by Law, with one great swing sublime ;
    Resting Himself in lonely joy apart :
    But to each pulse of life is beating heart.
    And, as a parent sensitive, is stirred
    By falling sparrow, or heart-wingèd word.

" As the Babe's life within the Mother's, dim
    And deaf, you dwell in God, a-dream of Him.
    Ye stir and put forth feelers which are clasped
    By airy hands, and higher life is grasped
    As yet but darkly.   Life is in the root
    And looking heavenward, from the ladder-foot,
    Wingless as worms, with earthiness fast bound.
    Up which ye mount but slowly, round on round.
    Long climbing brings ye to the Father's knee ;
    Ye open gladsome eyes at last to see
    That face of Love ye felt so inwardly.

" In this vast universe of worlds no waif
    Of spirit looks to Him but floateth safe.
    No prayer so lowly but is heard on high ;
    And if a soul should sigh, and lift an eye,
    That soul is kept from sinking with a sigh.

" All life, down to the worm beneath the sod,
    Hath spiritual relationships to God—
    The Life of Life, the love of all, in all ;
    Lord of the large and infinitely small.

" Birds find their home across the pathless sea
    By no hereditary memory.

"From land to land they move, their way illumed
By the inflowing Love that bore them, plumed
For flight, through which the Mother Bird is
  taught
To know which youngling had the last worm
  brought ;
The Insect led to garner food in nook
For young, on which it never lives to look.

" The veriest atoms, even as worlds above,
Are bridal chambers of creative Love,
Quick with the motion that suspends the whole
Of Matter spiral-spinning toward Soul.
A spirit of life rides every tiny grain
Of flower-seed flying through the air, for rain
And wind to feed until its heavenly Sower
Drops it to earth and it takes form,—a flower !
And nothing is, but groping turns to Him,
Like babe to bosom, though the sight be dim :
Nothing but what reflects in some faint wise
The image that is God in Angel eyes—
The Infinite One, whose likeness we but see
Glassed in the Infinite of Variety :
Just as the waters fix a fluttering beam,
Caught in this chamber, and, with golden gleam,
Throw on the ceiling, limned in little, one
Pale image of the glory of the Sun !

" No seed of life blown down a dark abysm
Of earth or sea but feels the magnetism
That draws us Godward ! Flowers sunk in mines,
Or plants in ocean, where no sunbeam shines,
Will blindly climb up toward their Deity,
Far off in Heaven, whom they can never see.

" *There is a Spirit of Life within the Tree*
That's fed and clothed from Heaven continually,
And does not draw all nourishment from earth.
It puts a myriad tender feelers forth,
That breathe in heaven and turn the breath to sap:
In every leaf it spreads a tiny lap
To take its manna from the hand of God,
And gather force for fingers 'neath the sod
To clutch the earth with; moulds, from sun and
    rain,
Its leaves; with spirit-life feeds every vein,
And through each vein makes wood for bough and
    bark:
Girth for the bole, and rootage down the dark.

" *So Man is fed by God and lives in Him:*
Not merely nourished by his rootage dim
In a far Past; a dead world underground,
But spirit to spirit reaches life all round.

" *Creative heat is current in the soul*
From ages past, like sunshine in the coal,
Some fire of heaven in fossil stored away,
But spirit-life yet kindles at the ray
Warm from our Sun that shines for us to-day!

" *Not in one primal Man before the Fall*
Did God set life a-breathing once for all,
He is the breath of life from first to last;
He liveth in the Present as the Past.
But ye, like rowers, turn your eyes behind;
Ye look Without, and vainly feel to find,
Raised in relief, like letters for the blind,
The substance of that Glory in the mind.

" *Hints of the higher life, the better day,*
Visit the human soul, outlining aye
The perfect statue now rough-cast in clay ;
And with a mournful sigh ye think and say,
'This is the type that was, and passed away !'
God holds a flower to you, it only yields
The fragrance fading from forgotten fields.
'Ah, only Eden could have wafted it !'
Immortal imagery His hand hath writ
Within ye is with revelation lit
By secret shinings of the Infinite.
'These are but glimmers of a glory gone !'
I tell you they are prophecies of dawn,
And glimpses of the life that still goes on.
Man hath not fall'n from Heaven, nor been cast
Out from some Golden Age lived in the Past !
His fall is from the possible Life before ye :
His fall is from the Crown of Life held o'er ye :
The falling short from an impending glory !
Ye stoop by Corpse-light, groping on the ground,
And lo ! the living God, a-shine all round !
Even while I speak there is a quickening,
The unrest of a world that feels the spring ;
The crust o' the Letter cracks ; new life takes
   wing :
A strong ground-swell will heave, a wave will
   break,
The Eternal grows more visibly awake.

" *Upon the verge of sunrise ye but stand—*
The door of life just open in your hand.
Behind you is the slip of space ye passed ;
Before you an illimitable vast.
Not backward point the footprints that ye trace

Of those who ran the foremost in the race,
With light of God full-shining on their face !
Look up, as Children of the Light, and see
That ye are bound FOR *immortality,*
Not passing FROM *it : Heirs of Heaven ye,*
Not Exiles.   God reverses human growth
For spirits ; they go ripening toward youth
For ever.   The fair Garden that still gleams
Across the desert, miraged in your dreams,
Smiles from the spirit, rather than the sod,
Wherever hallowed feet of Love have trod ;
Wherever souls yet walk and talk with God.
And Heaven is as near Earth now as when
The Angels visibly conversed with Men.
'Neath human roofs still stoopeth the Divine
Closer than ever ; makes the heart its shrine.

" God hath been gradually forming Man
In His own image since the world began,
And is for ever working on the soul,
Like Sculptor on his Statue, till the whole
Expression of the upward life be wrought
Into some semblance of the Eternal Thought.
Race after Race hath caught its likeness of
The Maker as the eyes grew large with love.

" You ask me ' how the lamp of life burns on
When all that visibly fed the flame is gone ? '

" Man does not live alone by visible breath,
And He who brings to life will lead through death.
Wait yet a little while, and ye shall see
The flame was breathed on ; fed invisibly :
And that its motion springs with force seven-fold
When the life-heat is clashed against Death's cold.

" *You think of spirit as prison-walled about*
By substance, marvelling how it can get out !
But to my vision radiates the soul
Through body ; by its pulses lights the whole
With life, and makes it luminous as the glass
Through which you see but only in spirit pass.
The wee babe nestled in the Mother's lap,
Feels her soul radiate in love, and wrap
It softly in the very heart of bliss,
And draw all heaven through it in a kiss.

" *As chalk is formed at bottom of the sea*
From life that sheds its shell continually ;
As bones are built up out of life's decay,
The body is shaped of substance sloughed away
From soul in ripening : 'tis a husk which yields
The earthy scaffold whereby spirit builds
Its heavenly house, that stands when the world-
　　crust
Is made of dropped and perished human dust.
Spirit is Lord and Master at the death,
As in beginning, of its house of breath.
And from it the new shape is surely given,
When visible form fades, cloud-like, into Heaven.

" *Man does not live alone by hunger and drouth,*
But by the breath which kindles from love's
　　mouth :
'Tis breathing spirit makes the body breathe,
And sets in outer type the life beneath.
So print makes visible the unseen thought
To pass away, the miracle being wrought.
Life is an inner energy, unfurled
In visible shows from an invisible world ;

Still fed and fed from that Almighty force
Of which no science yet hath grasped the source,
Whose infant germ from the dead seed reborn,
Is greater than a realm of ripened corn.
Like worlds warmed into being by their Sun,
Ye are embodied by the rays that run
Mysteriously across a gulf of night ;
A bridge of spirit laid in beams of light.
And that which is the centre of the blaze
Travels in life unseen along the rays.
The book will pass ; the living Mind works on ;
The Visible fades ; still shines the Eternal sun.

" I tell you these things are : I may not show
  You how : there's much the senses cannot know.
  Who knows the links of that invisible chain
  Which runs from soul to soul, from brain to
      brain,
  Whereby thought passes into other thought,
  And out of sound its silent shape is wrought ?
  You see the miracle done before your eyes,
  And in the flash of spirit to spirit dies
  The common daylight : visual sense is b'ind
  To see how Matter is made quick by Mind.
  And there's a power in the hidden soul
  To pass in at the eyes and print its whole
  Self, in a picture finished infinitely
  Beyond the portrait that the eyes can see.
  Eyes ne'er behold your own souls face to face :
  Your real selves invisibly embrace.

" You know not how a prayer ascends to God.
  You saw no ladder Angel-feet e'er trod

In answer; hear no door turn on the hinge
When heaven opens, or the hells impinge
Upon the soul with their suggestion dark.
Good spirits help, but how you cannot mark:
The bridge is still invisible that doth span
Your known and unknown: reach from God to
    Man.

" With labours infinite your Science seeks
Footing on inaccessible cloud-peaks.
Yet, must the Climbers know that there are things
Only attainable at last with wings;
That skies will not be scaled howe'er they clasp
The solid rock; that heaven thus mocks their
    grasp.
On these they may not speak the final word.
On these the great Hereafter must be heard.
At best Man doth but darkly draw his light:
Each step ye take, each secret wrest from Night,
Must furnish food for faith as well as sight.

" The more ye feel the chain whereby ye are spanned,
The more its missing links elude the hand.
So Saturn's perfect rings, when, closer seen,
Are broken with dark gaps of night between!
Nor can ye more than mark the Visible shine
And in the gloom accept the Hand Divine.

" Live fruitfully the life ye may possess
With rootage beyond reach of consciousness,
And wait till the Unseen in flower blows.

" To find what gems lie hidden where it grows
Ye must not pluck the plant up by the root.
Wait till its treasures hang in precious fruit.

Nor shall we see within the seed concealed
That world of wonder by the flower revealed !

" *There is no pathway Man hath ever trod*
By faith or seeking sight but ends in God.
Yet 'tis in vain ye look Without to find
The inner secrets of the Eternal Mind,
Or meet the King on His external Throne.
But when ye kneel at heart, and feel so lone,
Perchance behind the veil you get the grip
And spirit-sign of secret fellowship ;
Silently as the gathering of a tear
The human want will bring the helper near :
The very weakness, that is utterest need
Of God, will draw Him down with strength
    indeed.

" *Enough to know ye live because He lives !*
And love, because in love Himself He gives !
The gift is ever held sufficient sign
There is a Giver ! And if it be Divine
And like the Heaven ye dream, but may not see,
Giver Divine and Heaven there must be.

" *Lean nearer to the Heart that beats through night :*
Its curtain of the dark your veil of light.
Peace Halcyon-like to founded Faith is given,
And it can float on a reflected Heaven
Surely as Knowledge that doth rest at last
Isled on its ' ATOM' in the unfathomed vast
Life-ocean, heaving through the infinite,
From out whose dark the shows of being flit,
In flashes of the climbing wave's white crest :
Some few a moment luminous o'er the rest ! "

A A.

The voice ceased : the form faded in the beam
Of dawn, that swam down like the gladsome gleam
Of heaven to him who struggles, nearly drowned,
And melts to a gold mist the dim green round,
And draws him lifeward from the gulf profound.

PART VII.

Who hath not marked how graciously the Dawn
Comes smiling when some stormy night hath
　　　gone ?
As Beauty lifts the heaven of her eyes
Full on you large with their serene surprise
That you should dream such gentleness could
　　　dart
The looks that hurt you to the very heart !
Calm eyes, that through luxurious reaches roll
The richness of their rest upon the soul.

So comes the Morning ; new heavens rise above,
And open wider arms of larger love
Than ever : glad blue Ether, with the bliss
Of sunshine, laughs and kindles at its kiss.
There lie the tears of tempest, softly-bright
As Heaven had only rained in drops of light.
The air, an overflow of Heaven's own balm,
Nought but Earth's music breaks the divine calm.

Yet that same Morning looks on ruin and wreck,
And soothes a sea that lifeless swept the deck
Of some proud ship, and glorifies the wave
That landward heaves the mariner's glassy grave ;

Playfully rippling, shoaling goldenly o'er
Dead seamen dimly drifting to the shore!
Terribly innocent, Morning laughs on high,
While Ocean rocks them with its lullaby.

So came the Morning, smiling, crowned with
        calm,
After my night of trouble, breathing balm.
Fair Earth with all her night-long-tearful eyes
A-sparkle with the soul of new sunrise!
On every blade there hung a drop of dew,
And every drop a live star shimmered through :
All phantoms of the night by shadowy stealth
Retired with Darkness from our world of health ;
All life unshrouded, to Heaven's influence
        bare,
Took wings of morning in the open air.
Our world, a warm safe nest of happy souls,
Basked in the brightness as the lily lolls
In whiteness bosomed on the sunny stream,
Whose ripples lip her where she lies a-dream.

The stream, that crept a river of death by
        night,
Full of dark secrets, ran a river of light !
Such sense of rest to all glad things was given,
As earth were cradle to the peace of heaven.
A more than common freshness fed the breath
Of being ; there was no least taint of death.
My nightmare over, I would dream no more
Of murder and the charnel at life's core ;
Or nameless creatures that may haunt old
        graves
Bat-like, and flit from out lone, twilight caves.

Green earth, glad heaven, gladly vied to win
Thought out-of-doors, yet would it brood within,
Sullen and shy as fish that will not rise
To any tempting lure of feathered flies,
But haunt the pool where, horribly quiet, lies
A dead child, with its wide-awake blue eyes.

Lonely I wandered in my garden-ground,
Musing on Life, the Death's-head rosily crowned,
And of the mystery that shrouds us round,
And of the mournful possibility -
That, in some blindness, we may lose the key
Which to the keeping of each soul is given
To ope the door, and so be shut from Heaven;
Raking the ashes and the dust of death,
Long after we have done with human breath;
And of the features printed on my brain
In vision that would evermore remain,
And, any instant, sinister and swart,
From out the light, at turn of eye, might start;
And I should see him! as 'neath the Tunnel's
      arc,
Where, down the shaft, day lightens through
      the dark,
Some chosen victim momently may mark
His murderer, with those snaky eyes at work
Fixed on him; in whose spark malignant lurk
Cold fires of death drawn inward for the spring;
The dagger-flash leaps in their glittering!

So, till its horrors almost lived to sight,
My spirit brooded o'er the bygone night;
Reflecting all the strife in upper air,
As you have seen, by some sea-margin, where

The circling sea-bird hovers, dreamily slow,
In likeness of the wave that sways below,
The Spirit of its motion on the wing :
Over that night my mind kept hovering.
At length the growing image of my thought
To some such final shape as this was wrought—

From end to end of things we may not see,
Nor square the circle of Eternity ;
But, I can not believe in endless hell
And heaven side by side.   How could one dwell
Among the Saved, for thinking of the Lost ?
With such a lot the Blest would suffer most.
Sitting at feast all in a Golden Home,
That towered over dungeon-grates of Doom,
My heart would ache for all the lost that go
To wail and weep in everlasting woe :
Through all the music I must hear the moan,
Too sharp for all the harps of Heaven to drown.

I cannot think of Life apart from Him
Who is the life, from cell to Seraphim :
And, if Hell flame unquenchably, must be
The life of hell to all eternity !
A God of Love must expiate the stain
Of Sin Himself, by suffering endless pain ;
Sit with eternal desolation round
His feet ; His head with happy heavens crowned.

From Him the strength immortal must be sent,
By which the soul could bear the punishment.
I cannot think He gave us power to wring
From one brief life eternal suffering :
And prove the Infinite's own limiting !

If this were so the Heavens must surely weep,
Till Hell were drowned in one salt vast, sea-
    deep.
Forgive me, Lord, if wrongly I divine;
I dare not think Thy pity less than mine.

I cannot image Heaven as Triumph-Car,
That rolleth red and reeking from the war,
Upborne on wheels of torture whirling round
With writhing souls for ever broke and bound !

God save me from that Heaven of the Elect,
Who half rejoice to count the numbers wrecked,
Because, such full weight to the balance given,
Sends up the scale that lands them safe in
    heaven;
Who some fallen Angel would devoutly greet
And praise the Lord for another vacant seat,
And the proud Saved, exulting, soar the higher,
The lower that the Lost sank in hell-fire.

I think Heaven will not shut for evermore,
Without a knocker left upon the door,
Lest some belated wanderer should come
Heart-broken, asking just to die at home,
So that the Father will at last forgive,
And looking on His face that soul shall live.
I think there will be Watchmen through the
    night,
Lest any, afar off, turn them to the light;
That He who loved us into life must be
A Father infinitely Fatherly,
And, groping for Him, these shall find their way
From outer dark, through twilight, into day.

I could not sing the song of Harvest Home,
Thinking of those poor souls that never come ;
I could not joy for Harvest gathered in,
If any souls, like tares and twitch of sin,
Were flung out by the Farmer to the fire,
Whose smoke of torment, rising high and higher,
Should fill the universe for evermore.
I could not dance along the crystal floor
Through which the damned looked up at Para-
    dise,
For ever fixed, like fishes frozen in ice.

Such mournful eyes from out their night would
    gleam
And haunt for ever all my happy dream !
I could not take my fill for thinking of
Those empty places in the heart of Love.

The New World's poorest emigrant will lend
A kindly hand to help a poorer friend.
And I must pray to God from out my bliss
For those who are beyond all help but His—
Pray and repray, the same old prayer anew ;
Forgive them, Lord, they know not what they do.
Because they were so utterly accurst,
Self-doomed, that bitterness would be the worst.
O look down on them from Thy place above,
The look of pity, Lord, half-way to love !

Mere human love, in this, its narrow sphere,
Can never think of those it once held dear,
Who, down the darkened way will pull apart,
But with a pitying eye, an aching heart.

And still, as less the beckoning hand they heed,
The strength of Love grows with their greater
    need;
The less they heed, the more it yearns to save.
And shall this love be dwarfed beyond the grave,
To lose, on wings, its feet-attainèd height?
Better its blindness, than the eye of light
That coldly down on endless hell could glance
With all its mortal sympathies in trance.

Or will some Lethean wave the soul caress,
And numb it into dull forgetfulness;
Washing away all memory of distress
That others feel, while we but lift the hand
To pluck and eat the lotus of the land,
And those far wailings of the world of tears
Come mellowed into music for our ears,
With just the zestful dash of discord given,
That makes the pleasure pungent — perfects
    Heaven?

'Tis hard to read the Handwriting Divine;
The vanishing *up-stroke* so invisibly fine!
There must be issues that we do not see.
The whole horizon of Futurity
Is nowise visible from where we stand;
We are but dwellers in a lowly land:
We think the sun doth set, the sun doth rise,
And yet our world's but turning in the skies.
Seen from our lower level there must pass
Mysteries, so high and starry, we but glass
Them darkly, as we strain our mortal sight,
  While 'twixt our souls and them there stands
    the night.

And then we scratch upon our window-pane,
Dimming its clearness, and we are so fain
To read our own imaginations fond,
For the true figures of the world beyond.
We model from the human life, and so
Feature the future from the face we know.
'Tis always sunless one side of our globe,
And thus we fashion the Eternal's robe.
God made Man in His image, but our plan's
To mould and make God's image in the Man's;
And if my thought be human as the rest,
At least the likeness shall be Man's at best.

Our Science grasps with its transforming hand;
Makes real half the tales of wonder-land.
We turn the deathliest fetor to perfume;
We give decay new life and rosy bloom;
Change filthy rags to paper virgin white;
Make pure in spirit what was foul to sight.
Even dead, recoiling force, to a fairy gift
Of help is turned, and taught to deftly lift.
How can we think God hath no crucible
Save some Black Country of a burning Hell?
Or the great ocean of Almighty power,
No scope to take the life-stream from our shore,
Muddy and dark, and make it pure once more!

Dear God, it seems to me that Love must be
The Missionary of Eternity!
Must still find work, in worlds beyond the
    grave,
So long as there's a single soul to save;
Gather the jewels that flash Godward in
The dark, down-trodden, toad-like head of Sin;

That all divergent lines at length will meet,
To make the clasping round of Love complete ;
The rift 'twixt Sense and Spirit will be healed,
Before creation's work is crowned and sealed ;
Evil shall die like dung about the root
Of Good, or climb converted into fruit !
The discords cease, and all their strife shall be
Resolved in one vast peaceful harmony :
That all these accidents of Time and breath
Shall bear no black seal of a Second Death :
And, freed from branding heats that burn in
    Time,
The lost *Black Race* shall whiten in that clime :
All blots of error bleached in Heaven's sight ;
All life's perplexing colours lost in light :
That Thou hast power to work out every stain,
That purifying is the end of Pain ;
And, waking, we shall know what we but dream
Dimly, our darkness touched by morning's gleam ;
There is no punishment but to redeem ;
And here, or There, the penitent thrill must
    leaven
The earthiest soul, and wing it toward Heaven ;
That when the Angel-Reapers shall up-sheave
The harvest, Angel-Gleaners will not leave
One least small grain of good—and there are
    none
So evil but some precious germ lives on,—
The grimiest gutter crawling by the way
Still hath its reflex of the face of Day ;
And all the seeds divine foredoomed by fate
To bear blind blossoms here shall germinate,
And have another chance, in other place,
Where tears of gratitude and dews of grace

Shall warm and quicken to the feeblest root,
Till in Thy garden they are ripe for fruit :
For all who have made shipwreck on that shore
Another outfit and one venture more.
So shall we find the Dark of our old Earth
Twin with the eternal Daylight from the birth,
And trodden in the grave-dust we shall see
The serpent-symbol of Eternity,
That only maketh ends meet, head and tail,
A world all blessing with a world all bale.

Thus, in its maze, my mind went round and
      round,—
Like him, lost in the Bush, who thought he
      found
The pathway that he sought, because he beat
His track with constant tread of his own feet,—
As round the dew-drenched garden-walks I went
Till, pausing, all unconscious of intent,
Nigh where a greenery of Syringas grew,
And, shedding shadow round, there leaned a
      Yew,—
Sombrely-ancient watcher by the tomb !
A Nest of Thrushes the live heart o' the gloom ;
I saw the earth was cracked, where recent rain
Had crushed and crumbled in a new-made drain,
And human bones were plainly peering through,
As if Death grinned and show'd a tooth or two !
I searched, and, ere the ghastly work was done,
Had gathered half a tiny skeleton,
That had been once a Child.
                 And then it came
On me that in my dream I saw the same,
And had been warned to calcine them in flame,

And pound them small as is the finest rust,
And on the winds of heaven fling the dust.
I did it, and, although that soul, self-cursed,
Still walks the darkness, we had passed the
     worst,
And there was peace o' nights at the Haunted
     Hurst.

                                    1869.